ALL UNQUIET THINGS

ALL UNQUIET THINGS

Anna Jarzab

DELACORTE PRESS

Visit us on the Web! www.randomhouse.com/teens

Educators and librarians, for a variety of teaching tools, visit us at www.randomhouse.com/teachers

Library of Congress Cataloging-in-Publication Data
Jarzab, Anna.
All unquiet things / Anna Jarzab.—1st ed.
p. cm.
Summary: After the death of his ex-girlfriend Carly, northern California high school student Neily joins forces with Carly's cousin Audrey to try to solve her murder.
ISBN 978-0-385-73835-4 (hardcover)—ISBN 978-0-385-90723-1 (lib. bdg.)—ISBN 978-0-375-89407-7 (e-book)
[1. Murder—Fiction.   2. Social classes—Fiction.   3. Interpersonal relations—Fiction.   4. High schools—Fiction.   5. Schools—Fiction.   6. California, Northern—Fiction.   7. Mystery and detective stories.]   I. Title.
PZ7.J2968A1 2010
[Fic]—dc22   2009011557

The text of this book is set in 12-point Filosofia Regular.

Book design by Angela Carlino

Printed in the United States of America

10 9 8 7 6 5 4 3 2 1

First Edition

Random House Children's Books supports the First Amendment and celebrates the right to read.

For my parents,

in memory of Audrey Richier

This makes the madmen who have made men mad
By their contagion; Conquerors and Kings,
Founders of sects and systems, to whom add
Sophists, Bards, Statesmen, all unquiet things
Which stir too strongly the soul's secret springs,
And are themselves the fools to those they fool;
Envied, yet how unenviable! What stings
Are theirs! One breast laid open were a school
Which would unteach mankind the lust to shine or rule.

GEORGE GORDON, LORD BYRON
Childe Harold's Pilgrimage

It is indeed a mistake to confuse children with angels.

DOUGLAS COUPLAND
Hey Nostradamus!

{ Contents }

PART ONE

Neily

CHAPTER ONE

Senior Year

It was the end of summer, when the hills were bone dry and brown; the sun beating down and shimmering up off the pavement was enough to give you heatstroke. Once winter came, Empire Valley would be compensated for five months of hot misery with three months of torrential rain, the kind of downpours that make the freeways slick and send cars sliding into one another on ribbons of oil. On the bright side, the hills would turn a green so lustrous they would look as if they had been spray painted, and in the morning the fog would transform the valley into an Arthurian landscape. But before the days got shorter and the rain came, there was the heat and the dust and the sun, conspiring to drive the whole town crazy.

School was starting on Monday. I had two more days of freedom. I hadn't slept very much since Wednesday night; my palms were sweating, and everything ached with the ache that comes after a long hike and a couple of rough falls. My mother wanted to take me to a doctor for the insomnia, so the night before school started I didn't go home. Instead, I went to Empire Creek Bridge, where I thought I could clear my head. The bridge was a small, overgrown stone arch, a mimicry of ancient Roman aqueducts that was more about form than function, designed to accommodate one car at a time going one direction over carefully placed cobblestones. A narrow, slow-moving body of water ran beneath it, and clumps of oak trees rose up near its banks. The bridge was almost useless, but very picturesque. Along one side of it was a small ledge meant for pedestrians, and this was where I lay down so that I wouldn't get run over, and closed my eyes. I needn't have bothered. All night, not one car passed. I could have died on that bridge and no one would have known.

This is not to say that I wanted to die. I wasn't—and have never been—suicidal. The valley was blanketed by a late, torturous heat wave that made the shadows the only decent place to sit during the day, and the dry winds kicked up the dust, making me uneasy. I had grown up in Empire Valley and was used to these uncomfortable summers, but this time I had begun to feel a restlessness reverberating through my bones like the persistent hum of cicadas.

It had been a long, slow summer. I had spent most of it reading massive Russian novels on my porch, playing video games, and sleeping until noon. I didn't have a lot of friends and I didn't see much of anyone apart from my parents. I had plenty of schoolwork, too—my class schedule for the upcoming year promised to be brutal, with six AP classes and college application season right around the corner—but nothing seemed to be able to occupy me for very long. My mother had an easy explanation for my agitation—it was my senior year and I was under a lot of pressure, especially from my father, to chart my future—but it was more complicated than that.

There was another reason I had come to Empire Creek Bridge. The year before, almost to the day, a girl I loved had died on this bridge, shot in cold blood. The police considered the matter solved—there had been an arrest, a trial, a guilty verdict—but Carly's murder retained an air of mystery for me and so did the place where she died. I had so many questions, but nobody except Carly seemed capable of answering them, and by the time I had found her body she was already dead. Despite all the effort I had put into blocking that night from my mind and trying to forget, the murder still haunted me. I didn't know what help spending time at the bridge would be, but I had been drawn there throughout that boiling summer, and I thought it was best to go with my instincts, even though they never seemed to do me any good.

As the sun came up that Saturday morning, I sat watching the animals—deer, hawks, the occasional wild turkey—move around on the scorched foothills. Soon, a patrol car pulled up, its siren whooping to get my attention. I had already moved from the ledge down to the creek bank, and was splashing some water on my face. The doors slammed, and I could hear footsteps making their way behind me. I felt a hand on my shoulder.

"Neily Monroe?" The officer leaned over me. "Your parents are very worried. Did you sleep here last night?"

"Yeah," I said, though I hadn't slept at all.

"Bryson?" The other officer was on the bridge.

Bryson stood. "He's pretty out of it. We should get him home."

His partner came down and took a look at me. "You feel sick?"

I nodded.

"You look sick," he said.

"What are you doing here?" Bryson asked. "This is a park. You can't sleep in a park overnight."

I glanced around. "Doesn't look like a park."

"It is according to the city of Empire Valley." He looked at his partner for confirmation, but the other cop just shrugged. "Anyway, it's public property."

"I am the public," I said.

"You want to be a wiseass? We'll put you in the back of that patrol car and haul you down to the station if you keep that up." Bryson narrowed his eyes at me.

"Can't you just write me a ticket or something?" I asked. I put my hand to my forehead, suddenly dizzy. I was hungry, too, and already sweating from the heat. I wanted my bed.

Bryson recognized me then, as I knew he would. There were very few full-time police officers in Empire Valley, which had the lowest crime rate in the Bay Area, according to the *Chronicle*. Bryson had been in the station the night I found Carly.

"What were you doing out here?" he asked again, suspicious. "Does this have anything to do with last year?"

"I don't know."

The other cop, whose name tag told me he was Officer Lopez, put a hand on my shoulder. "Let's get you out of here."

I tried to follow him up the creek bank, but I couldn't keep my balance and fell flat in the mud. I thought it might be all right just to lie where I fell.

Bryson slipped his hands under my armpits and tugged at me. "Come on, Neily, you've got to help me here," he grunted, digging his heels into the mud. "Steady as she goes there, captain. Lopez, help me get him in the car."

"Maybe we should take him to the hospital," Lopez suggested, and Bryson nodded.

We drove along Empire Creek Road slowly. I let my eyes go lazy and the trees blurred together. The sun was no longer showing. A blanket of clouds had blotted it out. I couldn't help feeling relieved; maybe it would rain soon and the heat wave would end. I put my head back against the seat and closed my eyes.

At the hospital they must have given me some kind of sleeping pill or a tranquilizer, because I woke up at four-thirty on Sunday afternoon feeling gruesome. I stared at the ceiling, bringing the cracks and paint bubbles into focus. I was in my bedroom and could hear somebody moving around downstairs. It was probably my mother, but then there was a low voice, my father's voice. The fact that he had come meant that, to them, this was serious.

I got out of bed and pulled on a pair of jeans. The room was hot and stuffy, so I quit rummaging around for a shirt and returned to the bed to gather myself. When I had left the house, my room had been a disaster, per usual: clothes—clean and dirty—heaped in piles on the floor, papers strewn all over my desk, garbage spilling out of the trash can. My mother had been in here. She had cleaned.

I finally ambled downstairs, trying not to look so much like a zombie, although God knows for whose benefit. I caught sight of myself in the hall mirror and drew back; my skin was a pale gray, the color of chewed gum, and my dark, wavy hair, which needed a cut, was plastered against my face. There were red creases where my cheeks had been pressed against the pillows. I looked like I was about to hurl. The sedatives hadn't sat well in my stomach; it churned at the smell of brownies coming from the kitchen. My mother had gone on a rampage of nervous baking. The kitchen counter was covered with platters, each piled high with a different baked good. My parents were at the kitchen table, arguing.

I cleared my throat. They stopped talking about me and looked up.

"Oh, Neily, you're awake," my mother clucked, getting out of her seat and wrapping her arms around me. I swayed a little, still unsteady on my feet. She pressed her hand against my forehead. "How are you feeling?"

"Like I've been hit by a truck."

My father didn't say anything. He just stared at me like he didn't know who I was. The house seemed smaller with him in it; his self-righteousness was crowding us out.

"What's he doing here?" I asked, opening the refrigerator and getting a carton of orange juice. My parents had divorced when I was seven, and I could have counted on two hands the number of times my father had visited since he'd moved out. They had joint custody, which was strictly enforced by my mother. She insisted I visit my father every other weekend and sometimes on major holidays, but I don't think either of us enjoyed our time together much.

"I called him. I was worried."

"Well, I'm fine. He can stop pretending to care and go home now."

"Neily, he's your father—"

"Would you two stop talking about me like I'm not even here?" my father shouted, pounding his fist against the table. "I'm in the goddamned room."

"Sorry, I guess we're just not that used to it," I snapped.

"Well, our son's being an asshole. I think that means he's back to normal." My father got up and stood behind my mother. He had almost a foot and a hundred pounds on her, but since the divorce, whenever we were together, he'd started putting her between the two of us, as if daring me to try something. I wasn't huge, but I was agile and strong—I could've taken him.

"Kevin, don't."

"I guess I can be going now, since he's awake." My father picked up his suit jacket and tossed it over his arm. "Glad you're not dead, Neily."

"That would be more convincing if you weren't looking at the door when you said it!" I shouted after him. The front door slammed. I slumped against the refrigerator, suddenly too weak to stand on my own.

My mother rushed over and put her hand under my arm. "You're too hard on him. He rushed right to the hospital when I called."

"*I'm* too hard on him? Why is it that the only time you ever stick up for him is when I'm the one who's mad at him?"

"What are you talking about?"

"You're always bitching about him, but the one time I need you to back me up, you rush to his defense." I shook her off. "I don't need your help."

"Maybe you should take another sedative. Sleep a little longer. It might make you feel better."

"No."

"Or you could eat something? I could make you toast? The doctor said nothing heavy for a while after you get up, but I could make soup?"

When she's worried, my mother speaks only in interrogative sentences. "You know what, Mom? I'm fine." I headed toward the stairs.

"Suit yourself. But if you're fine, then you can go to school tomorrow. Senior year. Go, Gaels!" My mother made a half-hearted fist in the air and gave me a small smile.

Senior year at Brighton Day School. Go, Gaels.

We lost a classmate last year, but you wouldn't know that from the way everyone was acting. It was all business as usual, laughing and showing off after a summer of leisure and pleasure. The big news on the quad was that Cass Irving got a new car, a black Mercedes SLK, and Lucy Miller had hooked up with a college guy down in Cabo San Lucas. Adam Murray, the tough, good-looking son of a cardiothoracic surgeon and his bombshell second wife, was the center of attention as always. The go-to guy for drugs at Brighton, Adam took top billing on the roster of the school's popular crowd. He seemed to command the school without ever really having any interest in it. He cared about nobody and nothing but himself.

Carly Ribelli, the girl who died, had been many things. She had been my first friend at Brighton, and my first girlfriend. It had ended badly, and I had never forgiven her for it. Carly had been smart, the brightest girl in our class. But she had also been reckless and damaged and lost, and the people she trusted to fix all of those problems had only made them worse. When I first met her, I had known none of those things, saw none of it coming. In retrospect, it was all there, down in the dark, cavernous part of the heart where anything might lurk, but when I met Carly she was, for all intents and purposes, an entirely different person than she was on the night she died, and I blamed Adam and his crew for that.

I would say that Carly fell in with the wrong crowd, but the truth is that there was no falling, no tumbling, no deceit on the part of the wrong crowd involved. Carly sought them out. *She* wooed *them,* anxious for something more than after-school study sessions and People with No Problems. Overnight, seemingly, she developed an affinity for kids with sharp edges. For Carly, this sort of social mobility involved ascension rather than collapse—these wastrels she wanted so desperately to befriend were not the gutter junkies teetering on the brink of expulsion, or the emo hipsters who sat behind the library at lunch smoking clove cigarettes and wanking about bands no one had ever heard of. Her target was Brighton royalty.

My classmates disgusted me most of the time, now more than ever. I knew that it was hypocritical—after all, I was one of them—but I couldn't help it. I felt bad for the Brighton Fund kids, students whose grades and standardized test scores were their free ride into the school but who were teased mercilessly for their lack of status. Every day at Brighton was a reminder of what I didn't want to be, what my father had tried so hard for years to make me become. By the time Carly died, I was already straining at my ropes, desperate to escape but incapable of finding a real way out, or too cowardly to try.

Brighton was in the foothills, with Empire Valley proper spread out beneath it. The rich kids all lived in the mansions bought with medical millions. Their fathers cured the sick in the valley, then scurried like cockroaches to their brightly lit palaces at the end of their shifts. My father, however, was an executive at a local software company, not a doctor—it was one of the many ways I didn't quite fit in.

I had a half hour to kill before first period (physics, advanced placement), so I headed to the library. There was a corner where nobody ever went, with a table and chairs. I'd been using it as my makeshift study since I started at Brighton four years before. Carly used to sit there with me; we became friends over that table. Like every other place on campus and in town, it reminded me of her. I could imagine her sitting there without even closing my eyes, hunched over a notebook, her face a mere inch or two from the page, long dark hair spilling over her shoulders.

This morning, Audrey Ribelli had beaten me there. Audrey was Carly's cousin, and was in the same year as us at Brighton. Shortly after Carly's murder, Audrey's father, Enzo, had been arrested for the crime. Audrey's maternal grandparents—with whom she was now living—had pulled her out of school. They were afraid, I'd heard, that she would be tortured if they forced her to return, which was probably what would have happened. As it was, I couldn't believe she was sitting here as if no time had passed, as if we were friends.

"What are you doing here?" I asked. Audrey and I hadn't been on good terms since the end of our freshman year. There was no reason—at least, none that I could think of—for why she was sitting at *my* table, waiting for *me.* It had to be some sort of joke.

"I'm back." She closed her book, putting a yellow note card in as a placeholder. "Try not to look so disappointed."

"You have no idea what you're in for," I told her. "They're going to crucify you."

"I'm not afraid of them," she said.

"Well, you should be. If you think they're going to let you forget whose kid you are, you're delusional. You'd be better off anyplace but here."

She looked at me squarely, unafraid, and for a moment I wondered if she really was prepared for how she would be treated.

"I don't understand you," I told her, shaking my head. "If I were you—"

"You're not me," she snapped.

"Thank God."

"I had to come back."

"I don't see why."

"That's what I came to talk to you about."

"Not interested. It's your problem. But don't say I didn't warn you." Which was probably more than I owed her.

She hesitated. "I heard about your . . . weekend."

"How?"

She shrugged. "People talk."

"Not to you."

"They'll talk to anyone with ears to hear. Word gets around. Are you okay?"

"I don't know why everyone is making such a big deal out of this. I'm fine."

She gave me an exasperated look. "Picked up by the police, Neily? Taken to the emergency room? In case you can't see them, those are red flags."

"I have a mother. I don't need you to worry about me."

"If you say so." She reached into her pocket and pulled out a chain-link bracelet, placing it in front of me on the table. "I thought you might want this."

The bracelet was silver, with a tag the size of a quarter inscribed with the initials CCR in a Gothic script. It had belonged to Carly; it was the gift I had given her for her fourteenth birthday.

"Where did you get this?" I asked.

"It was in the box of personal effects the police returned to my uncle Paul after the trial," Audrey said. "Carly was wearing it the night she died. You didn't notice that?"

"That's impossible."

"Not impossible," she said, getting up out of her chair. "True. Keep it. She would've wanted you to have it."

"Why would she . . . ?" I sat down, fingering the bracelet almost absently, lost in thought.

"I don't know. I thought *you* might."

I shook my head wordlessly. I couldn't imagine why Carly would have been wearing the bracelet on the night she died; she hadn't worn it, that I knew of, since we'd broken up the year before her death.

Audrey started to walk away. I looked up sharply and asked, "That's it?"

"That's it." Audrey looked as if there was something else

she wanted to say, but apparently thought better of it. "See you around, Neily."

"Yeah," I muttered, still clutching the bracelet in my fist. "See you."

When I got to my locker, it was almost time for the bell to ring. I had shoved Carly's bracelet in my pocket, aware, however obscurely, that it had no answers for me. Instead, there were only questions: Why had Carly been wearing it the night she died? And why had Audrey returned it to me now, under the pretense of simply wanting me to have it? I was sure it was a pretense, that there was an ulterior motive to her appearance in the library. I considered that maybe she had not come to give something to me, but to receive something—assurance, perhaps, that her decision to return to school had been the right one. Or that, even though her friends may have deserted her, I was someone she could count on.

Most of the other students were already in their first-period classrooms. My locker should have been empty except for a couple of books, but there was a folded piece of paper at the bottom. I held it up as if it were wired with explosives, carefully unfolding it.

It was a bad scan of a newspaper article that ran a year ago to the day. The picture that accompanied the item, Carly's last yearbook photo, was blotched and wrinkled, as if somebody had hurriedly shoved it into a copy machine. The bell rang, but I didn't feel like going to class. I shoved my books in my locker and sat down on a bench to read the clipping. I had read it before; I had read it about a hundred times. I was familiar with the details, but I couldn't help it.

EMPIRE VALLEY TEEN SLAIN

EMPIRE VALLEY, Calif.—Police are looking for any witnesses who may have information regarding the murder of 16-year-old Carly Ribelli.

The victim died of multiple gunshot wounds to the chest on Empire Creek Bridge late Sunday night. Authorities place her time of death at approximately 8:45 p.m.

Ribelli attended Brighton Day School in Empire Valley. She was the only child of surgeon Paul Ribelli and his late wife, Miranda.

The victim received a significant inheritance after the death of her grandmother. Police suspect that her uncommon wealth might have been a motive for her murder.

That was all the article had to say: Carly, her age, her parentage, her murder, and her money. Everything that mattered. Carly's inheritance came from her widowed grandmother on her father's side, who, due to some rift nobody really liked to talk about, skipped her two sons in favor of her granddaughters—Carly and Audrey—when it came to bequeathing her fortune.

There were two details that never made it into the papers;

they had nagged at me from the very beginning, but the police had suppressed them, perhaps because they didn't fit perfectly with their theory. The first was the complete lack of fingerprints on Carly's cell phone, which had been found in the front pocket of her jeans. The second was that, along with the gun that had killed her, a waterlogged digital recording device like the ones used by journalists had been dragged up from the bottom of the creek bed. Carly had owned one exactly like it, and when her bedroom was searched for evidence it had not turned up. It was obvious, at least to me, that the recorder belonged to her and that she had had it on her the night she died.

This was an early article, written before the police officially stated that they had a suspect in custody, before they arraigned and charged Audrey's father, before the town was invaded by a media circus and Carly's face was splashed all over the front page of every rag in the country.

I was the only person connected with the tragedy who didn't talk to a single reporter.

CHAPTER TWO

Eighth Grade—Fall Semester

I was admitted to Brighton for my eighth-grade year a few weeks after school had started. My parents had been trying to get me in for years; at first, they had assumed it would simply involve filling out some forms—my father was an alumnus, after all—but they had underestimated how popular private education had become in the East Bay after the toll that decades of education cuts had taken on the public school system. Brighton was filled to capacity. Eventually, however, a letter arrived congratulating me on my admission. Upon reading it, my father said, with a wide smile, "Somebody must've gotten expelled."

The Friday before I was supposed to start, Mr. Finch insisted on meeting with my parents and me. Back then, Finch's office was across the hall from where it is now. He was vice principal at the time, and his superior, Dr. Darling, was more of a phantom presence than an actual person. For all intents and purposes Finch ran the show. My father talked about him like they were old Brighton comrades, but the truth was that Finch hadn't attended Brighton, or any school even remotely like it—he was a proud graduate of PS 145, then rough-and-tumble Bushwick High School in Brooklyn, New York, before going on to Columbia and Yale. He was a wrong-tracks success story, and he meant for people to know it.

Finch was a broad-shouldered man who stood about six foot four and terrified the living daylights out of prospective students, and sometimes their parents. Our apprehension was largely unnecessary; unless a student was trouble, Finch was pretty fair. He especially loved the really smart Fund kids, doted on ███████ him of himself. They were ten███████se. For so many students, Br███████h liked those who saw it more a███████

I was ███████ite my father's wealth. Being wa███████have rejected me was more tha███████everything in my life had been rather compulsory—no-cut sports were forced to take me, even sometimes to play me; the Catholic grade school I was attending couldn't afford to turn me away; even my interpersonal relationships were either determined by genetics or engineered by a gaggle of socializing mothers. But Brighton had wanted me. I was chosen.

Overnight, fear and guilt had hardened into a block of pure anxiety. On the way to Brighton, my mother asked several times what was bothering me, but I couldn't articulate it. I certainly wasn't excited to see my father. I still suspected I might not live up to the expectations set by my acceptance to Brighton. I had been a standout student at my old school, but even my intelligence could be matched, and if there was any school in northern California where I could go from brilliant to ordinary it was Brighton. My father wouldn't stand for ordinary.

Like many California high schools, Brighton was a compound of low, squat buildings arranged around a quad where the students hung out between classes and ate lunch. At its inception, the school was modeled after the more traditional private schools on the East Coast, but the sixties and seventies had given it a hippie glaze. About fifteen years before I started classes, the board of directors had all the old brick buildings torn down and replaced with hip, sleek concrete ones with lots of sea green glass. The landscaping had been allowed to grow semiwild, in keeping with the natural environment of the foothills, and was only trimmed back twice a year—on Parents' Day, and right before graduation. Adjacent to the quad stood the library, which was surrounded on all sides but one by covered banks of lockers.

As I walked between my parents toward the building where Finch had his office, I saw Carly. I had no idea who she was, of course. It was lunchtime, and most students were milling around several outdoor tables, laughing and gossiping, teasing one another and eating. We walked around the quad at my request, passing through a smaller courtyard where there were only a few tables, all but one of which was empty. That's where Carly was sitting. She was reading, dark hair cascading over her shoulders, one leg tucked under the other, lips slightly pursed, a half-eaten apple in her left hand. Her right hand was holding the book open at the spine. I can't explain it, but I office was across the hall from where it is now. He was vice principal at the time, and his superior, Dr. Darling, was more of a phantom presence than an actual person. For all intents and purposes Finch ran the show. My father talked about him like they were old Brighton comrades, but the truth was that Finch hadn't attended Brighton, or any school even remotely like it—he was a proud graduate of PS 145, then rough-and-tumble Bushwick High School in Brooklyn, New York, before going on to Columbia and Yale. He was a wrong-tracks success story, and he meant for people to know it.

Finch was a broad-shouldered man who stood about six foot four and terrified the living daylights out of prospective students, and sometimes their parents. Our apprehension was largely unnecessary; unless a student was trouble, Finch was pretty fair. He especially loved the really smart Fund kids, doted on them, because they reminded him of himself. They were tenacious, grateful, eager to please. For so many students, Brighton was seen as a right—Finch liked those who saw it more as a privilege.

I was certainly one of the latter, despite my father's wealth. Being wanted by someplace that could have rejected me was more than a little thrilling. Until then, everything in my life had been rather compulsory—no-cut sports were forced to take me, even sometimes to play me; the Catholic grade school I was attending couldn't afford to turn me away; even my interpersonal relationships were either determined by genetics or engineered by a gaggle of socializing mothers. But Brighton had wanted me. I was chosen.

Overnight, fear and guilt had hardened into a block of pure anxiety. On the way to Brighton, my mother asked several times what was bothering me, but I couldn't articulate it. I certainly wasn't excited to see my father. I still suspected I might not live up to the expectations set by my acceptance to Brighton. I had been a standout student at my old school, but even my intelligence could be matched, and if there was any school in northern California where I could go from brilliant to ordinary it was Brighton. My father wouldn't stand for ordinary.

Like many California high schools, Brighton was a compound of low, squat buildings arranged around a quad where the students hung out between classes and ate lunch. At its inception, the school was modeled after the more traditional private schools on the East Coast, but the sixties and seventies had given it a hippie glaze. About fifteen years before I started classes, the board of directors had all the old brick buildings torn down and replaced with hip, sleek concrete ones with lots of sea green glass. The landscaping had been allowed to grow semiwild, in keeping with the natural environment of the foothills, and was only trimmed back twice a year—on Parents' Day, and right before graduation. Adjacent to the quad stood the library, which was surrounded on all sides but one by covered banks of lockers.

As I walked between my parents toward the building where Finch had his office, I saw Carly. I had no idea who she was, of course. It was lunchtime, and most students were milling around several outdoor tables, laughing and gossiping, teasing one another and eating. We walked around the quad at my request, passing through a smaller courtyard where there were only a few tables, all but one of which was empty. That's where Carly was sitting. She was reading, dark hair cascading over her shoulders, one leg tucked under the other, lips slightly pursed, a half-eaten apple in her left hand. Her right hand was holding the book open at the spine. I can't explain it, but I knew at first sight that we were two of a kind. Sitting alone like that, reading—that was the way I got through school.

My father stopped for a moment to point out the direction of the field house, because I was considering running track, but I left the job of listening to him to my mother and kept my eyes on Carly. She was pretty, but not so gorgeous that you couldn't look at her. Her face was round, her body soft and curvy, but those eyes were sharp and focused, the eyes of a person who saw the value of things. She took a large bite out of the apple and wiped away the juice with the back of her hand. She looked up, and our eyes met; her expression was the sort that you see on the face of someone who remembers you fondly, even if many years have passed since you last met.

Mr. Finch greeted us far more formally. For an administrator of a school where students were instructed to address teachers by their first names and dress to express themselves (although there was a dress code in place to prevent actual nudity), he was much stiffer and more conservative than I had expected him to be.

"Neiland, you go ahead and have a seat across from me there," he said, pointing to a chair.

I cleared my throat. "You can call me Neily," I told him.

Finch nodded and leaned forward in his chair. "Do you like St. Mary's, Neily?"

I looked at my father, who nodded encouragingly. I turned back to Finch and shrugged. "It's all right."

"Your father tells me that it's not intellectually stimulating or academically challenging enough for you. Do you think that's a fair assessment?"

"Sure." I was bored at St. Mary's and I was desperate to go to Brighton, despite my anxiety, but I had a hard time understanding exactly why we all needed to be in this office, why my father was showing me off like some trophy he'd won. I was uncomfortable being the center of attention. I didn't want to discuss *me*—I didn't want to discuss anything, really, with Finch or my parents. I just wanted to be let off the leash.

Finch's eyes flickered over to my father, who rolled his own and shook his head slightly. Finch sat back in his chair. "Well."

I glanced at my mother. She gave me a small smile and jerked her head slightly toward my father. Fine. I was glad to have him continue to speak for me, to settle everything so I could get on with what I wanted to do.

"The thing is, Mr. Finch—I think we spoke about this on the phone—Neily's schoolwork and test scores put him in the ninety-ninth percentile of children his age. We don't want all of his potential to go to waste in some parochial school when it could be so much better realized here," he said.

"I see," Finch said, trying not to look too enthusiastic. "We do have a place for him, as you probably gathered from the letter I sent you. Brighton is an excellent school; our resources are greater than most other institutions', and our students have a wide range of scholastic aptitudes and a large variety of interests. We also have a handful of very gifted students for whom we've developed a far more innovative program of study. I think it may suit Neily perfectly—if he's willing to participate."

My father beamed at me. "What do you think, Neils?"

"What sort of a program?" I asked.

"It's very independent," Finch said. My mother shifted in her chair. "I oversee the students' progress, assign them work, make sure they're following the curriculum that has been developed for them. They are supervised at all times during the school day, but aren't lectured to or tested as often as the other students. I believe—and most of the faculty agrees with me—that children who are so far advanced should be given space to learn, rather than strict guidelines to follow."

For the first time, my mother spoke up. "I'm sorry, Mr. Finch, I don't mean to be rude, but do you really think that giving Neily so much freedom will accelerate his learning? Can you honestly expect thirteen-year-olds to buckle down and do their work when there's nobody breathing down their necks?"

Finch looked at her blankly. My father frowned. "Mrs. Monroe, I assure you, the program has been in place for nearly ten years now, and not once has it failed a student. I will gladly put you in touch with parents whose children participated, and you may ask them any questions you like."

My mother nodded. "Yes, please. I'd like to do that."

"Mom, come on," I protested. I had my own reservations about the program as Finch had explained it. I was worried about making friends—if I was on my own ninety percent of the time, when would I meet people, who would I hang out with?—but I understood perfectly what Finch was getting at. This was a highly specialized, elite, and unconventional program, and he thought that *I* was smart enough to handle it. The part of me that was flattered, and the part of me that felt it was important to live up to the expectations of others, had won out, however marginally, over the part that was afraid of once again being the smart, odd boy who sat by himself during recess.

"Cathy, I don't think that's necessary," my father said firmly.

But my mother stood her ground. "I would like to speak with a parent. I'm sure Mr. Finch understands that."

"Absolutely." His face, however, said otherwise. "I'll have my assistant e-mail you a list."

My mother smiled, satisfied. My father looked angry, but I wasn't worried. The parents would tell my mother exactly what Finch had, and I would be allowed to make my own decision—to make my father's decision, rather. I didn't mind. For the first time ever, I was looking forward to school, and that had to mean something good.

Finch rose and shook my father's hand. "Now, would you like to meet one of the others?"

The program was small, consisting of roughly a dozen students grades seven through twelve. We were supposed to attend two regular classes a day, and the rest of our time we spent in the library or empty classrooms, toiling away at our independent study projects. Each of us was assigned an academic mentor (Finch, for some reason, intended on being mine) and required to participate in one cocurricular activity, the implication being that things like student council would properly socialize us. The day I paid my visit to Brighton, the rest of the students were scattered here and there around the school—in gym class, or in a session with their mentor, or off studying something complicated somewhere private. Carly seemed to be the only one that Finch could locate.

We toured the campus, trailing far behind my parents and Mr. Finch. Carly was not shy with her feelings about Brighton and the program.

"I'm glad you're here," she said, "because I can tell you're smart. I've been at Brighton since kindergarten, and almost everybody is worthless. I keep telling Finch I'm going to drop out and go to Carondelet when I finish middle grades."

I couldn't imagine this girl at a strict Catholic high school, but it occurred to me that she dressed sort of like she already attended one. Though Brighton students didn't wear uniforms, she had on a navy blue skirt that hung about two inches above her knees—when she bent down to pick up a book she had dropped, I noticed that she rolled it at the waist to shorten it, just like the girls at St. Mary's—a crisp white short-sleeved button-down shirt, untucked, and scuffed black Doc Martens with white socks. Several of the top buttons of her shirt were undone and she wore a white tank top underneath that skimmed over the top of her breasts, providing a peek of cleavage every once in a while when she moved. The girls at St. Mary's had just started to look like this the year before, coming back from the summer all tanned and curvy, to the overwhelming approval of us guys. But despite her appearance, Carly was in all other ways nothing like the girls at St. Mary's. First of all, no girl at my old school had ever gotten this close, close enough that I could smell the spearmint from her gum on her breath, or notice the way the hair around her temples was curling up slightly in the heat. Second, she was easygoing and calm, and she made all my anxiety melt away with one well-placed eye roll and a friendly smile.

"Would you really change schools?" I asked.

She shook her head and smiled. "No. My dad wouldn't let me. I just say it for the reaction. One thing you'll learn is, even though he tries to be intimidating, Finch doesn't treat us kids in the program like regular students. He yells at us more, but he lets us get away with more, too."

Carly was the only child of a doctor and his wife; the Ribellis seemed to have a reasonably happy marriage, no doubt lubricated by money. Her mother didn't have a job, preferring to spend her time on charity work: "Which you can't blame her for," Carly said, as if I had suggested otherwise.

She asked what my mother did, and I told her, "Nurse," adding "pediatric" a second later because it made my mother sound like she loved children, even though she'd only had one.

"Cool," Carly said. She asked where I went to school now, and I told her.

"Do you like it?"

"Not really."

She pushed a long, stick-straight piece of hair behind her ear. "Where do you live?"

"In the valley, with my mom. Off Argot Canyon Road."

She nodded. "There's a really great restaurant down there."

"The Calamity Diner," I said.

"Great burgers. We should go sometime." From the way she said it I knew we would. That was the thing about Carly and me—we fit from the very beginning. We were friends in an instant, and despite everything that happened later, it was something I don't regret, because it has never happened to me again.

I looked down at the book she was holding. "What are you reading?"

She glanced at it briefly, as if she'd forgotten she had it. "Oh. It's just an old book of short stories."

"By who?"

"Edgar Allan Poe."

"Ah."

She held up her hand to shield her eyes from the sun. "I think we lost them."

We had reached the student parking lot on the edge of campus. "Maybe we should go back," I said, not meaning it.

"If you want. Do you have somewhere to be?"

"My parents called me out of school," I told her.

"That's not really what I meant." She reached back and gathered her hair into a ponytail, twisting it up into a knot, then letting it fall. "You should come over to my house. We can hang out. I mean, it's boring, but it's not school. My mom'll take you home later."

"Don't you have class or something?" I asked.

"Finch'll let me go home early," Carly said. "I've been staying late this week doing extra algebra tutoring. That's one of the perks of the program—flexible hours."

I thought about what my mother would say about this particular perk. "Okay," I agreed, knowing my parents probably wouldn't go for it.

But they did. My father thought it was a great idea, and my mother, though no doubt secretly dismayed, put up a great front. This way, she could finish her shift this afternoon, she said, even though I knew that she had been investigating movie times in the newspaper that morning—I had found a few matinee showings circled, films I had mentioned wanting to see.

It turned out that Carly lived down the street from my father's McMansion in the hills. Not wanting to trespass on Mrs. Ribelli's goodwill, he offered to pick me up from her house when I was ready to go home and then deliver me back into the arms of my mother. It was a ridiculous business, this attempt at politeness and civility; my father was a performer, and I was the ventriloquist's dummy. I didn't know it at the time, but Carly was about to change all that.

CHAPTER THREE

Senior Year

Harvey Rosenberg was the only person at Brighton who talked to me now without needing a reason. He was on scholarship, and he lived in a house near my mom's in the valley. Harvey had transferred in the middle of sophomore year when a Brighton Fund spot finally opened up, so while he knew who Carly was, he had no real connection to her and no personal interest in her death.

I had quit the independent study program the previous September, one of the few decisions in my life so far that was both right and my own. Harvey and I ended up in all the same classes. I was comfortable around him, and we got along well. He was very smart and an all-around good guy—generous, laid-back, and friendly. He had a girlfriend, a blandly pretty brown-haired junior named Jules Grover. They were constantly groping each other at the lockers. She stayed away from me, though, and encouraged him to avoid me as much as possible, but Harvey wasn't the sort of person who dabbled in rumor, or even heard what people were saying for the most part. He was a life raft in a sea of assholes.

Harvey sought me out at the break, wondering where I'd been. Since I was late for class, I had found a shady place underneath the bleachers to read and wait out first period. "Hey, where were you this morning? Phyllis assigned lab partners."

"Oh yeah? Who'd you get?" I didn't want to tell him about the article.

"You, you moron. She almost didn't let me because you were missing, but I turned on the charm and she was conquered. Although," he continued, "she advised me to inform my partner that AP does not stand for 'absences permitted.' So, in other words, show your ass up from now on."

"Will do. Any homework?"

Harvey scoffed. "Please, dude, this is *Phyllis*. We're supposed to split the atom before Thursday."

"Copy the syllabus for me during your office hour?"

"Fine. Are you coming to our next class, or you planning on spending the whole day wandering campus? Because if that's your intention, I would suggest going home."

"Thinking about it," I said, squinting into the sun.

The newspaper article was in my back pocket. I don't know why I didn't just throw it in the trash. I had considered who might have been behind the little gift. At first I wondered about Audrey, but chucked that idea almost immediately; we weren't on the friendliest terms, especially considering how cold I'd been to her that morning in the library, but she wasn't the type to put energy into unnecessary malice. Finally I figured it must have been someone from Audrey and Carly's old group of friends, specifically BMOC Adam Murray. He disliked me on principle, considering me one of the eggheads he was, by virtue of his popularity, bound by duty to hassle whenever it was convenient. But he had another big reason to give me a hard time: He was Carly's boyfriend right before she died. He was the guy she dumped me for.

Ever since Carly's murder, rumors had run rampant about me. Even though someone else had been tried and found guilty, there were always whispers: *How is it that he was the one who found her? What was he doing there? Didn't they used to go out? What if he killed her?* There was no doubt in my mind that Adam and the rest of Carly's old friends—if you could call them that—were the ones who started people talking. I would've been more upset, but the unintended effect of the rumors was that they gave me what I wanted—my privacy—because very few people wanted to hang out with or talk to me after that. Except for Harvey. His willful ignorance of any and all school gossip was a fireproof blanket wrapped around my shoulders, one that I accepted with no hesitation whatsoever. It was worth coming to school to be reminded of that.

"What's up, man? You're clearly not on today. Somebody forget to flip your switch this morning?" Harvey asked.

I shook my head. "No sleep."

"Video games?" Harvey said, nodding his head in a show of sympathy.

"Yep," I lied.

"Same here. But I got a latte before school, so I'm alert. You should look into large doses of caffeine, my man, if you're going to maintain the virtual lifestyle. I do a run every morning if you ever want me to pick you up something." He gave me a soft punch in the shoulder. "I'm going to catch up with Jules on the quad before nap time. Save me a seat in the back."

We had AP English next (nap time for Harvey, who favored the hard sciences), so I headed over to the humanities building, hoping that they'd fixed the Coke machine over the summer. They hadn't. I was early for class; even Carmen, our teacher, wasn't there yet. I took a seat near the door, as far from the blackboard as possible, and put my bag on the one next to it.

Carmen came in first, her arms full of books, several of which toppled to the floor as she crossed the threshold. I picked them up for her and placed them on her desk, where she dumped her own armload. Wheezing from the effort, Carmen smiled her thanks at me and I headed back to my seat.

"Wait, Neily!" she called. I turned.

"Take one," she said. I took a book off the desk and looked at the spine: *Crime and Punishment*.

"This should be fun," I said.

"It will be hell. But you'll thank me later."

"Might as well give me one for Harvey while you're at it," I said. Carmen handed me a second copy as other students began to file in. "Not that he'll read it."

"Defamation of character," Harvey protested from behind, which made Carmen laugh.

The last person to stroll into class was Audrey. I was surprised to see her there. I'd never had an advanced class with her, ever, as she wasn't an AP sort of girl. Even Harvey, oblivious to almost everything, leaned over to me and asked, "Is she lost or something?"

She walked with the air of a visiting dignitary and surveyed the room, scoping for a good seat. The first place she looked was straight to where Harvey and I were sitting, but the back row filled up the fastest in every class at Brighton and there were no empty seats. Finally, she was forced to take one up front.

Halfway through class the second-period office aide came in quiet as a cat and handed Carmen a small blue slip of paper. Seeing the color, I knew it was for me.

"Neily?" Carmen waved the piece of paper. I gathered my things from around my desk and went up to the front to retrieve it.

"You're excused," Carmen told me unnecessarily. When you get a summons from the school psychiatrist, it's never a question of whether or not you're excused.

Eighth Grade—Fall Semester

My anxiety returned as Carly and I made our way up the drive of her very large, very elegant home. It looked nothing like my father's house, which was ostentatious and cold, the embodiment of new money. People sometimes say that all California money is new money, but there is a difference between the people who know how to hide it and the people who don't even know it's something to be ashamed of. Still, I cringed the way I always did when I went to visit my father, and felt the icy blast of separateness travel up my spine. *You don't belong here,* everything—every object, every room, every piece of art or furniture—seemed to be saying. *This is not your place.*

Miranda, Carly's mother, tried her best to set me at ease. She welcomed me warmly, brought me into the kitchen to point out where they kept the snacks and the sodas, then took off for parts unknown, pausing to rumple Carly's hair and say, "Have fun, kids," before disappearing.

The afternoon consisted largely of Carly and me watching television, but mostly I just watched her. When she became absorbed, her face, usually so animated, would go absolutely still, and she would purse her lips. I would always catch her doing this when we were reading. Once, I pointed it out to her, and she tried very hard not to do it again. That was the funny thing about her—she never seemed to give much of a damn about what anybody thought. But she did—she really, really did.

After an hour or so, it occurred to me that I might want to see the rest of the house. It didn't look like Carly was going to offer to give me a tour, so I asked her where the bathroom was— "Down the hall, to the right, past the fountain"—and then marveled inwardly a little at the idea of a fountain in the Ribelli's front hall.

In actuality, the fountain was less like the Trevi of my imaginings and more like a piece of tin mounted on the wall, with water running over its surface in whispering rivulets. Miranda Ribelli was sitting in the living room, which was on the opposite side of the hall, reading a Michael Crichton novel and sipping a glass of white wine. I went into the bathroom and ran the faucet, staring at myself in the mirror.

My hair needed a cut—it always did. I looked myself over from head to toe, wondering what Carly saw when she looked at me. What I saw was unpromising—a gangly boy, tall and lanky, with arms that were strong but lacked tone and a countenance that lacked conviction. I had no idea who I was, despite

33

all the people in my life telling me, and you could see it in my face. That was the part of me that I wanted to hide from Carly, who seemed so sure of herself.

When I came out of the bathroom, Miranda (who from that day forward insisted that I call her by her first name) was gone and the coast was clear.

The floors were hardwood, so I removed my shoes, set them by the front door, and padded up the stairs in my socks. I had no idea what I was looking for. In the hall, on a long credenza, there were photos of Carly as a baby—chubby-cheeked, blue-eyed, and, amazingly, blond. By the time she was walking, her hair had darkened; in the photo I picked up, she looked to be about two years old. She was toddling forward, arms outstretched for something uncaptured. As I walked down the hallway, I watched Carly grow from an affectionate child who pressed kisses against her mother's cheek to a contemplative six-year-old who was most often shown reading a book to a proud nine-year-old holding up a trophy won in a horseback riding competition. Obviously, someone in the house fancied himself or herself a photographer. The most recent spatter of portraits could be most appropriately titled Carly in Nature—Carly picking apples, Carly petting a sheep, Carly reading in a tree, Carly swimming in a lake. They all seemed to have been taken in the last year or so.

I heard water running in the walls, and took this to mean somebody had flushed a toilet or run a faucet nearby. Not wanting to be caught snooping, I opened the first door I saw. I thought it was a guest room because it was so neat, but in moments I realized that it was, in fact, Carly's own bedroom.

Instead of the requisite pink, Carly's room was done up in hues of light blue and green. Everything was perfect, as if it was a professional job, which, I reasoned, it probably was. Later, Carly would tell me that before marrying her father, Miranda had been an interior decorator at a well-respected design house in San Francisco. She seemed as proud of that fact as Miranda seemed of her daughter's fourth-grade dressage trophy—that is, hugely.

Carly's bedroom was practically the size of the living room in my mother's house. She had a large four-poster bed, which was covered with a blue, green, and white patchwork quilt and piled high with pillows. There was a light green love seat pressed up against the wall in one corner, and a matching arm-chair with an ottoman. Carly had a large white rolltop desk with what looked like a brand-new laptop and state-of-the-art speakers sitting on it, and a smaller white vanity with a large mirror that was littered with female mysteries. The walls were painted sky blue; I'd find out later that it was the only room in the entire house with carpeting.

"My sanctuary." Carly was standing in the doorway, shoulder mashed against the doorjamb, arms crossed and eyebrow lifted. "Are you lost?"

"N-no," I stammered, trying to think up a good excuse for being in her bedroom uninvited. There really wasn't one. "Yes. I'm lost."

She shook her head and smiled. "I don't believe you. It's nice, huh?"

"Uh, sure."

"I hate it," she confided. "It's like a Laura Ashley catalog threw up in here. But my mother insisted. She thought it was *so me.*"

"It isn't?" The room was bright and confident and per-fectly collected, which was how Carly seemed.

"Oh, God no. This is Easter on morphine. Pastel paradise." She shuddered.

"Why don't you say something?" I asked.

She shrugged. "My mother really loved the idea. She designed the whole room. It'd break her heart if I told her I hated it."

It struck me how kind and mature that sentiment was, abnormally so for someone our age. I fought with my mother over everything, from school to the intramural sports she was constantly trying to sign me up for to what brand of hot dogs we bought at the supermarket. It never occurred to me to shut up and deal with some things in order to protect her feelings or make her life more bearable.

"You're nice," I said, lamely. But it was how I felt.

"Thanks." She grinned. "Now get out of here. I can't believe I caught you snooping."

When my father picked me up that night, I could tell he had had a martini or two and was feeling affable. As I climbed into the car—he hadn't bothered to come to the door, preferring to honk instead—and buckled my seat belt, he asked, "How was it? Did you have fun?"

"Yeah," I said, when what I really meant was, *I never want to go home again.*

Senior Year

The school psychiatrist's office was a fascinating spectacle of ego in bloom. The good doctor, who insisted we call her Harriet ("Like all the other teachers"), kept her office impeccably neat. Her books, all academic texts and journals, were arranged alphabetically by title on frequently dusted shelves; her walls were covered with every diploma, certificate, award, and letter of recognition—framed—that she had ever received in her short career; every object in the room was turned ever so slightly toward the one chair that sat on the opposite side of the desk. It was as though Harriet wanted the student, her patient, to feel like he or she was the center of everything. It might have reassured some, but I found it vaguely unsettling, so when Harriet's back was turned I liked to subtly shift a few of the items to take off some of the pressure.

Harriet had no photos of friends or family to indicate that she had a private life, but whether it was a matter of personal taste, or an effort to make herself seem a little more human for our comfort, or just a sad attempt at cultivating an eccentricity, every spare inch of Harriet's desk was covered with seashells. I would guess that, on average, Brighton students spent eighty percent of their time staring at the seashells and wondering if their presence was some kind of test.

"Are you still having nightmares, Neily?" Harriet tilted her head slightly and gave me a tight smile.

I'd been seeing Harriet more or less regularly since Carly died. Everybody, from my parents to the principal, insisted on it. They said I needed therapy to help me cope with the tragedy, with everything I saw. By the time she died, I hadn't spoken to Carly in almost a year, but by discovering her body on the bridge that night, I had accidentally stumbled into the middle of something devastating, and people were worried.

"They're not nightmares," I told her. "They're just dreams."

"The dreams, then—are you still having them?"

I shrugged. "Sometimes." *Every night.*

"And the sleeping pills I prescribed for you aren't helping?"

"No." They did me no good sitting in the back of my medicine cabinet, hidden behind a box of Band-Aids.

"Are you even taking them?"

I hesitated. "No."

Harriet sighed heavily, like I'd let her down. "Why not?"

"I don't want to become dependent on them. That happened to a kid I knew." *On television.*

"I wouldn't have suggested you take them if I didn't think they would help you," Harriet said. "If you take them responsibly and don't abuse them, then there shouldn't be a problem."

I shrugged. I wasn't really interested in the sleeping pills. Yes, I was having trouble sleeping, and yes, that was partly due to the fact that I often experienced nightmares, many of which involved Carly and any number of absurd dream-scenarios connected to her death and the memories of finding her body. I didn't know what the dreams meant—I don't even know if I believe that dreams can *mean* anything—but I wanted them to go away on their own, I didn't want to drug them into submission. To me, that just seemed like putting a lid on a problem and expecting it to go away, which in my experience rarely works. That, combined with how I felt the day before when the sedatives from the hospital had worn off, convinced me I was not the sort of person who would benefit from the use of sleeping pills.

Harriet put down her pen and leaned forward just slightly. "Can I be completely honest with you?"

"Sure." I doubted that she was capable of complete honesty, but I was eager to hear her evaluation of me. After all, I'd been seeing her for over a year and she had never given me any feedback other than a prescription for Ambien.

"I'm worried about you."

I scoffed.

"It's been over a year since it all happened and you don't seem to have come to terms with the loss in any significant way. That concerns me."

"Yeah, well, it's kind of hard to get over something like that."

"I am aware of that. No one is suggesting that you should just 'get over it'—trauma like you experienced isn't commonplace. It takes time."

"That's exactly what I just said."

"The problem is that you're not trying to work through what happened. Instead you're trying to bury it inside of you, which is counterproductive to the healing process."

"Wow," I said, picking up a seashell from her desk and tossing it from palm to palm. "That's deep."

"I'd prefer it if you wouldn't touch my things," she said, holding out her hand for the seashell. I gave it over without argument, squinting at her.

"Maybe you could use some therapy yourself, Harriet."

She ignored me. "I believe I was saying that it's unhealthy to try to push things deep inside of you instead of letting them go. You'll never move on that way." She took in a deep breath and sat back in her chair. This is how I knew the clincher was coming. "Then again, maybe you don't want to move on."

I slumped in my seat and heaved a melodramatic sigh. "There it is."

"Why do you keep punishing yourself?"

"You think I'm responsible for what happened?"

"No, but it's obvious that you do."

"That's crazy. I don't blame myself. Enzo Ribelli killed Carly, and he's in jail. What have I got to feel bad about?"

"Okay, maybe you don't realize it, but I think that the nightmares are definitely a sign of latent guilt. The sleeping pills are a temporary solution, because you need sleep to live. But if you want the nightmares to stop, you'll have to face whatever it is that's causing them to manifest."

"They're just dreams."

"Right." She glanced at her watch. "It looks like we're out of time for today. We'll pick this up again next week."

"Can't wait," I remarked, getting up and slinging my bag over my shoulder. "How long am I going to have to keep coming here?"

Harriet paused. "I don't know. I'll have to speak to your parents about that."

"Great."

I opened the door and turned to leave, slamming into Audrey on her way in. The contents of my backpack went skittering across the hallway. Audrey and I bent down to gather them up.

"Oh, hi!" she said brightly, but falsely. She handed me a stack of notebooks.

"Sorry," I mumbled.

She shook her head. "No problem."

"Everything okay?" Harriet called.

Audrey smiled anxiously and shifted from one foot to the other. "Weekly appointment," she said.

Harriet appeared at the door. "Hi, Audrey. Come on in." She shot me an impatient smile. "Class, Neily?"

"Yeah." I glanced at Audrey one more time and started down the hall.

The last words I heard Harriet say to Audrey: "I'm so glad you decided to start seeing me."

"So, what words of wisdom did the headshrinker have for you today?" Harvey asked, falling into step beside me as I made my way to my next class.

"Huh?" I wasn't really listening. I was considering the odds of running into Audrey outside of Harriet's office. I mean, the school had approximately five hundred students, so the odds of running into anybody anywhere on campus were pretty high if you did the math, but still.

"Blue slip. Harriet the Spy? They should really stop color coding—everybody knows when you've been called to her office," Harvey said.

"Yeah, right. Weekly checkup. Pretty standard."

"I don't mean when *you've* been called to her office," Harvey backpedaled. "I mean, you know, anyone. Lots of people get blue slips."

"Don't worry about it, man. Hey—what do you think about Audrey being in Carmen's class with us?" I asked.

"Uh, I don't know. I wasn't aware I would be expected to form an opinion."

"Off the top of your head."

"It's weird. Don't you think it's weird? Wasn't she always moping around in the dumb classes, with Cass and Adam and . . . all them? I mean, we only overlapped for like six months in sophomore year, but wasn't that the way it was?"

"That's what I was thinking. Padding the resume in preparation for college applications?"

"I guess. Although I always thought it was a foregone conclusion she was going to USC, since her grandmother donated, like, a *building* or something."

I shrugged.

"Why?"

"No reason. Thought it was weird."

"Well, I agree. It is weird."

It got weirder in AP government, when Audrey came in halfway through class and took the last remaining seat in the front row for the second time that day. Harvey, who was sitting in front of me, turned around and raised his eyebrows. I did my best to look uninterested.

Chapter Four

An hour later, I sat alone with my lunch. I was twisting off the stem of an apple when Audrey emerged from the library and took a seat at an empty table. I shifted to get a better view. She put down her tray and pulled a book from her bag, the same book that she had been reading in the library that morning. She didn't appear to have noticed me, and she rarely looked up from whatever she was doing to glance around. Over the course of the hour, not one person came up to talk to her. The rest of the seats at Audrey's table, as at mine, remained vacant.

The past year had been hard on Audrey. Her father's arrest and conviction for Carly's murder had been disastrous, especially since she and Carly had been so close. She and I had been friends briefly at the beginning of high school, and I remembered her as quiet, well behaved, smart but no genius like Carly, with very little interest in really trying. Her family situation, even back then, was considered amply tragic; Enzo, notorious in Empire Valley during his youth, was an alcoholic and compulsive gambler who squandered his wife's trust fund at the Indian casinos, and Audrey's mother had left for good when Audrey was in the sixth grade. When Enzo had brought his daughter back to Empire Valley, the town was simultaneously scandalized and relieved: scandalized that Enzo Ribelli was once again living within their borders and relieved that his daughter had been returned to the bosom of her more responsible and upstanding family members. When she moved back to town, Audrey was showered with both pity and praise, for about ten minutes before everyone forgot about her and all they could talk about was Enzo's latest exploits.

Carly took it upon herself to befriend Audrey and put every bit of effort she could spare into understanding, loving, and sympathizing with her. This was the summer before our freshman year, soon after Carly's mother was diagnosed with the ovarian cancer that killed her less than a year later. Their connection wasn't anything I particularly understood, but it was real and strong and largely unaffected by Carly's later transformation. I hadn't hung out with Audrey since the end of our freshman year at Brighton—since Carly broke up with me, in fact—and I certainly wasn't interested in striking up an acquaintance now, even though we seemed to be fellow outcasts.

Apart from the obvious, Audrey's penance for being the daughter of a murderer was social ruin. She was bearing up as well as could be expected. I could barely remember her from the previous year—in my memories of the police investigation, depositions, and trial, she hovered only at the very periphery, if I could recall her presence at all. Audrey fascinated the papers. I assume it was because she and Carly were like sisters, roughly the same age, and both students at Brighton. The word used most often in the articles to describe her was "stoic," so that is how I pictured her: silent and stone-faced, absorbing everything.

For cousins, Audrey and Carly looked nothing alike. Carly had inherited her mother's creamy Irish skin, straight dark hair, and brilliant china blue eyes, the envy of every girl in our class. She was much shorter than Audrey, petite and curvy and certainly eye-catching, but there was no doubt that Audrey was the gorgeous one. Audrey was solid, tall, and athletically built. Her skin was darker, always a little tan courtesy of her Italian blood, but she had gotten her mother's blond hair, green eyes, and flushed, heart-shaped face.

Through a combination of good looks, patience, and plain dumb luck, Audrey managed to attract the attention of Cass Irving, the most popular guy in our class and a very promising basketball player. Only a few days after Carly's murder, Cass—under pressure from his parents and his friends to disassociate himself from Enzo's daughter—unceremoniously cut his ties with Audrey. He might as well have taken her out to sea and thrown her overboard; the friends her relationship with Cass had attracted dispersed quickly, and though I suppose that I should have admired Audrey's resilience, at the time I felt as though she had gotten what was coming to her. I certainly didn't feel sorry for her. I guess I thought things would inevitably get better once she moved into her maternal grandparents' mansion in the hills, reminding everyone that she was actually part of Empire Valley's elite, but that never happened. She had been tutored privately throughout the trial last year, but now she was back and I hadn't seen one person make an effort to speak to her. Her old friends appeared to be giving her an extremely wide berth. It was strange seeing Audrey without a swarm of people. She didn't seem built to be a loner.

When the bell rang for sixth period, Audrey closed her book, got up, and disappeared into the cool darkness of the science building. I gathered my things and ran after her.

"So, I have a question," I said, falling into step beside her.

"Sure, go ahead."

"How did you get into AP English? I didn't even know you could read."

She stopped and turned to stare at me, her expression not so much offended as bemused. "Does it bother you?"

I hesitated before saying, "No, why should it?"

She shook her head and continued walking. "Finch let me into AP classes because of all the work I did last year with my tutor. Caring about school isn't exclusively for the brain trust, you know, Think Tank."

"Don't call me that." Think Tank was what Audrey and Carly's dumbass group of friends—Adam Murray in particular—called me.

She shrugged. "Mind if I go to biology now? It's the first day—I want to get a good seat."

"Sure, fine. Be my guest," I said sarcastically.

"Don't worry, Neily," she said. "It has nothing to do with you."

"I didn't think it did," I lied.

When I got home, my mother was already at the hospital. She had left me a frozen packaged casserole to heat up and a note saying my father had called to check in. When my father was on a paternal kick, it was better to let my mother answer the phone, or let the call go to the machine. That way, he was able to prove he cared without ever having to speak to me. The presence of a middleman assured him that yes, he was a good father, but circumstances beyond his control had made me unavailable to him. Then we both got what we wanted.

I took an energy drink out of the refrigerator and popped the tab. There was plenty I could do, but I didn't feel like it. The thing was, I didn't feel like much of anything. Even wasting my time watching television didn't seem remotely appealing. I lay on the couch, draining can after can of Red Bull, listening to cars peel out on the street and neighbors arguing on their front lawns.

The couch also offered an excellent vantage point from which to look out the window and observe the comings and goings of the neighborhood, something I took advantage of. For about an hour I stared out at a car parked across the street. It was a nice car, a BMW, painted an understated shade of dark blue—not the sort of vehicle I often saw pull up within twenty blocks of my driveway. And as the light shifted, I began to notice something moving, a shadow—there was someone in the car. And they had been sitting there for a while. I thought back to earlier, when I arrived home. Had I seen the car then? Or did it appear later?

It took me a while, but eventually, after dredging through my memory bank, I recognized the vehicle. I was unsure of what to do next. I didn't want to be paranoid, but wasn't there something illegal about following a person home from school and sitting outside their house for hours at a time with no clear and upright motive for doing so? I was certain I could make a case for it somehow. So I went to the kitchen, picked up the phone, and reported Audrey's car to the police.

CHAPTER FIVE

My mother still insisted on driving me to school, even though I had told her over and over again that I was fine. I was early, which often happened when I got a ride, so I went to the library as usual. I expected to see Audrey sitting in Carly's old seat again, but she wasn't there. I was relieved, but also a little disappointed. I had provoked her, and I was looking forward to seeing what she would do next.

Before class I got ahold of Harvey and copied his homework. Harvey normally didn't care that I kept things close to the vest, but he was still human. He did sometimes betray a casual interest.

"I called your cell this morning but it went straight to voice mail."

"You did?"

"Yeah. I was on my way to Starbucks and wanted to check in, see if you wanted something."

"Sorry. I didn't even hear it ring." I didn't remember putting my cell in one of my pockets, but I patted them down anyway just to make sure. I figured I must have left it in my backpack.

"No problem. You were probably on the other line with 1-800-HOT-GIRLS or something."

I smiled and shrugged. "I can never get Natasha to shut up. I keep telling her I've got to go to school, but she won't let me off."

"Imaginary girlfriends are such a drag."

He grinned and held up a sketch he'd been working on of Phyllis, our physics instructor, complete with horns and a tail. "Nice, huh?"

"Perfect likeness. Except that you forgot the fangs."

In AP physics, just as we were sitting down to a chapter on vectors, a slip came for me via the office aide. This time it was yellow, which meant that I had been summoned to the principal's office, to see Finch.

Back when Finch was only the vice principal, he spent most of his time devising a scheme to oust Dr. Darling, his predecessor, whose outward hostility and indifference toward all students made it abundantly clear that he had no intention of living up to the tender disposition that his name suggested.

I never officially met Darling, but many of my earliest Brighton memories are shadowed by Finch's presence. Eventually, Darling retired, and there I was, heading to meet with Finch in the principal's office, just as he'd always dreamed.

I handed my slip to the receptionist, who barely looked up from her computer screen. "He's waiting for you," she said. "Just a heads-up, he doesn't look happy."

"What's new?"

I barreled into Finch's office unannounced and planted myself in front of his desk. "If this is about my grades, I remember our three-hour parent-teacher conference last June and I am perfectly aware that my GPA is on eagle-eyed watch. Now that I've boiled this scolding down to its essential elements, am I free to go?" I knew I was just asking for trouble, talking to Finch like that, but my relationship with His Majesty, King of Brighton, was unusual. My stint as his program mentee had forged a more casual, almost familial bond between us, one that I had simultaneously resented and exploited since leaving the program.

Finch looked up, not amused. "Sit down, Neily."

I flopped down in a chair. "So I can assume that something other than my 'disappointing academic performance' last year earned me a yellow slip this morning?"

"I found out about your little episode last weekend," Finch told me, scrawling his name on a piece of paper and putting it aside.

"From who?"

"Your father."

"Figures." I leaned back and stared at the ceiling.

"He's very worried about you and thought that I, as your mentor, should know about it."

"Jesus, you're not my mentor, Finch. It was nothing. A blip. I wasn't getting any sleep and I just fell off the grid for, like, a day. But I'm back, and I'm fine, and I even completed all of my summer assignments, so unless you called me in here to give me a gold star and a pat on the back for finally listening to you, I'd like to return to class now. I'm missing vectors."

"I should think that your mental health would be more of a priority to you under the circumstances, Neily. Aren't you sick of parading around like what happened doesn't bother you?"

"I'm fine. That's what I told Harriet, and I'm not going to change my story and sob my heart out on your shoulder just because you put your 'I care' face on all special for me this morning."

"You need to let people help you," Finch said, struggling to sound sympathetic. "You need to really talk to someone instead of using humor and sarcasm as a defense. If you keep holding on to everything that happened, you're never going to move forward the way you need to."

"For Christ's sake, close the textbook and open your ears. *I'm. Fine.*" I leaned forward and said it slowly. He stared at me without blinking. "I'm just tired of everybody treating me like I'm some kind of mental patient. I don't owe you an explanation, and I don't need your sympathy or your support. If anybody needs to move forward and stop holding on, it's you." I got up and headed for the door.

"I'm just looking out for your best interest."

"Yeah. Keep telling yourself that."

Eighth Grade—Fall Semester

Carly and I spent long hours in the library, at a little table in the back near the stacks that Carly called the Nest. Our supervisors—teachers who had offered to oversee our progress in various subjects—would drop by for fifteen minutes each sometime during the day, to give us new assignments, hand back old ones, and gather up our completed exercises. Finch himself paid us several visits a day, mainly to make sure we weren't goofing off, and Gert, the librarian, was supposed to keep an eye on us the rest of the time. We took gym and music appreciation with the other students in our grade, but mostly we just sat in the back and practiced looking bored. God, were we insufferable then—no wonder everybody avoided us.

We worked hard. There was more pressure than either of us really understood, but we could feel it bearing down on us all the same, pushing up against our backs. Every once in a while, Carly would stand over me, resting her chin on my shoulder while she read what I had written; sometimes, she would hand me something, or take something from me, and her fingers would comb my palm; once, she got up to go to the bathroom and rumpled my hair as she passed, just to rile me; in these moments, the pressure would lift.

It had only been a few months since we met, but it felt as though we'd known each other since we were children. We hung out together after school every day. Most of the time, we would walk the mile or so to Carly's house and do our home-work together or just hang out before I got a ride home. Some-times, though, we would go to the bridge.

Carly liked Empire Creek Bridge. Of the two ways to get to

her house, it was the quickest, and the less traveled. We hardly ever saw anyone there.

One day we were hanging out on the bridge, just before dark, a time when the valley gets rosy and dim. I had to be home in a half hour for dinner; soon, Carly and I would trudge up the hill together, and my father's housekeeper would drive me back to my mother's on her way home.

We were leaning against the bridge wall, next to each other, talking. I don't recall the conversation; I suspect it must have been a pretentious, faux-intellectual discussion that amounted to little more than meaningless navel-gazing. To annoy me, Carly hoisted herself up on top of the wall, which was high enough to reach my rib cage while I was standing. Crouching, she reached out her hand for me to catch.

"Help me up."

I did as she asked, briefly considering the danger involved in such a venture. The bridge was not so high, but it was a good ten feet from the lip of the wall to the bottom of the creek. I was afraid she might fall. But Carly stood, occasionally tottering, as if she had just stepped off a boat, before steadying herself. She looked over her shoulder at me and beamed.

I laughed and let go of her hand. "You better watch yourself or you'll fall," I warned her.

"I won't fall," she told me. "I've got excellent balance."

I snorted. "Whatever. Just be careful."

"Aren't I always?"

"No."

Carly seemed to believe she was invincible. She'd twisted her wrist the month before in gym class, taking the only girl on the Brighton football team head-on in a field hockey match. Then there were the late-night joyrides in her father's Lexus even though she hadn't properly learned to drive (and, to be honest, wasn't very good at it). I stopped riding with her when she nearly sideswiped a semi coming off the freeway. When I asked her why she took the car, she just shrugged and said, "I like to drive." That was the way Carly was, whether I liked it or not. Her easy life and her parents' leniency made it possible for her to get what she wanted most of the time, but if this made her spoiled and slightly selfish, at least there was no guile or malice behind it. She rarely took what she wanted at someone else's expense, but if it benefited her and hurt no one—well then, she figured, what was the harm?

"Well, no use in starting now. I'm going to dive." She kicked off her flip-flops and stretched her arms out over her head.

I must've looked horrified, because she laughed, the sound echoing off the trees and the hills and the stone of the bridge. It was starting to get chilly, and perhaps part of my terror could be attributed to thoughts of how cold the creek water would be, but mostly I was thinking about Chris Whitman.

Chris had gone to parochial school with me, and in fourth grade he took a sharp, running dive into the shallow end of a friend's pool, smashing his head and snapping his neck. He died six months later when his parents pulled the plug. After what happened to Chris, I couldn't think about pools without hearing the crunch of bone against concrete.

"Just—don't, Carly," I pleaded. "You could really hurt your-self."

She bounced a few times on the balls of her bare feet and jerked forward to fake me out. I flinched and she frowned at me.

"You don't trust me?"

I shook my head.

"Well, that's ridiculous," she said, and leaped off the bridge.

I lurched toward the wall and peered over the side. She hadn't dived; she had jumped—thankfully, because a broken leg was preferable to a broken skull. I had no idea how deep the creek was, but it couldn't have been more than a few feet—five, maybe, if she was lucky. According to my instantaneous calculations, that jump might have been long enough to do some serious damage.

It seemed that I arrived on the bank of the creek in a split second, before Carly even surfaced. I ditched my shoes and began to wade in, mud and weeds oozing between my toes. When she came up, spurting water, I held my breath. At first she was silent, and I feared the worst—that she had hurt herself badly and was in shock. But then she turned her head and smiled at me.

"See? I'm fine!"

"You sure?" I called out as I approached her. The water was up to my chest, but Carly was significantly shorter than me. "No broken bones?"

"No," she said, her teeth chattering. "The water is *freezing*." She smoothed back all her hair from her face and spat. "And it tastes like mud."

"It's creek water. What did you expect it to taste like?" I reached her with a couple of freestyle strokes.

"What are you doing in here? Why didn't you just wait for me up there where it's dry?"

I shrugged.

"Did you come in to save me?" she teased.

"Nope. Just came to keep you company," I said.

She smiled. "Let's get out of here before one of us gets hypothermia."

Senior Year

After class, Harvey and I walked together to the lockers, where he planned to spend the ten-minute passing period sucking face with Jules. I had everything I needed, but was interested to see whether the new day had brought another article from my secret admirer. My locker was empty except for a few moldy library books at least two years past their due dates. I wasn't disappointed—I had enough reminders as it was.

I slammed my locker door shut as hard as I could to get Harvey's and Jules's attention, but they were lost. "I'm going to class," I announced. No answer. I shrugged and walked away, unable to resist knocking Harvey's shoulder with my bag as I passed. And still they were undeterred. I admired their tenacity.

I was early. I thought I would be the first one in the classroom, but Audrey was already there, sitting in the farthest back corner. Seeing her reminded me of something. I patted the front and back pockets of my jeans, then dropped my bag on a back-row desk and started rifling through it, pulling out notebooks and loose paper, pens and pencils, a couple of tattered paperbacks, my physics book. I emptied the whole thing out, made a big production of it, ran my hands through all the pockets. It wasn't there.

"Something wrong?" Audrey asked, glancing at the door as people began to file in.

"No," I told her. "I just lost my cell phone."

"Oh. That's too bad."

She had stolen it. I was pretty sure about that. My bag had fallen open when we bumped into each other yesterday outside Harriet's office; my stuff had been dumped all over the floor. It would have been so easy for her to pick it up and slip it in her pocket without me noticing. I couldn't think of any reason why she would want my cell phone. I couldn't think of a reason she would want *anything* of mine, actually, but I was sure it had something to do with the fact that she had suddenly started turning up—in my classes, outside Harriet's office, not to mention last night on the street where I live. And the fact that she had returned Carly's bracelet to me had to mean *something,* too—I wasn't entitled to it, it didn't belong to me, and if she didn't want to at least strike up some sort of friendship, then there was no need for her to go out of her way to hand it over. Then again, cell-phone theft was hardly the way to make friends with somebody, and she certainly knew that. As much as I hated it, I was interested in finding out exactly what sort of goal all these various intrusions served, but it was clear from the way she had just reacted that I was going to have to ask her directly. I resolved to do just that.

~~~~~

I caught up with Audrey after school on her way to the parking lot. I didn't know what I planned on saying, but when she finally noticed me the words sort of tumbled out of my mouth.

"Where's my cell phone, Audrey?" I asked.

She gave me a blank look. "I don't know what you're talking about."

"Bullshit. You stole it when you bumped into me yesterday, and I want it back." Apparently I was going with an aggressive approach. I immediately regretted it; she was less likely to be forthright if she thought I was trying to intimidate her.

She stared at me, and for a second I thought it might have worked. It hadn't.

"That was a clever little stunt *you* pulled," she said coldly.

"Don't change the subject." I shook my head. "Besides, I don't even know what you're talking about." I was committed to my strategy now; if she could invoke plausible deniability, so could I.

"You're an asshole."

"Those are some pretty harsh words, coming from a stalker."

"I'm not a stalker." She smirked. "I can't believe you had the balls to call the cops on me. It's like I've stepped into a parallel universe or something and you're AlternaNeily."

"If you're not a stalker, what were you doing parked outside my house for hours?"

"Research."

"What do you mean, 'research'?" I asked, a little thrown. Audrey just shrugged.

"Whatever. Cell phone. Now." I held out my hand, which she ignored.

"Why would I have your cell phone?"

"Actually, the question is, why would you *steal* my cell phone?"

"I. Don't have. Your cell phone. Maybe you dropped it or left it at home or something." She gave me a phony smile, clutching her books to her chest like a beatific Norman Rockwell child.

"Cute. But I know you do. And if you'd rather me not make a scene here, we can always take this up to Finch's office. You know how much he likes a good afternoon he-said-she-said."

She narrowed her eyes at me, hesitating. I could tell she was weighing her options. If she told me what she wanted with my cell phone now, she risked deflating all the curiosity she had built up in me; on the other hand, if she kept playing dumb, I might actually take the matter to Finch—less because I wanted to rat her out than because I was bored.

"Suit yourself. It's fine, I've got all day," I said, taking off in the direction of the administration building and hoping she didn't call my bluff. The last thing I wanted to do was talk to Finch. The less attention he paid me, the better.

"Neily," she called after me. She didn't sound frazzled or upset, just irritated. I turned and watched as she fished around in her shoulder bag. She pulled out my cell phone and presented it in her palm.

I reached to take it from her, but she yanked it back.

"I'm going to need you to answer a few questions first," she said.

"You can't just take something that belongs to me and hold it ransom," I said, knowing that—of course—she could.

"Can and have. Now, why don't I give you a ride home and I'll explain everything on the way." She slipped my phone into her back pocket, virtually ensuring that I wouldn't reach in and grab it. Virtually.

"I'm not getting into a car with you. You might drive me down to Tijuana and sell me into white slavery."

"Yeah, because I'm sure there are a lot of people who would pay good money for you. Come on. It'll be painless, I promise."

"Painless?"

She hesitated. "Well, not really. But it'll be quick. Okay, that's not true either."

"You should go into sales or something. Give it to me."

"Come on, Neily. Aren't you the least bit interested in what I have to say?"

"You mean, in what you have to ask me? No." We were playing a game here, and we both knew it. The thing was, since her return to Brighton, Audrey had actually started to interest me. That was unexpected, but sort of exhilarating. I hated to say it— even to think it—but she reminded me, just a little, of Carly.

"You are such a bad liar. You might want to work on that."

I stood there for a minute, thinking it over. I really didn't want to take this to Finch—it was such a hassle, even though I was guaranteed to get my property back. I did need a ride home, and how bad could her questions be? And if I didn't get my phone back then, I'd just call the police on her again.

At that instant, Adam Murray charged between us, knocking Audrey's books to the ground and smacking me in the shoulder with his backpack. "Out of the way, Think Tank," he muttered, heading in the direction of his cronies, who were lounging by their cars.

I bent down to help Audrey with her stuff, picking up a red notebook, which she snatched out of my hand.

"Hey, don't touch that," she said, righting her things and standing back up.

"What's that, your diary?" I scoffed. And maybe it was, but I couldn't have cared less. In saying that, I had just reminded myself of something: *Carly* had kept a diary. I don't know for how long, but at least since her mother passed away—it had been one of Harriet's therapeutic suggestions.

"What?" asked Audrey, noticing the look on my face.

"Nothing," I said, feeling the possibility like a dull thud in my chest. Carly might have written about me in her journal—things that might illuminate how she had felt about me. If I were just able to read it, at least my lingering questions on that subject would be put to rest. The problem was, the only way I was going to get my hands on it, if it even existed, was through Audrey.

"Fine," I said. "I'll answer your questions."

"Fine?"

"You sound surprised."

"Honestly, I thought you'd be harder to convince. Come on, your chariot awaits."

"Uh, Audrey?"

"Huh?" Then she saw it. Her car, a sweet-sixteen present from her grandparents, was sitting in its spot, smeared with egg and blanketed in toilet paper. A throng of Audrey's old friends—Adam Murray, Lucy Miller, and her ex-boyfriend Cass among them—were lolling around on the lawn, laughing. Audrey drew a deep breath and squinted. Inside she was boiling, I was sure, but she knew as well as I did that a public display would only make things worse.

She turned to me and smiled. "You think anyone noticed I'm back?"

I stared at the car, suddenly bitter on her behalf. The sense of entitlement, the lack of empathy, the fucking *balls* of Adam and his friends had always pissed me off, and even though I tried to remind myself that Audrey had been one of them once, had stood by and watched them humiliate other people just as they were humiliating her now, I did feel a little bit sorry for her. "Don't let them get to you. You have just as much right to be here as they do."

"I know that."

"I'll help you let the air out of Cass's tires," I offered.

"Look at you, getting all fraternal."

"What's that old saying? An enemy of my enemy is my friend?"

"Touching. But revenge isn't my style. I just want to clean this up and get out of here."

"All right. Come on—I know where the janitor keeps the extra paper towels."

After wiping down the windows, we settled into Audrey's BMW and went screeching out of the student parking lot like we were trafficking stolen goods.

"Are you kidding? Do you have a death wish?" I snapped as Audrey cut off two cars on her way to the left-hand turn lane.

"Not really. I'm just impatient."

"Yeah, well, I've got time, so I'd appreciate it if you delivered me to my house in one piece. Seriously, I feel like I'm in a scene out of *The Italian Job*."

"I loved that movie."

"I'm sure you did. So, when do I get my phone back?"

"I told you."

"Okay, go ahead, ask your questions. Wait. Are we using *Jeopardy!* format?"

She stared straight ahead, watching the road for the first time since I buckled my seat belt. "It's about Carly."

I didn't say anything. I had expected this, of course—giving the bracelet had not been a meaningless gesture, as I had rightly assumed—but all I could think was, *Please, can we just not talk about this?*

She sighed. "Can I safely deduce from your silence that you're not going to do a tuck-and-roll right out of the car?"

"Deduce away," I said sullenly.

"I did steal your cell phone."

"Obviously."

"But I had my reasons."

"Crazy people always do. Did your neighbor's dog tell you to do it?"

"Look, after the trial, when the police department released all of Carly's personal effects, her father gave them to me. He said he couldn't stand to look at them. That's how I got the bracelet I gave you yesterday, and that's how I got *Carly's* cell phone."

"Illuminating. So?" I'd put the bracelet in my pocket again this morning. I didn't really know what to do with it—I certainly didn't want to just put it away somewhere and forget about it.

"Her last outgoing call was to you."

"I know that, and so does the rest of the world. Did you miss that day of the trial, or are you just playing dumb?"

"I remember. She left you a message. But they didn't play the tape in court. I never heard the message itself, just your interpretation of it."

"Well, believe me, if I was lying the DA would have called me on it. Why do you need to hear it, anyway? Do you get kicks chasing ambulances, too, or do you just fill all your empty hours nowadays playing *Cold Case* with a murder that's already been solved?"

"I wanted to see if you'd kept the message. Saved it, in your mailbox."

"Why would I do that?"

"I don't know. Because you were unhealthily fixated on her?"

"That is not true!" I slammed my fist against the door.

"You seem awfully worked up," Audrey said. "What's that quote from *Macbeth*? Something about protesting too much?"

"Shut up, Audrey. So, what, you got me into this car so that you could hassle me about Carly?"

"I don't recall holding a gun to your head."

"Look, just give me my cell phone, take me home, and we can each go back to pretending the other doesn't exist. The last thing anybody needs is a rewind of last year."

"Why are you being so defensive?" I didn't answer. She glanced at me and her jaw dropped. "You *did* save the message, didn't you? What, did you download it onto your computer or something? Forward it to another digital mailbox? What? Neily, I have to hear that message."

"I did not save it. As soon as the detective had a copy, I deleted it. If you want to hear it, you'll have to break into the evidence room in the Empire Valley Police Department." I couldn't even look at her.

She pressed her lips together and let out a deep breath through her nose. "Fine." She reached into her pocket and tossed the cell phone at me. "Don't help."

"Help with what?" I turned toward the window and watched the woods go past. "Forget it. I don't care."

"I don't think my dad killed Carly. And I would *really* like to prove it."

I considered my words carefully. Audrey was a bitch, but

her life hadn't been easy since Carly died. There was quippy, and there was cruel.

"Look, Audrey, I know you don't want to believe it—"

"Wanting has nothing to do with it. I *don't* believe it." She looked at me earnestly. "And I don't think you do, either."

"What makes you think that?"

"Because you don't really act like someone who's got all the answers," she said. "I've been watching you, Neily."

"That's creepy."

"And I can tell that behind that weak Holden Caulfield affectation is a spongy, leaking heart desperate for some sort of closure."

I looked out the window, at the houses whipping past, willing her to stop talking. I had never felt completely comfortable around Audrey, even when we were supposedly friends. This was not a new side to her—she was always trying to get a reaction, like a child poking at a sleeping dog with a stick. It was something she and Carly had in common, but when Audrey pried it was like chipping away at a wall; when Carly had been like this, it was as if she were throwing a stick of dynamite and waiting for the explosion.

"I don't blame you for wanting to believe it," Audrey continued. "It's human nature to go with the solution that suits us, to lock away the threat and try not to think about it ever again. But that's not *life*. Life is messy."

"No kidding."

"I need you to believe me."

"Why? Why do you care what *I* believe?"

"Because I want you to help me."

I leaned my head back. "God."

"What?"

"Look, you do whatever you want, but I think it's totally stupid to convince yourself that the truth is inconsequential if you don't like it. So thanks for the invite, but I'm going to take a pass on the amateur sleuthing."

"You're honestly telling me that if I'm right, if my dad is innocent and the real killer is out there somewhere, you'd rather my dad rot in prison while someone else gets away with murder?"

I hesitated, my mind a whirlpool of possibilities. "We can't do this, Audrey. We're not cops, we're just kids."

"I don't know about you, but I stopped being a kid the night I found out my best friend was dead and my dad was about to go to prison. I'm not playing, Neily. This is not a game to me." She shook her head. "And if I can't convince you of that, then I won't be able to convince anybody."

"I'm sorry," I said quietly.

"I'm disappointed in you. I thought you cared about Carly."

"I did! I mean, I do."

"Then why won't you help me?"

"Because!" I shouted. She jumped, and I strained to keep it together. "Because if you're right, and your father *is* innocent, and that message Carly left me the night before she died has something to do with it, then that means it's all my fault."

"What are you talking about?"

"I could've answered the phone, I could've listened to the message, but I didn't. Not until it was too late. I was still angry, and I didn't want anything to do with her. Every day I think about what might have happened if I had answered the phone or called her back right away. Part of me thinks she'd still be alive."

"You don't know that."

"It doesn't matter what you, or I, or anyone knows. If we do this, if we dig everything back up again, all we'd be doing is tearing out our own stitches."

"Don't you want to know for sure?"

"I don't think I do."

"Is this why you're having nightmares?"

I glared at her. "How do you know about that?"

Audrey averted her eyes. "Harriet stepped out of the office for a minute during our session and I might have caught a glimpse of your file."

"Audrey, you're such a bitch! That's my *private* file. You had no right to look at it."

"It was sitting right there on her desk—how could I not? If you were me, you would've done the exact same thing, and you know it, so don't give me that judgmental look."

She had a point. But I had another question.

"Why are you doing this now? If you're so sure your father's innocent, why wait a year to start looking into it?"

She pressed her lips together, taking a long pause before answering. "I didn't believe him at first. As soon as I got over the shock of it all, I bought the DA's story just like everybody else. But the longer I sat in that courtroom, the less sure I became, and when I went to see him last month I realized that I wasn't angry at him anymore because I *knew* he hadn't done it. He tried so hard to convince me, and I tried so hard to resist believing him, but I couldn't keep it up."

She finally looked over at me. "I had to fight with Grandma and Grandpa to come back to Brighton. They think it's going to be hell, and maybe it will be, but I know this is where the answers are. Do you remember what the psychiatric expert said at the trial?"

"Yeah," I said grudgingly. "He said that Carly's murder seemed like a personal crime. He was almost a hundred per-cent certain that whoever killed her had known her, and hated her."

"Exactly. And practically every single person who could possibly fit that description goes to our school. Do you see now why it's so important that I do this?"

I nodded. "Okay," I told her, after a very long silence. "I'll help you."

Chapter Six

My mother forced me to spend my first weekend back at school with my father. I hated being at his house. The only reason I went at all was because my mother was afraid that if my relationship with my dad disintegrated to the point that we were no longer on speaking terms, he wouldn't pay for me to go to college. College was my ticket away from Empire Valley, and there was no way I was going to pass up a blank check, even on principle.

My father wasn't home when I got to his house on Friday afternoon, so I threw down my bags in the foyer and grabbed a beer from the fridge in the garage. The man hadn't really parented me since I was very young, and I tended to get away with most things when I was there. At first I tried to push my boundaries, but my father was neither home enough nor interested enough to care, and as long as he could convince himself I still respected him, he pretty much stayed out of my way.

I had just settled down in front of the TV when the doorbell rang.

"I want you to come with me," Audrey said as soon as I opened the door. Even though I had agreed to consider her argument, we hadn't really had time to talk since Tuesday afternoon when she drove me home. The first week back from summer vacation at Brighton was called Hell Week for a reason—instead of easing us in gently, the teachers liked to overload us with as much work as possible to "catch us up."

"How did you know I was here?"

"Your mom told me."

"Figures. Okay, what do you want?"

"I'm going to the bridge, and I need you to be there."

"Why?"

"I want you to tell me everything that led up to you finding Carly. I need to be able to see it in my mind."

I hesitated. Going back on my own was one thing, but going back with Audrey? I had reservations.

"I thought you were in this with me."

I drew in a deep breath. "Okay. Just let me get some shoes on. I'll be out in a second."

When I got into Audrey's car, she gave me a sympathetic look.

"Are you scared?"

"No. Why would I be?"

"It must've been horrible for you. Coming across her body like that."

"Just drive," I said, looking out the window so that I didn't have to meet her eyes.

"I wonder how long it took the police to decide you had nothing to do with it."

"I'm doing what you want me to do, so stop taunting me."

"I'm not taunting you, I'm just thinking out loud."

"You're trying to get a rise out of me." I glanced at her. "And you have that look."

"What look?"

"That Carly look, the look she used to get when she was sure she'd caught you in something."

"I don't remember her having any *look*," Audrey said, but I remained unconvinced. Audrey was far and away the person at whom Carly's look was most often directed. She and Carly had been like sisters, and, like sisters, they had gotten on each other's nerves on a daily basis. They had picked fights and argued over stupid things. Maybe *that* was why Audrey needed me around—she needed somebody to fight with.

"You're trying to figure out if *I* did it. Just go ahead and admit it so we can get this little farce over with."

"That's what some people think," she said carefully.

"What people?" I knew, of course, but I wanted to hear her say it.

"Carly's old friends."

"You mean *your* old friends? Those idiot robots don't think," I scoffed. "It doesn't match their outfits."

"It does make a little bit of sense."

"How?"

"Carly broke up with you in, admittedly, not the best or most mature of ways," Audrey said, staring intently at the road.

"You should know."

She shifted in her seat. "You were angry, rightly. For all anybody knew, you spent the last year of Carly's life obsessing over her, watching her, fantasizing about her."

"That's not how it was."

"That's what you say. Carly's not going to contradict you, she's dead."

"Carly and I broke up at the end of freshman year. Why would I wait until more than a year later to do something about it, if that was the way I wanted to handle it?"

"Lack of opportunity?"

"How would I have gotten her down to the bridge?"

"I don't know. Maybe you convinced her to meet you there."

"You've seen her cell phone—five missed calls from me on the day she died, not one of them answered. How do you think I got ahold of her?"

"Calling the house, e-mail, IM, singing telegram, telepathy? You tell me."

"If you really believed all this, you wouldn't be sitting here with me right now," I pointed out.

"I would if I were stupid."

"But you're not. And anyway, that doesn't explain how I shot her with your father's gun. Coming from my mother's house, I wouldn't have driven down Empire Creek Road to the bridge; I would've driven up Argot Canyon. There's no way I could've known your dad was there, let alone had the presence of mind to *frame* him. Because that's what you're implying, isn't it?"

Audrey chewed at her thumbnail. "Yeah, you're right." She shrugged. "Oh well. It was just a theory."

"It was a crap theory."

Empire Creek Bridge, where I found Carly's body, was down the hill from my father's house, and as Audrey had no respect for stop signs we reached it in very little time. It was just as quiet as always, only the ambient noise of cars rushing past one another, past the town's four freeway exits, on their way to other parts. Rush hour started early in the Bay Area, and everybody was aching to get home. I thought of those signs you sometimes see on apartment buildings near the freeway, signs that read something like IF YOU LIVED HERE, YOU'D BE HOME BY NOW. They had always seemed more like a threat to me than an enticement.

We were both silent. After all, what were there to say but insubstantial things? Audrey bent down, perhaps looking for some blood that had been carelessly left behind, or maybe a clue of some kind. But there was nothing, of course. It had all been washed away, cleared up, cleaned out by the police. I wondered why she hadn't been here since Carly died, but then I reminded myself that such a grim pilgrimage isn't exactly everyone's preferred way of remembering the dead. It wasn't as if Audrey was here to erect a memorial or say a prayer; she was looking for insight. For her, this was business. I couldn't help but admire that a little, and envy it.

Audrey stood up and brushed her palms together. She squinted into the sun, shading her face with her hand. "I guess there's nothing here."

"What did you expect to find?" I asked.

"I don't know. Nothing, I guess. I just wanted to be able to picture it."

I nodded, shoving my hands in my pockets. "Can we go now?"

"Not yet. I want you to tell me how you found her."

"Is that really necessary?" That night played itself over and over again in my dreams. I had no desire to relive it in my waking hours.

"Yes."

"You were at the trial. You heard my testimony. Don't you remember?"

She shook her head. "I don't remember most of that. It was . . . unreal."

"I know what you mean."

"Come on, Neily."

I took a breath and let it out slowly. The air was uncomfortably warm. The hills behind Audrey looked like dunes, and for a moment they ceased to appear solid. The light and the shadows cast by shifting clouds made them seem soft and shapeless, mountains of sand. I lowered my eyes to Audrey's face, which was ripe with expectation. That she was relying on me was strange, that she seemed to trust me even stranger. I wondered if maybe she hadn't come to me reluctantly, and out of necessity, simply because it wasn't in her nature to be alone in the world. I could see the weakness in this need to be liked, to be an integral cog in a group dynamic or even just one person's life—it was something I had long suppressed in myself—but I pitied Audrey for feeling it and especially for betraying it to me, so I did what she asked.

Sophomore Year—End of Summer

At two-thirty a.m. on Friday, Carly had called me. I didn't even have to look at the screen to see who it was; I knew it was Carly because she had programmed my phone to play Cyndi Lauper's "Girls Just Want to Have Fun" when it recognized her cell and home numbers, and I hadn't changed it. I was up reading, but I let the call go to voice mail. It took all my willpower to do so. Audrey was right about one thing—at the time that Carly died, I still had her under my skin, but I knew better than to get drawn into all that again. I thought I was protecting myself, but I was also punishing her. If I was expendable to her to the point that she hadn't even tried to preserve my friendship, then she had no right to call or talk to me. I had made that clear to her, or thought I had. So I went to bed and tried not to think about it, failing miserably.

Later that morning I broke down and listened to the message.

"Neily—Neily!—why aren't you answering your phone? I've done something terrible and I need you to pull me out of it—I need you to tell me what to do. I know you hate me—you have a right to hate me. It's my fault you do and I'm *sorry,* but I've gone and screwed everything up. I said I would keep a secret for a friend, but I didn't. You have to understand, I just didn't know, and everything blew up at the party, I finally know the truth and I have to do something. Somebody has to pay for what happened to us. You have to tell me what to do. Please—"

There the message cut off, whether by her own volition or the arbitrary nature of cell-phone technology—or by someone else's doing—it was difficult to say. Carly's voice was garbled, and I thought maybe she was messed up on something. Later I learned from the police that Lucy Miller had thrown an End of Summer party that Thursday night (her parents were coming home from Europe on Saturday), and Carly had been in attendance. Her set drank heavily, and I knew that she had at least toyed with drugs—provided oh-so-generously by Adam Murray—so she could've been high as well. I couldn't really parse the message, but I figured it had something to do with her friends. She had told a secret, started a fight, and in her state she thought I could help her figure out what to do about it. This was probably just a drunk dial she would regret after she sobered up. I kept telling myself to ignore it, but the tone of the message worried me. Carly seemed frantic and upset. Against my better instincts, I gave up pretending not to care and tried calling her.

I phoned Carly four more times that day, but every time it just went straight to voice mail. I became increasingly concerned for her as the day wore on and possibilities ran through my head. I had once promised her that I would always help her if she asked, and I had ignored that promise earlier. The guilt I felt about not answering her call out of some sort of frigid pride weighed heavily on me. After everything, I still wasn't capable of abandoning her.

The fifth time I called her, around nine p.m., was no different. She didn't answer. For some reason, it didn't occur to me that she might be avoiding my calls; I came up with all sorts of other explanations, like she'd left her phone in the car or at the party the night before. Finally, I decided that the best plan was just to see her. At least then I could tell if she was all right. If she didn't want me around, she wouldn't be shy about it, but at least I would know.

Empire Valley is practically dead after dark, and the hills

aren't that far from my mother's house. I drove up Argot Canyon Road, which runs perpendicular to Empire Creek Road, where, as it later turned out, Enzo Ribelli's car had been parked. The two roads meet just ten feet from the bridge, so I made a quick right onto the creek road and then a left onto the bridge. I was crossing it when my headlights picked up something crumpled in a patch of grass near the wall. I thought it was a dead deer and took out my cell phone to call animal control before I realized that it was a human body.

I remember putting down my phone and getting out of the car. I didn't think to call 911 until after I saw that it was Carly. I had no idea I was looking at a corpse. I ran over and turned her face. Her eyes were open, and blank. Her lips were already blue. I let her face fall to the side again—I couldn't stand to look directly at it—and lifted her halfway off the ground. With my fingers I fumbled around on her neck until I found her artery; she had no pulse. She was covered in blood, and now so was I. I laid her down and went to the car to call an ambulance. When I hung up, I returned to Carly and crouched at her feet, my back against the wall. I didn't have to wait long. Within five minutes I was in the rear seat of a squad car, headed for the police station.

Senior Year

"They questioned me for three hours," I told Audrey as she snapped some photos of the spot where I found Carly. "Then they let me go."

"Did they think you did it?"

"I don't think so. The coroner said she died less than two

hours before I found her, and I was at home all evening, which my mother verified. Besides, wouldn't make a lot of sense for me to go to all the trouble of disposing of the gun just to call 911 myself and wait for the police."

Audrey pulled an overstuffed file folder out of her shoulder bag and removed a small stack of papers from it.

"What's that?"

"A transcript from your interview with the police the night Carly died." She held it out to me. "Do you want to see it?"

I shook my head. "No thanks, I was there. If you have my interview, what do you need me for?"

"I wanted to hear it from you."

"So you're trying to see if what I tell you matches what I told the police?"

"Maybe."

"So you don't trust me." I guess it made sense. I still wasn't quite sure I trusted her, either.

"No, I do. But it's been a year—something new might have come up."

"What are you doing with copies of the case file? Did you walk into the police department and steal it?"

"No, my dad's defense attorney gave it to me," Audrey said, putting the file away.

"Because you asked nicely?"

"Because Dad told him to. They've been friends since high school. I have copies of everything the police ever turned over to him."

"And you're sharing all of this with me because . . ."

"You were Carly's friend—you cared about her. Even she knew that. Otherwise, she wouldn't have called you after Lucy's party."

"If you say so." I had wondered if maybe it was more than that. Knowing that Carly had been wearing my bracelet the night she died had stirred up hope that she might still have had feelings for me.

"I say so." Audrey flipped the page. "You still remember the message she left you by heart, huh?"

"Some things you never forget."

"Indeed." She paused. "Now all we have to do is figure out what it means."

"Maybe it doesn't mean anything." Somehow I had fallen into the position of devil's advocate, and I was so invested in my role that I was starting to say things that I didn't even believe.

"I don't think so. She wouldn't have called you out of the blue if it wasn't something serious."

"Why didn't she call *you*?"

Audrey shrugged. "We weren't really getting along that well before she died. We fought a lot, about stupid stuff mostly. She thought Lucy and I had something to do with that rumor going around that she was pregnant. She wasn't, and we didn't—at least, *I* didn't."

"Were you at Lucy's party?"

"Yes, but Carly wouldn't speak to me. I left early, right before her big argument with Adam. Cass told me about it the next day." There was a hint of sadness in her voice when she mentioned Cass. It was refreshing to know I wasn't the only person still obsessing over a long-ago breakup.

"What was their fight about?"

"Cass said that Carly thought Adam was cheating on her," Audrey said. "He didn't mention a name, so I guess Carly didn't know who."

"Do you know what time she left? Or who drove her home?"

Audrey shook her head. "No. I didn't think to ask. I assume she drove."

I nodded. "The thing is that Carly sounded angry on the message, but she also sounded *guilty*. And scared. What could have happened at the party to make her feel that way?"

"I keep asking myself that same question. She was reacting to something for sure."

" 'Somebody has to pay for what happened to us,' " I quoted.

"I can't figure out what that means. Who could have done something to you *and* her? You didn't even know the same people anymore."

"Adam Murray," I said in a low voice, almost to myself.

"What did Adam ever do to you?" I glared at her. She gave me a wide-eyed, haughty look. "He stole her from you? Is that what you think?"

"Well, he did."

"Sure, partially. But he didn't drag her kicking and screaming. She left you and went to him of her own free will, Neily. The sooner you accept that, the better."

"I know," I said sharply. "I know that. But maybe Carly found out he was cheating on her, like Cass said, or maybe he did something worse. It's possible."

"I guess so." Audrey leaned against the bridge's stone wall. "Though I can't see why she'd be freaking out about Adam's infidelity. All his boys screw around like that. Except Cass, I mean, but he doesn't really count."

"Why not?" I asked. "He's one of the boys."

She shook her head. "He's Cass. He's different. A childhood

friend, but only part of Adam's crowd when he wants to be. Same goes for me. Or, went for me, I guess."

"Oh, okay," I said, rolling my eyes. "But you said Carly and Adam fought about him cheating on her."

"Well, Cass wasn't sitting there watching the argument play out like a prize fight," Audrey said. "He probably missed most of it. He told me that they took it into a room and closed the door, but everyone could still hear their muffled shouting through the wall."

"What else could it have been?"

"I have no idea."

"So what do we do now?"

"I guess we start asking questions."

CHAPTER SEVEN

Eighth Grade—Spring Semester

One afternoon, right before spring break, I had to go to the dentist instead of Carly's house. When I told her, Carly shrugged and said that it was just as well. Her mother had an appointment, and she was going along. She looked strangely put out, and I had the ego to think it was because of me.

"Cheer up," I said, poking her softly in the shoulder and flashing her a grin. I had had a crush on her for months and was constantly trying to find ways to touch her, to be close to her, without creeping her out. She never seemed to mind. "There's always tomorrow. And the day after that. And the day after that. And—"

"I get the idea," she said, slamming her chemistry book shut and standing up.

"Where are you going? We have forty-five minutes left before last bell."

She glared at me and snapped, "I don't care."

Before I could really wrap my brain around what had happened, she stormed off. I called her name, but she didn't turn around, just said, "It's not always about you, Neily," loud enough for the entire library to hear. Gert glared at me from behind the circulation desk.

"It wasn't me!" I insisted, but all that did was earn me another dirty look.

* * *

My mother and I ordered pizza that night, for once eschewing all pretenses that she might actually cook. Usually, she banged around in the kitchen for about a half hour, searching the cabinets for something half decent to make before giving up and ordering takeout or microwaving something frozen. The only thing my mother could do well in the kitchen was bake.

When the doorbell rang, my mother shoved a twenty in my hand and said, "Tell him to keep the change."

But when I opened the door, Carly was standing there, clearly distraught.

"You're not the pizza guy," I said.

She looked as though she'd been crying. Unsure of how to react, I peered past her at the darkening street. "How did you get here? Did you walk?" It would've been a long walk.

She shook her head. "My dad dropped me off. I need to talk."

"What's going on? I don't—did something happen to you?" I asked. She dropped into my arms so suddenly I barely caught her. "Carly. What's wrong?"

For a few moments, all she did was press her face into my shoulder. When she finally lifted her head, my T-shirt was wet and so were her eyes. I ushered her out onto the porch and shut the front door, gesturing to a bench where we could sit and talk.

"What happened today?" I asked. I meant the library—I thought her current state of upset might have something to do with our fight.

"My mom had an appointment," she said, biting her lip.

"I know, but you didn't have to leave like that. You could've talked to me about it."

She shook her head. "My mom was having these pains, in her stomach, kind of. It had been happening for a while, and since she's always had indigestion, she thought it was just getting worse, that it might even be an ulcer. My dad examined her and wrote her a prescription, but the medication wasn't helping, so two weeks ago she went in for a more thorough exam. We got the results today."

I pulled back a little, afraid to look at her. I wanted to stop her from saying what I knew was coming, to keep deluding myself that she was angry at herself for blowing up at me and was here to apologize. But she surged forward.

"It's—um—it's cancer?" She wiped at her eyes. "Ovarian cancer. And they kept giving us all these odds and numbers, so when I got home I looked it all up and I realized what it meant. And my dad, you know him, putting a positive spin on it, but he's a doctor, he knows. It's not—well, it doesn't look good."

I put my arm around her shoulder. I couldn't think of anything else to do to comfort her. What words? I had none.

"And the thing is, they kept saying how if they had just caught it sooner, they'd be able to do more for her. It's not fair! She's always taking me to doctors—orthodontist, dentist, dermatologist—dragging me to yearly checkups. And all this time, she's been the sick one, and she never did anything to take care of herself." Her hands dropped into her lap. "I don't want to lose my mom, Neily."

My mouth hung slightly open, like I was getting ready to say something important. What I wanted to say was: I'm so, so sorry. But instead I said, "I love you." Only then, when I said it out loud, did I know that it was true.

Carly threaded her fingers through mine and I squeezed her hand. She said it back to me, and I was relieved in a way that I wasn't expecting. I didn't know that I needed her to say it until she did. I was so grateful; I leaned down and kissed her fearlessly, which was unlike me. When she kissed me back, I brought my hand up and cupped the nape of her neck, pulling her hair with my clumsy fingers. I tried to back off, to apologize for hurting her, but she kept me close, kissing me softly at first, then hard and fast until the lines between us blurred.

Senior Year

After we were done at the bridge, Audrey dropped me off at my father's house. As I climbed out of the car, she thanked me for my help.

"I think this goes without saying, but please don't tell anyone I'm doing this," she requested.

"I won't." *Who would I tell?* "Hey, Audrey?"

"Uh-huh?"

"Don't be stupid."

She gave me a sarcastic thumbs-up and started backing up.

"Wrong finger!" I called after her.

When I walked through the door, I noticed that someone had cleared my bags out of the foyer. I found my father in the kitchen, flipping idly through *Time*.

"Hey, son," he said amiably. He pointed to my beer, which was sitting out on the counter. "Did you have a bad day or something?"

"Let me think—is it a weekday? Then, yes."

"Where were you just now?"

"Skeet shooting."

"No, really."

"Really. I'm getting good."

"Fine, don't tell me. When do I get to meet your new girlfriend?"

"She's not my girlfriend," I said quickly. "And you were, what? Spying on me? Is your shoe also a phone?"

"I wasn't spying. I was guessing. So who is she?"

"Nobody. Just this girl from school. We were working on a project."

"Oh, a *school* project," he said, putting on his best Knowing Father look. I liked to think he spent time practicing it in the mirror.

"When did you get so interested in my comings and goings, anyway?"

He looked away, as if embarrassed, and shrugged.

"Dad, what do you know about Enzo Ribelli?"

He thought for a moment. "You mean besides the fact that he murdered a girl down the road from my house?"

"Yes, besides that," I said blankly.

"I didn't know him personally. But if memory serves, he and his brother, Paul, didn't really get along. They grew up here, you know. We all went to Brighton together."

"Yeah, I know." It was part of the Legend of Kevin Monroe.

"When we were at Brighton, Paul was the hotshot. He was three years younger, but he got better grades and was a great football player. Enzo didn't even really try, but you could tell it bothered him, all the attention Paul got. All Enzo came out of Brighton with was a substance abuse problem."

"Things haven't really changed much."

"No. They haven't."

"When they arrested Enzo, did you think he was guilty? I mean, did it make sense—just the person he was?"

"Well, there was this one incident in high school—but it might have been an exaggeration, and my memory's sort of fuzzy on the details."

"What happened?"

"Enzo had this girlfriend a grade lower than him, really pretty. Anyway, one day she came to school with a black eye and by the time the day was over everybody was saying that Enzo had hit her and that her father was going to press charges."

"Did he?"

My father shook his head. "I don't think so. She changed schools soon after that." He narrowed his eyes at me. "Why all the sudden interest in ancient history, Neily? Did something happen at school today?"

"It's nothing. Never mind." I went to the fridge, got another beer, and went up to my room.

⁓⁓⁓

Audrey caught up with me after second period on Monday.

"I'm late for class," I told her, slamming my locker shut and walking away. She followed me. "How is it that my coldness is not putting you off?"

"I thought you were going to help me," she said.

I stopped and faced her. "I changed my mind. Your father—he hasn't exactly built up a reputation for honesty and nonviolence. Maybe you believe him, but that doesn't mean that I have to."

"You've got to be kidding me."

"I am known for my sense of humor." I slipped past her and into the men's bathroom, thinking that was the only place that she wouldn't follow me. I was wrong.

"Unbelievable!" she shouted. The door swung open and hit the wall.

"You're lucky we're the only ones in here, or else this would be very awkward for you."

Audrey ignored me. "Do you *know* what people say about you?" she asked sourly, crossing her arms.

"Do you know what people say about *you*?"

"They say you were infatuated with Carly. They say you were stalking her. Everyone who hasn't mentally crucified my dad thinks *you* killed her. How does that make you feel?"

I turned on her, furious. "Is that really what you think? Can you honestly look me in the eyes and tell me that you believe I could've done something that evil?"

"Everybody has a dark side, Neily," Audrey said. "Even you."

"I don't care what people say," I replied. "Is that all you've got?"

Audrey grabbed my arm. "I'm going to visit my dad this afternoon and I want you to come. If I can't convince you that he's innocent, maybe he can. And if you don't believe me after that, I promise I'll leave you alone."

She looked desperate. Despite my instincts, I felt sorry for her. Though what my father had told me about Enzo had raised my suspicions back up to orange alert levels, I still believed that there were questions that hadn't been answered, avenues that had yet to be explored. I was sure that Carly's diary held the key to her true feelings for me, but it also occurred to me that it might hold the key to other things as well, and staying on Audrey's good side was necessary for getting my hands on it.

"Fine. But you're lucky I don't have a life, or I would have been able to come up with an excuse."

"Good. We'll go straight there after school, then."

"Fine," I said.

"Fine," she said. She glanced around as it finally sank in that she was in the men's bathroom. "I better get out of here." She pulled open the door and nearly collided with a freshman whose locker was near my own.

"What the—?"

"Sorry," she said, grimacing at me as she slipped past him out the door.

The freshman glanced at me. "Should—should I go?"

I waved him on. "Just do your business," I said. When he

had disappeared around the corner to the urinals, I bent over a sink and stared at myself in the mirror. There was nothing in the world that I wanted less than to get tangled up in all this, but I had no choice, not until I had the answers to the questions the police and prosecution had never asked: What had happened to Carly at the party the night before she died? Why did she leave me that message and what did it mean? And, most important, the answer to one final question: Had Carly still been in love with me?

~~~~~

Enzo Ribelli was being held at San Quentin. I'd never been to a prison before and I was just a little excited, not that I would've admitted it.

"Do you go see your dad a lot?" I asked Audrey as she drove.

She narrowed her eyes at me. "So we're friends now?"

"Just making conversation." I leaned back. After a moment, I asked, "Are you going to answer my question?"

"About once a month. I'm the only person he'll see."

"So what makes you think he'll talk to me?"

"He will if I ask him to."

"Not to seem insensitive, but for that brief moment when you and I were friends, you didn't seem to care too much for your father. Now that he's in jail for murder, you're suddenly a devoted daughter?"

"Do you blame me? He drank and gambled away everything he and my mother had—you would cringe to think of what we had to make do on because of him, Mr. Moneybags."

"You should talk," I said.

"Yeah, *now* I have money. But I grew up moving from

apartment to apartment in the middle of the night because my dad would default on the rent—we would go days without heat or electricity while he disappeared on a bender. My mom left us—left *me*—because she couldn't stand it anymore. Hasn't been heard from since."

"Did he ever . . . ?" I let my voice trail off, certain my question was inappropriate.

"Hit us? No, not me. But he slapped my mom around once or twice when he was piss-drunk, which was enough."

I didn't know what to say. However cold my father could be, my childhood had been cake compared with what Audrey went through. I nodded sympathetically and let her talk.

"But he's my dad, and he's innocent. If I don't stand by him, nobody else is going to."

"That's really decent of you, Audrey."

"It doesn't hurt that I believe him. If he had done it, I don't think I could've forgiven him. Carly was practically my sister."

I nodded. "I know."

"What about you?"

"What about me?"

"Has anything changed between you and your dad?" Audrey asked, eyes on the road.

"No, but next time I go to his house for court-ordered visitation, I'll let him know you were asking about him."

"Well, at least he's not in prison."

"If he was, I guarantee you that I wouldn't be trucking it all the way out to the Q just to see him."

She stiffened and glared at me. "You know what? The not-talking thing—that was working out really well for me, so if we could just get back to that, I'd appreciate it."

"Fine by me," I said, lowering my seat until I was lying down. As we passed a sign for the Richmond–San Rafael Bridge, I closed my eyes and settled back for a short nap.

Eighth Grade—Spring Semester

Things got worse for Miranda Ribelli over the next few months. When school ended for the summer, she was already far into her first round of chemo, and her hair was falling out in large clumps. She couldn't eat much without throwing up, and Paul was constantly taking her to the hospital so that she could be hooked up to IVs and pumped full of nutrients. Carly was beside herself, but instead of talking about it she committed every second to the program, completing assignments faster than I did and asking for more and more work.

"Don't you sleep?" I asked her a few weeks before school let out.

"Not much," she told me, rubbing her eyes. "Sometimes my mom needs me at night."

"Maybe you should talk to your dad about getting her a nurse."

"Why?" She frowned. "What does she need a nurse for? She's got me."

"Yeah, but you have school and your dad is always at work— it just seems like it's too much to ask of you. You're only one person."

She shrugged me off. "I can do it. It doesn't bother me."

"Well, it bothers me." She was so tired. Her face was full of anxiety—she never smiled anymore, and she wouldn't let me hold her as much as she did after we first got together. She seemed to be pushing me away, and as much as I felt for her I couldn't help fearing that she was no longer in love with me.

Her bottom lip dropped a little. "Excuse me?"

"You're never around, and when you are, you're tired and cranky." I knew I was saying all the wrong things, but they just kept pouring out of me like a faucet somebody had turned on. "You never talk to me."

"That's because you're impossible to talk to."

"How's that?"

"Whenever I want to talk about my mom, you nod and tune me out, like I'm some kind of song you're afraid of getting stuck in your head. You don't *listen*. If it doesn't have anything to do with you, you don't want to hear about it."

"That's not fair." But maybe it was. I had always thought of myself as a good listener, the sort of person you could depend upon and lean on, especially when it came to Carly, but the truth was that I had very little experience dealing with illness and the possibility of death. I didn't know what to say or how to say it, when to give her space and when to push her to confide in me. I was hopeless, and I knew it.

"And when you do listen, you keep telling me it's going to be okay—like, what if it's *not* okay, Neily? What then? What if she dies? What if she dies and you've been sitting here the whole time telling me that everything's going to be okay?"

"What do you want me to tell you? Tell me what I can say to make you feel better."

"I don't want you to tell me anything—I want you to listen to me."

"Well, I'm listening now." I took her hand.

"That's not good enough. You can't just be there for me when it's convenient for you, or when I tell you that you're doing a lousy job at it. I'm going through enough of a hard time as it is, and I can't be worrying about your feelings. It's too much, Neily."

I nodded. "I'm sorry."

"Yeah. I know." She wiped at her eyes. "I need some time alone. To spend with my mom."

"Okay. Whatever you need." It killed me to say it. Part of me sensed that we were moving toward something dense and ugly and all too real, and that I had no power to stop it.

I left Carly alone for that entire weekend. As difficult as it was, I didn't call or e-mail or send her any text messages. When I saw her at school the following Monday, I feared it was all over. We stood at opposite ends of a bank of lockers, staring at each other. I wanted to approach her, but I knew that she had to make the first move. When she eventually did move, she tried to brush past me, embarrassment and regret etched all over her beautiful face. Unwilling to let that be the end of it, I caught her wrist as she passed and pulled her toward me, leaned down, and kissed her deeply. She kissed me back, throwing her arms around my neck. When we came apart, I pressed my forehead against hers and said:

"I love you, please don't be mad at me. I'm sorry."

"No," she said, shaking her head. "*I'm* sorry. I love you, too."

I smiled and kissed the tip of her nose. From behind us came the sound of a throat clearing. We both looked to the side

95

and saw Finch standing only a couple of feet from us, glaring his disapproval. Wordlessly, he lifted his finger skyward, and at that exact moment, the bell rang.

"That's enough," he said. "You're both officially late for class. And I will be by the library later *to check up on you,* if you know what I mean."

"Ten-four," I said. Carly smiled at him sheepishly.

"This better not be how you spend all your time these days," Finch said, stepping back as we scooted past him on our way to music appreciation. "I don't want to have to split you two up."

~~~~~

By the time school ended for the summer, things were looking better—Miranda was responding to the chemo, and Carly's mood had taken an upswing. Paul had engaged a nurse for his wife, and the whole family was feeling good enough to take a night off from hospitals and IVs and worry and go out to dinner for Carly's fourteenth birthday. Miranda invited me over Paul's objections. It wasn't that he didn't like *me,* Carly insisted; it was just that he didn't approve of his daughter having a serious boyfriend at such a young age. My mother had similar concerns, but she mostly kept them to herself; Paul was not as subtle.

The fine dining options in Empire Valley being limited to fast-food restaurants and one moderately priced steak house, Paul took us all up to San Francisco in his brand-new Mercedes. Bored with the innumerable Italian, Mexican, and seafood restaurants the city had to offer, Paul had chosen something different—a tiny, family-run Polish restaurant in

West Portal that doubled as an art gallery. Halfway through our pierogi appetizer, Paul announced that he had news.

"I don't know how much this will interest *you*, Neily," he said, taking a swig of Polish beer. "But Enzo's coming back to town, and he's bringing Audrey with him."

"Enzo? Really?" Miranda seemed surprised. "Why?"

Paul shrugged. "Now that it looks like Hilary's gone for good, I guess he wants to bring Audrey closer to family. My mother called this morning and told me. She teamed up with Hilary's parents, Louise and Charles Jordan, to put a down payment on a house in the valley for them, and they're moving in next week sometime."

I leaned over to Carly and whispered, "Who's Enzo?"

"My uncle," she said. "Dad's brother. Audrey is his daughter. She's our age."

"Oh." It was the first I'd heard of either of them. "Are you close?"

"Not really. They've lived in Portland since we were babies, and they don't visit that often." She glanced up and noticed her dad staring at us. "Tell you later."

Once we were back at her house, Carly gave me Enzo's entire sordid history. After graduating from Brighton as one of the marginal one percent of students who don't go on to a four-year college or university, Enzo Ribelli had careened from failed scheme to failed scheme for almost ten years, sporadically attending classes at the local community college while dabbling in everything from construction to starting his own lawn-mowing business before hooking up with Hilary Jordan, a USC junior, during her summer vacation. The day before Hilary was supposed to go back to school, she found out that she was pregnant; she and Enzo married quickly, and he moved down to Los Angeles with her. In her fifth month, Hilary suffered a painful miscarriage, but somehow she and Enzo stayed married.

Several years later, two weeks after Miranda had Carly, Hilary sent word that she had also given birth to a baby girl. For a while, the families made an effort to keep in contact, if only for the sake of the children, but Enzo eventually moved his wife and daughter to Oregon, ostensibly for some job, and the lines of communication collapsed. Now the only way Carly's parents got news from Enzo was through Paul's mother. The last time they had heard anything was when Hilary had abandoned her husband and daughter two years earlier. Audrey's grandparents on both sides were sending money every month, but it had recently become clear that it wasn't being spent the way it was meant to be, so they had finally convinced Enzo to bring his daughter back to Empire Valley.

It was hard to figure out how Carly felt about Audrey moving to Empire Valley. I tried to draw her out, but she was inscrutable. Later, when we were sitting on the porch, Carly pressing her cheek and shoulder into my chest, I asked her flat out what she was thinking.

She lifted her head. "About what?"

"Your cousin coming to town. You seem upset."

"I'm not. I just don't know her very well, and my dad is going to expect me to help her out at school. Mams says she's not a very good student." Mams was what Carly called her father's mother. Her mother's parents lived in Connecticut, and the Ribellis weren't nearly as close to them.

"You're worried that Paul's going to make you tutor her?" I raised my eyebrows. That didn't sound like Carly.

Her shoulders drooped, and she sat up. "Maybe you should go home now. It's getting really late. I'm tired."

"Carly—" I held fast to her wrist.

"Neily, let go."

"No. Carly, this is getting ridiculous. Ever since we found out about your mom, you've been so weird with me. *Talk* to me."

"Don't say 'we' like it's the same for you and me," she warned. "You stay up half the night holding her hair back while she throws up from the chemo, then you get to say things like 'we.' "

"I would help if you asked me to," I told her. "I'd do anything. I've been trying to give you more space, but if you need me I'm here."

Carly brushed at her eyes. "I know."

But I felt like I had to keep saying it. "No matter what happens, I'm always going to help you if you need me." It was these words I remembered the morning of the day Carly died, the ones that made me call her back, seek her out. I wanted to be the sort of guy who made good on his promises.

"What can I do?" I asked her.

She shook her head. "I'm fine."

"Come on. There has to be something."

Carly looked at me. "Well, maybe you can help me with Audrey."

"How?"

"I have a feeling it's going to be really awkward with her," Carly said. "Her dad and my dad have been on bad terms since they were kids, and I haven't seen her for a really long time. I'm afraid she'll hate me."

"Why would she hate you?"

Carly shrugged. "I don't know. People tend to."

"People don't hate you." It was true, Carly and I didn't have many friends at Brighton, but that was as much our fault as anybody else's. Our contact with other students in the program was sporadic. As for the nonprogram students, we knew them from elective classes and cocurriculars, but only in the most casual way. Honestly, on the whole I would've said that people hardly gave us a passing thought, and my mother had always told me that people have to care about you to hate you.

"Do we go to the same school?"

"People don't hate you," I repeated. "They're intimidated by you. They know that you're smarter than they are."

"Well, I don't want Audrey to feel that way about me," Carly said. "I want her to like me."

"And how am I supposed to help with that?"

"Be friendly to her. Maybe punch me in the arm when I'm being too clever or too patronizing," she suggested light-heartedly.

I laughed. "I'm not going to punch you."

"Pinch me, then," she joked.

"We need a signal that doesn't involve physical violence, or you're on your own," I said, kissing her.

"Okay." She pursed her lips in thought. "How about if you tap your nose with your finger if I'm being obnoxious?"

"Sure. That I can do."

"Why are you smiling?"

"No reason."

"Tell me."

"It's just very you. Secret gestures and everything." I reached into my pocket and pulled out a small blue box. The white ribbon that the woman in the jewelry store had tied around it was a little smashed. "Happy birthday, Carly."

She took the present and slipped the ribbon off with excitement. She brought out a little blue velvet bag and dumped its contents into her hand. There, glinting in the fading light, was the bracelet. I had saved up my allowance for several months in order to afford it and had the store engrave it with her initials.

"Do you like it?" I asked softly.

She lifted her eyes to mine. "I *love* it," she said, putting her arms around me and giving me a soft, tender kiss. I felt a tear fall from her cheek onto mine. She wiped it away with her thumb. "It's wonderful." And Carly smiled—for the first time in a long time—a big, genuine smile.

Chapter Eight

Senior Year

Twenty minutes after we arrived at San Quentin, we were seated in a room filled with inmates and their visitors, separated from Enzo Ribelli by a small table and a thick plate of fiberglass.

"Neily," he said. "What are you doing here?"

I jerked my thumb at Audrey. "Ask this one. The last thing I remember was my Coke tasting funny—when I came to, we were pulling up to the gate."

"Audrey?"

"I wanted him to hear your side of the story," Audrey said.

Enzo sat back in his metal chair and stared up at the ceiling, letting out a deep breath. I didn't know him very well.

When Audrey and I had been friends, her relationship with Enzo had been in tatters. He was almost never at home, and Audrey spent most of her time at Carly's house; she even had her own bedroom there. I probably hadn't seen him more than a half dozen times, but I knew his face from the media—scores of old photos filtered into the local news stations and the newspapers, each one showing a man who, thanks to the ravages of destructive habits and a life of hard knocks, had changed a lot since high school—and during the trial. But prison life seemed to agree with him. His formerly chiseled face was still scored with deep wrinkles, his head was completely gray, and there were bags under his eyes, but he seemed healthier. Gone were the alcoholic abdominal bloat and hollowed-out heroin cheeks—he was well fed, clean, and sober. It even looked like he'd been working out. You could say what you wanted about our correctional system, but imprisonment had improved Enzo's life to a certain degree. It was freedom—or his inability to control himself when he had it—that had destroyed him.

At first, Enzo seemed reluctant to open up old wounds, but I suspected that Audrey was talking to him about Carly's murder every time she came to visit. He was probably used to going over it again and again—she could be very persistent. Finally, he nodded and heaved another deep sigh.

"Okay."

"From the top," I said.

❦

Enzo had just been fired from a construction site in San Ramon for being drunk on the job ("I'm not proud of it," he interjected bitterly, as if I had somehow implied that he was). It was just after noon, so, not knowing what else to do with himself, he went to a bar where they knew his name and he had a tab. Once there, he installed himself in a corner and didn't leave until the proprietor kicked him out at five.

"From there, I went home, drunk as a skunk," Enzo said. "Audrey was sick in her room, napping. I lay out on the couch and fell asleep for a couple of hours. I got up at seven-thirty and ate some leftover pizza. Then I went down to the 7-Eleven to pick up some beer. I thought Audrey might be up by the time I got back, so I headed to the creek."

And that's where, Enzo said, he passed out. "I'd been drinking already, and it didn't take me very long to mow through that six-pack. I was tired, so I closed my eyes. Next thing I know, an officer is knocking on my window and yanking me out of the car."

"You don't remember anything?"

He shook his head. "No."

"Well, what about your gun? They found it in the river, and they matched it to the bullet that killed Carly. I think that's what they call 'incontrovertible evidence.' "

"I used to keep the gun in the house, but every once in a while—" Enzo clenched his hands into fists. "Every once in a while I would take it with me. Just in case."

"In case what?"

"I don't know. In case I got into a fight. In case somebody tried to rob me. Listen, Neily, I was so messed up, I couldn't think straight. I couldn't keep a job. I couldn't take care of my daughter or myself. I didn't put very much thought into what I might need the gun for—if I got it into my head that I needed it, I'd bring it with me."

"And did you bring it with you that night?"

Enzo shrugged. "I don't know. I don't remember bringing it, but how else could it have gotten all the way out there? There's a lot I don't remember."

"When you did bring it with you, where did you keep it?"

"Sometimes I left it out on the passenger seat, but mostly I put it in the glove compartment. You know, to be safe."

"What if you didn't bring it with you?"

"You mean, what if somebody stole it from the house?"

"Yeah. It could happen, right?"

"Sure."

"Did you keep it locked up?"

Enzo shook his head. "No, I usually kept it in the top drawer of my dresser."

"I used to lock it up," Audrey said.

I turned to look at her. "What?"

"You didn't usually keep it in the dresser, Dad. You usually kept it lying around the house. When I would find it, I'd pick it up with a pen or something and put it away in the china cabinet, the one with the lock."

"What did you do with the key?" I asked.

"She used to put it on top of the china cabinet," Enzo said. "Audrey also used to hide booze in there. What, did you think I didn't know?"

Audrey sighed and shook her head. "Whatever. The point is, a lot of people knew what was in that cabinet and where the key was. I threw something like four parties the year before Carly died. All of my friends knew—Carly included—but it's not like it was a very creative hiding place. Anybody with half a brain could have found it. And when I was out, Dad almost never locked the door, even when he left the house. The gun— that's the easiest thing to rationalize away."

"Is there anything else you remember about that night?"

"Not a thing."

"Then I guess we should discuss motive, if that's all right with you."

Enzo met my eyes directly. "Sure. What do you want to know?"

"Well, they said you killed Carly over her inheritance. Is that true? Were you angry about the money your mother left Carly?"

He shifted uneasily in his seat. "I wasn't happy, I'll tell you that. I mean my mother knew I was hard up for cash—I had been for ages—and she just skipped me. It was a slap in the face. Sure, she left Audrey plenty, but I couldn't touch that money."

"She didn't leave Paul anything either," I reminded him.

"That's bullshit," Enzo said dryly. "Paul passed on an inheritance before my mother died—he helped her write her will, for Christ's sake. She left him some furniture and a couple of expensive paintings—things he asked for. He told her to put the rest of his share into trust for Carly. That was his choice. I didn't get a choice."

"And this shocked you?" I asked. "You weren't exactly the ideal son."

"You're right. You're absolutely right, and I know that now. But you asked if I was angry about the will, and I'm being honest when I tell you I was. I was furious. I thought that at the very least my mother ought to have left me her jewelry. She had some extremely pricey stuff, things that I valued as a part of my childhood. But she left it all to Carly—it was part of the deal Paul made with her."

"Including the necklace?" I asked.

"Yeah."

The necklace was high-quality, a half-carat diamond on a platinum chain that Carly had worn constantly since her grandmother died. I remembered jealous girls remarking on it at school—sure, most of them were rich, but none of them had jewelry like that. Overnight, Carly had become much more than a doctor's daughter—she was an heiress, a wealthy woman in her own right, and that necklace was proof.

The necklace was the reason that Enzo was supposed to have killed Carly. The story the DA told was that Enzo had somehow arranged for Carly to meet him at the bridge—maybe he had given her a sob story and begged her to help him out financially, maybe he had lured her there under false pretenses, or maybe, most remotely, they had met by sheer chance. Since Enzo never did confess, that bit was pure conjecture. In any event, they met, they argued, and Enzo pulled out a gun. He shot her four times in the chest, grabbed the necklace, dumped the gun in the creek, and stumbled back to his car, where he slipped into an alcoholic stupor. The necklace was found lying in the mud next to the vehicle. The district attorney claimed that Enzo had dropped it getting into the car.

"The thing is, they found it on the passenger's side. I was passed out behind the wheel—what's the likelihood that I would have crawled through the passenger's side to get to the driver's side?"

"That is tricky."

"Tricky? It's ridiculous. The point is, they convicted me based purely on circumstantial evidence."

"And the gun."

"But the gun is also circumstantial, if you think about all the opportunities other people would have had to steal it."

"You had a motive."

"The truth is, Dad knew that if things got really bad—if we were in danger of losing the house, or he was about to get his kneecaps broken because of some gambling debts—I would have given him the money," Audrey said, speaking up for the first time in a long while. It was a bit unsettling; it was unlike her to be so quiet. "It wasn't like I didn't have it to spare."

"Exactly," Enzo said. "And I knew that."

"So? They're saying you killed Carly over the necklace. *That* was in your possession," I pointed out.

"It wasn't in my possession, it was on the ground next to my car. How long would it take for somebody to throw it out of a passing vehicle or drop it as an afterthought? A few seconds, tops." Enzo leaned back and grimaced. "I don't even know why I'm trying to convince you anyway—who do you think you are?"

"Dad," Audrey said firmly, "I'm going to find out who put you in here, and Neily's going to help me. He's the only ally I've got."

Enzo nodded. "Fine. But that's all I have to tell you. I didn't do it, and there are plenty of people who could have framed me."

"Like who?" I asked.

"I don't know. Anybody in town with a decent brain and motive," Enzo said.

"Well, in a town full of Ivy League–educated doctors and their spawn, that really narrows it down," I said.

"Look," Enzo told Audrey, "don't go playing Nancy Drew. I don't want you finding out who really killed Carly. That's a job for the police."

"Because they did such a good job the first time," Audrey said.

"I mean it, Audrey," Enzo said. "Whoever killed Carly did it maliciously, and they'll do it again if you give them half a chance. You're the only thing in the world that matters to me. Don't do anything stupid."

Audrey nodded. "Okay."

"Neily." I looked up. "Don't let her do anything stupid."

"I'm sure she won't," I said. Audrey gave me a nod, and I knew it was time to go.

As soon as we left the prison, Audrey's cell phone let out a deafening peal.

"I have a voice mail," Audrey said, stopping to listen to the message. When it was finished, she sighed. "It's from my uncle Paul. He wants to see me."

"Why?"

"He wants me to start going through Carly's stuff."

"What do you mean?"

"Unofficially, all of the things Carly owned belong to me now. Paul called the house a few weeks ago to ask me to take what I wanted before he gets rid of it, but I haven't had time lately."

"You inherited Carly's stuff?"

"Not exactly. Technically, minors aren't allowed to enter into contractual agreements, so if you're under eighteen you can't inherit money or property or will any money or property to anybody else. So when Mams died a couple of years ago, all her money was put into trust for me and Carly—we each got our own, with Paul as the executor of both trusts."

"So your dad couldn't get his hands on your money?" I guessed.

"Exactly. Mams was a sharp woman. Paul gave Carly and me allowances out of the trusts, but I think he still felt uncomfortable with the fact that my dad might be able to access my money if something were to happen to me. He made us write statements of wishes and had them notarized so that if either of us were incapacitated or . . . worse, he could use them to protect our assets from anyone who might sue for them."

I nodded. "So what did Carly's letter of wishes say?"

"Well, you know Carly. She never wanted to make things easy."

I gave a short, involuntary bark of laughter. "No kidding."

"Paul's plan was to have Carly leave most of her money to him," Audrey said.

"Well, that's a little creepy. What parent expects to outlive their child?"

Audrey shrugged. "I guess it made sense to him, since she wasn't married and she had no children. Plus he would get it anyway, as her next of kin and executor of the trust. By the end of the process, I was pretty sure Paul would kill us both himself. I left most of my money to my dad, which was exactly what he was trying to prevent."

"Did your father know that?"

"Of course!" Audrey said.

"Just asking." That really did throw a wrench into the Enzo-killed-Carly theory—if he was going to kill someone for money, why not kill the daughter who wanted him to have everything if something happened to her? "What did Carly want to do with her inheritance?"

"Carly refused to take any of it seriously. *She* insisted on leaving all her money to the SPCA."

"The fights between her and Paul must've been epic."

"Oh, believe me. There have been civil wars with less bloodshed."

"So who won the argument?"

"Carly, of course. He got her to agree to leave him a quarter of what she had, but the rest is going to homeless dogs and cats around the country."

I smiled in spite of myself.

"What's that look for?"

"Nothing. It just sounds a lot like her."

"Since she was underage none of this is actually binding, but I don't think Paul had the heart to go against her wishes after what happened. Anyway, Carly and I left our stuff—our 'material possessions,' I think was the wording—to each other."

"So now you have to go through it and decide what to keep?"

"Apparently."

"That should be fun," I said, staring out the window.

"You're coming with me, you know," Audrey said.

"Uh, no. Why would I do that?"

"Because I'm asking you to, as a favor." She took a deep breath and let it out. "Look, Neily, I know we're not best friends, but—"

"We really don't have to have this conversation."

"Do you believe that my dad killed Carly?"

Did I? I had always had my doubts. As messed up and pathetic as Enzo Ribelli had been, he didn't strike me as sinister, and he certainly seemed sincere now. I wasn't naïve enough to think a look of innocence and regret couldn't be faked, but Audrey's arguments made a certain amount of sense. "No. I don't think he did."

"So, are you willing to help me dig up some evidence that could prove he's not guilty?"

"But your dad *just* said—"

"He's only trying to protect me," Audrey interrupted. "But he can't do that from inside a jail cell: I'm willing to risk it. Are you?"

I hesitated. "I guess," I said. This could not possibly turn out well. Logically, I knew it was ridiculous, the idea of Audrey and me playing amateur detective like characters on some TV show. But my synapses were firing with rabid curiosity, and each moment passing felt like a moment lost. If Enzo Ribelli hadn't killed Carly, that meant somebody else had, and that person was still out there, still living, still breathing fresh air. And of all the things that pissed me off, that was the only one that seemed worth fighting to change.

"Good enough. That makes us a team." Audrey gave me a small smile. "I need you to come with me. I haven't seen Paul in a really long time and I don't think I can face him alone."

"Just so you know, he's not a big fan of mine."

"Yeah, but who is, really?"

CHAPTER NINE

Freshman Year—Fall Semester .

My first impression of Audrey was of a girl eager to please. Everything about her—her clothes, her hair, her makeup, her flashing smiles and easygoing attitude—seemed calculated to force people to like her. It was clear from the first moment she arrived that Carly was the person she was most desperate to impress.

Carly and I had a summer tutor, but we only spent about three hours a day working on our curriculum. The rest of the time, we were at the Ribelli house, trying to amuse ourselves in between helping Miranda with whatever she needed. Audrey came over a lot in the afternoons, when we had finished studying. For a while, Audrey and Carly were trying so hard to make themselves likable that it seemed to me they might miss each other. I liked Audrey well enough, or maybe it was just that I was amenable to anything that cheered Carly up, and Audrey was, if nothing else, full of high spirits. I wouldn't say we were close, though—friendly, but not joined at the hip.

The summer moved slowly, crumbling away at the edges until school finally came. It annoyed Audrey that we were throwing her to the wolves, hiding away in our cozy library corner while she was left to navigate the halls and classrooms of Brighton all by herself. She said something to Carly, and Carly agreed to take journalism with Audrey during fourth period. I declined an invitation to join them—the class was a complete blow-off, everybody knew that, and it would be filled with wall-to-wall Brighton assholes, people I had no desire to be around.

I was bent out of shape about the journalism class—more than I should have been at the time, although, looking back, less than I ought to have been. But Carly loved it. She had never shown much interest in writing or investigation before, but suddenly all she could talk about was her articles and applying to journalism schools when she graduated.

"I was thinking about Columbia," she gushed one morning. "Or maybe Northwestern. I can't make up my mind."

Without looking up from my chemistry book, I said, "You know that we're freshmen, right? You've got a couple of years to make a decision."

"Well, not if I graduate early."

"Are you serious?" I shook my head. "Do you really want to be one of those freakish sixteen-year-old geniuses who can't even live in the dorms?"

"You're right. It's much better being a freakish sixteen-year-old genius here." She rolled her eyes. "Anyway, Villette says I'm a good writer."

"The journalism teacher's name is 'Villette'?"

"Yeah. What's wrong with that?"

"Nothing. Except that 'Villette' is not a real name."

"Sure it is."

"No, it's not."

"It's a creative name. Much better than Carly, anyway."

"I like your name."

"Don't you ever get tired of that?"

"What?"

"Never mind." She opened up her books and turned away from me.

"No, tell me. I want to know what you meant by that."

Carly sighed. "I just meant that you're awfully judgmental for someone so obsessed with the idea that he's being judged by the world."

I tapped my nose twice and she smiled sheepishly. "I'm sorry. That was out of order."

"It's okay," I said. It was yet another indication that I was starting to lose her.

Audrey ate lunch with us every day. We had our own table near the edge of the quad, and they would join me there after journalism class. One afternoon in early November, both of them were late. I was sitting by myself, reading a Neil Gaiman novel my mother had given me for my birthday and absentmindedly poking at a bowl of cafeteria chili. I heard Carly laugh, and looked up. She was standing in front of the science building, clutching a stack of books to her chest and rubbing one foot up and down the back of her other leg. Her long hair had been pulled back into a low ponytail when she left the library for class, but now it was loose, falling over her face and shoulders in a soft cascade. She was smiling with teeth, smiling at Adam Murray.

Her body language was all over the place—flattered head dips, nervous hair tucks, flirty smiles. I squinted into the sun, shading my eyes with my hand to get a better look. I had never seen her act so childish before, like an awestruck fan meeting a teen idol for the first time. When they finished their conversation, Adam gave her a hug and a big toothy grin. She nearly sailed over to me.

"Hey," she said, sitting. I leaned in to kiss her, but she bent down to fish around in her bag for something.

"Carly." She looked up.

"Oh, sorry." She gave me a quick kiss and flipped open her French book.

I shook my head slightly, trying to convince myself I wasn't jealous. "What was that about?"

"What?"

I gestured at Adam, who had joined his posse in the middle of the quad.

She shrugged. "Oh, that. Why is it so weird that Adam Murray would want to talk to me?"

"He hardly knows you," I pointed out.

"What are you talking about? He's known me since kindergarten."

"Okay," I said slowly, "but he's never had a conversation with you before."

"So?" she said. "There's a first time for everything. Lucy Miller talked to *you* in computer lab yesterday and you don't see me getting all jealous about it."

"She asked to borrow my pencil," I said. "She wasn't all over me like Adam was with you just now."

"He was not all over me," she scoffed.

"Uh, then what was this?" I asked, giving her a big bear hug and shaking her.

"He was just being friendly," she said, laughing as I released her.

"Way *too* friendly," I muttered.

"Seriously, Neily? You have no reason to be jealous." She leaned over and kissed me, nuzzling my nose with her own. "Besides, Adam only wanted to talk to me about Audrey."

"Really? Why?"

"Well," she said, whispering conspiratorially, "it turns out that Cass Irving has a crush on dear old Aud. He's taking her to the Loon on Friday night." The Loon was Empire Valley's outdoor mall and entertainment center. Its actual name was Luna Gardens—an odd name considering that the only bits of greenery in the whole place were wads of spearmint chewing gum, and the moon was often blotted out by the glare of thousands upon thousands of watts of neon light—but nobody I knew ever called it that.

"Really?" I was surprised, but then again it wasn't hard to see. Audrey was hot, approachable, and agreeable. The Brighton social scene had given birth to stranger couples. "Good for her, I guess."

"You guess? Cass is really sweet and cute, and Audrey could use something good in her life."

"So good equals a guy?"

"Exactly."

"You girls and your priorities."

"Look, Audrey's not stupid, but she's never going to find real pleasure in school, and she's hopeless at sports. Sometimes the only thing a girl's really good at is guys. And if I'm in the position of helping her out in that area, then what's the harm?"

It seems so funny now, remembering this, but what Carly said about Audrey was true. She was a very good girlfriend to Cass Irving. That Friday night at the Loon turned into a pretty serious relationship for them—one that lasted for almost two years.

⁓⁓⁓

Somewhere around Thanksgiving, Miranda Ribelli's health took a turn for the worse. The chemo that had given us all so much hope had stopped working, and the cancer was spreading more quickly than the doctors could burn or blast it out of her. She'd been forced to have a radical hysterectomy after her diagnosis, but now the disease was invading her other organs, devouring her from the inside. She went into the hospital for an indefinite stay at the beginning of December, and by New Year's Day she had died.

They held the funeral at the cemetery adjacent to the Catholic church in the valley. After the Mass and burial, people returned to the house for a reception arranged by Mams. The venerable dowager floated around in a cloud of sticky perfume, presiding over the event like the First Lady at the White House Christmas party, giving Carly plenty of time to slip away from the crowd of those offering condolences. Audrey was there, but Enzo was conspicuously absent.

I found Carly upstairs, curled up on her perfectly made bed, clutching a pillow to her chest. I leaned against the door-jamb and said, "Hi."

She drew in a deep breath and rubbed an eye with the heel of her hand. "Hi."

"Can I come in?"

"Sure."

I sat on the edge of the bed and stroked her hair. She closed her eyes, tears dripping onto the pillow. "I'm so sorry," I said, knowing how stupid it sounded, how small.

"Thank you," she said quietly, her voice muffled by fabric.

"Is there something I can do?" I asked.

She nodded and reached out her hand. I took it, and she tugged at it, drawing me closer so that I was lying down next to her. She shifted over to make more room for me. I leaned in and kissed her, pressing my lips softly against hers. She put one hand behind my head and rolled over onto her back, wrap-ping her other arm around my waist and pulling me on top of her.

"Are you sure?" I whispered.

"Yeah," she whispered back. "I'm sure."

I leaned down to kiss her, feeling the warmth of her skin rise up to greet me as our lips met. She tugged my bottom lip gently with her teeth and her fingers snaked over my shoul-ders, pulling my suit jacket off and letting it drop unceremoni-ously. She untucked my shirt and slowly, deliberately slipped each button from its hole until it came off and joined my jacket on the carpet.

It was at this point that I hesitated. She had undressed me—shouldn't I undress her? But she was grieving—we were both grieving, only she had the look of someone who had just seen her dog shot in front of her, that great love mixed with horror mixed with rage mixed with sentimentality and loss. Wouldn't it be wrong of me to do this, wouldn't someone else—someone outside the situation, an adult, my mother—call this "taking advantage"?

I stopped kissing her. "Carly, I don't want to take advantage."

She narrowed her eyes at me. "What?"

"You're—"

"Don't tell me what I am," she said sharply, turning her head away and sighing. She stared out the window, at the deep gray, funereal sky, then turned back to me as if renewed. "I need this," she said. She ran her hands up and down my back. "Don't you?"

"No," I said. "But I want it. I just thought that you needed more time."

She shook her head. "Well, I don't." I touched her chin, ran my thumb up and down her jaw. She was trembling. "Are you afraid?"

I swallowed hard. "No."

She smiled. "Me neither." She kissed me again. We sank into each other. I savored everything, like the last deep breath you take before plunging into the ocean. The smell of her skin, the feel of her breath on my face, the force of her arms around my neck—every sense was amplified a thousand times, and my mind raced with a million fragmented thoughts. Here was Carly, the girl, if you'll pardon the cliché, of my dreams, and here I was, finally doing what I'd wanted to do for months, for over a year if I'm honest. I tried not to think about the consequences of our actions—consequences that, in hindsight, would be drowned by waves of other emotions, anyway—but to keep focused on Carly and what she needed.

CHAPTER TEN

Freshman Year—Spring Semester

For a while, things with Carly and me were calm. That isn't to say that things were easy—Carly was still reeling from her mother's death, and her normally wry, pleasant everyday attitude was now punctured with long silences, sudden crying jags, and erratic bouts of inexplicable anger. We had only had sex a couple more times since January, but it seemed to make our feelings toward each other more tender, our behavior more understanding, and our gestures more loving.

Other changes crept in as well. Whereas Miranda's diagnosis had transformed Carly into a softer, more sentimental version of herself, Miranda's death hardened her. She was sharper with her father and Audrey, and delinquent in her studies. Audrey, unaccustomed to such harsh treatment, sought my opinion on it regularly, to my dismay.

"I just don't understand why she acts like this," Audrey complained one day at lunch when Carly was home from school with a stomachache. Ever since hooking up with Cass in November, Audrey had been neglecting our lunch table for his, and Carly was giving her the cold shoulder as punishment. "She's being so mean."

"She's hurting," I said, shrugging. Audrey's confidence made me uncomfortable; I felt as though, by saying anything, I was conspiring against Carly. And anyway, I didn't really have time to mediate their stupid girly problems—I had plenty of schoolwork to keep me occupied. "You have to be patient with her."

"Easy for you to say," she pouted. "She's great to you."

"I just know when to shut up."

"What's that supposed to mean?"

I sighed. "You always want to argue your way out of a fight with Carly. That's not smart. Whether or not you think you're right, you shouldn't participate."

"So I should sit tight and say nothing while she accuses me of things I didn't do?" Audrey insisted.

"If you want to preserve your relationship, you might want to get over the need to have the last word," I advised.

"That's it?"

"I don't know what else to tell you."

She grimaced. "I hate when people say that."

I shouldn't have been so dismissive of Audrey, because later, when Carly began to act similarly toward me, Audrey wasn't disposed to offer me any solace. But by the time I had become desperate enough to seek Audrey's sympathy, things had gotten completely out of my control.

As the months passed, Carly and I began to fight. She darted away from me faster than I could pursue her, and soon I started to see her less frequently outside of school. Entire weekends would go by without a phone call, and I would go places in town—anywhere, really, that she might have gone—in the hopes of running into her, of catching a glimpse of her as if she were some rare bird in the jungle.

I knew what she was doing. She told me herself.

"I missed you this weekend," I said to her one morning, catching her hand. "I called you. Where were you?"

She shrugged. "I went out with Audrey and her friends."

"What, you mean Cass and all them?"

"Yeah, Cass and Audrey and Adam and Lucy," Carly said, acting as though it were no big deal.

"Adam? You're hanging out with *him*?" I bit the inside of my mouth anxiously. "I wouldn't do that, Carly. He's bad news. You know, he's a drug dealer."

She shook her head. "He's fine. He's great, actually."

"You aren't—doing drugs, are you?" I asked cautiously.

"Excuse me?"

"Hey, I had to ask." I held my hands up in surrender.

"Oh, really? What is that, like, Question Number Five in the Jealous Boyfriends' Handbook?"

"You're avoiding the question," I pointed out, knowing what *that* meant.

"That's because it was offensive," she snapped. "I don't do drugs, and, in case this was Question Number Six, I don't *cheat.*"

"I wasn't accusing you of—"

"Yes, you were, or you were about to. Either way, I can't have this conversation with you now. We'll talk later."

"Yeah, we will," I said stiffly. We turned our backs on each other and walked off in opposite directions.

Things steadily deteriorated. Carly spent more time with Audrey and her group, and I started to hear people whispering about her and Adam Murray. Adam was by far the worst person I had ever met, and it made me sick to think of her with him, but every time I asked her about it she brushed off the rumors, telling me that I was being paranoid.

"We're just friends," she would tell me. She had started dressing differently—she wrote off her old clothes as frumpy and put thousands of dollars of tight, expensive jeans and low-cut tank tops on her father's credit card. She cut her hair, which had once reached way past her shoulders, and started highlighting it—streaks of mustard yellow, which looked like tarnish over her natural dark color. She began to wear more makeup, and one day I mistook her for Audrey from far away. She took it as a compliment.

Then she stopped talking about her mother. Right after Miranda died, we would have long conversations where Carly would tell me stories about what it was like growing up. Miranda had always seemed kind and generous, but Carly remembered her differently—a little judgmental, cold on occasion.

Everything Carly did as a child was meant to impress Miranda, every decision was weighed against what her mother would do or say. Carly missed her mother desperately, but part of her resented being left behind, and that part refused to canonize Miranda just because she was dead.

But now, when I tried to bring her mother up, Carly would give me a dark look, like I had betrayed her.

I let it go on far longer than I should have, but it's not hard to see why. Carly wasn't just my girlfriend; she was my best friend. She changed my life. The shy, anxious, and lonely boy I used to be had grown confident because of her; I began to see value in myself because she saw value in me, and if all I had to do to keep the illusion of that feeling was turn my head and ignore who she was becoming, well, that was something I was willing to do. It wasn't easy at first, but then I started running; I pushed myself harder and faster every day, and the pain and exhaustion of suddenly becoming active after years of sloth was a welcome distraction from my tangled relationship with Carly.

About a month before the end of our freshman year, however, things started getting better. Carly spent more time with me than with anyone else; her partying days were a thing of the past, and she assured me that she was on my team again. She didn't go back to the way she used to dress, but she toned down the makeup and let the highlights grow out, and she started working hard in school again. I felt that I could finally stop worrying about what was happening to her, because she had come back to me.

I don't know how she convinced me to go to Cass Irving's School's Out for Summer party. I wasn't used to denying Carly anything, but it wasn't something I would ever agree to under normal circumstances. I hated Cass and Adam and their whole gang, and I could think of nothing worse than hanging out poolside with my classmates while they puked in the bushes. But I wanted to make Carly happy.

"It'll be fun," she promised, brightening when I said I would consider it. "Don't think too hard—just say yes."

She even drafted Audrey for the cause. "You should come to Cass's party, Neily," Audrey said to me suddenly in the hallway the day before school let out for the summer. "Cass's brother, Jerod, is coming up this weekend from L.A. and promised to buy all the alcohol—he's getting us three kegs. It's going to be so great."

"Sounds like it," I said, unconvinced.

"You need to lighten up," Audrey told me, leaning up against a bank of lockers. "You're always so serious. How much fun is that?"

"Tons, actually. You people are idiots, and I get to sit back at a distance and watch all your stupid drama unfold."

"That's pathetic."

"It was a joke, Audrey. I don't care what you guys do. Have your party, drink your three kegs—I just don't want to be a part of it." I closed my locker and walked away.

"That may be true," Audrey said, following me. She leaned in and lowered her voice. "But if you don't start spending time doing what Carly wants, you're going to lose her, and you'll have nobody to blame but yourself." She smiled and shrugged. "Have a good summer, Neily. Maybe I'll see you at the party."

In the end, I was convinced. Carly bought me a shirt for the occasion, one of those trendy faded, slightly wrinkled T-shirts with a moose screen-printed on the front. It was brown, and it fit, so I didn't say anything, but looking at my reflection depressed me. Carly had a full-length mirror on the back of her bedroom door, and she positioned me in front of it, turning me around with her hands. I looked at myself and considered how much I had changed since I met her. I had grown about seven inches in those two years, now standing six foot two, and I had gained weight, mostly muscle from all the running and lifting I was doing in gym. Carly had convinced me to get my hair cut, and she seemed pleased with the result.

"You're handsome," she said. She put a hand on my shoulder, and we both gazed at my reflection. Carly smiled a little and kissed me. "I'd almost forgotten."

"What?"

She shook her head. "Nothing. Ready to go?"

I shrugged, throwing on a hoodie for warmth. "I guess."

"Just give me one sec," she said, unclasping the bracelet I had given her and putting it away in the bottom of her jewelry box. It was the first time she'd removed it in a year and a half.

"Hey, why are you taking that off?" I asked, kind of hurt.

"All the other jewelry I'm wearing is gold—it wouldn't match," she told me, as if it were completely obvious. How was I supposed to know you couldn't wear gold and silver at the same time?

As we walked out the front door, I asked, "Where did you buy this shirt?"

"Abercrombie," she said.

"Did you know that Abercrombie used to sell sporting

goods? Back in the eighteen hundreds," I told her. "Now they sell fake thrift-store T-shirts at fifty bucks a pop. It's truly tragic."

"Fascinating," she said. A car pulled up in the driveway, brights blazing. We shielded our eyes with our hands and walked over to the driver's side of the car.

It was Adam Murray. I glared at him as he rolled down the window of his mother's brand-new green Durango. He wasn't even old enough to drive. "What are you doing here?"

"Just came to give you two a ride," he said, answering my question but looking at Carly. She smiled at him and looked over at me.

"No, man," I said. "We're just going to walk."

"Well, I'm here now," he snapped. "Just get in, Think Tank."

"Actually . . . ," I began, unsure how I was going to finish that sentence without physical violence. I'd never wanted to hit somebody so badly as I wanted to hit Adam Murray.

"Come on, Neily." Carly pouted. "You really want me to walk all the way to Cass's house in these shoes?" She was wearing four-inch heels.

"Fine," I said.

"In the back, Think Tank," Adam called out. Carly jumped into the shotgun seat, and I did what he told me.

"What are you even doing driving?" I asked peevishly to the back of his head. "Aren't you fifteen?"

"I'll have my permit in a few months, and my mom could give a shit," Adam said, taking a turn sharply. He glanced at Carly. "How you doing, Car?"

"Fine," she said sweetly. "Everything's fine."

"You hear about Luce?"

"No, what about her?" Carly leaned in, eager to soak up the gossip.

"She's got some kind of boyfriend, some college guy. Her parents caught them doing it in their bed last weekend, and now she's grounded. Can you believe it?"

"She's not coming?" Carly asked.

"Fuck no, she's coming," Adam said. "You think being grounded could keep Killer Miller from having a good time?"

Carly laughed. "So true."

"Killer Miller?" I asked.

"You know Lucy Miller," Carly said dismissively.

"Yeah. Okay, whatever."

To get to Cass's house, we had to pass the overlook. It was a long stretch of road that skirted the edge of the foothills, offering a view of the valley unimpaired by trees. A blond girl whom I recognized as the daughter of one of my father's neighbors was walking her dog, a slightly overweight beagle, along the edge, but other than that the overlook was empty. The sun had set less than an hour ago, and the whole valley lay below us, glittering like a jumble of Christmas lights. I could have stood there and picked out my mother's house by following the freeway as it cut through town and headed off in the direction of the Livermore wineries.

"Wow," Carly whispered, as if she had never seen it before.

"Yeah," I said. "Sometimes I forget how nice this place can be."

Adam scoffed. "Whatever, dude."

Set way up in the foothills, Cass's house had its own view. By the time we reached the place, the party was in full swing, and one of the kegs was already empty. Adam and Carly went through the door side by side, because this seemed to be the order of things—their scene, their grand entrance, with me trailing behind looking stupid. Once we were in, Carly turned around, as if suddenly remembering me, and announced that she was getting a drink.

"You want one?" she asked, eyes roving, completely uninterested in the answer. She was looking for people she knew, her new friends.

"Carly," I began, but a look from her silenced me and she traipsed off in the direction of the kitchen. Adam had disappeared into the crowd in the living room, a mass of bodies undulating to the pulsating tune coming out of the state-of-the-art sound system. Cass, our host, came down a flight of stairs and spotted me standing near the front door.

"Uh, Nick, right?" Cass asked, as if we hadn't gone to the same school for two years. The bastard knew my name.

"Neily," I said, because making an issue out of it when he was deliberately trying to make me feel unwelcome wasn't going to do any good. "I came with Carly."

"Oh, right. You haven't seen Audrey, have you?" he asked. I shook my head.

"Well . . . see ya." He clapped me hard on the shoulder and walked off.

Standing there in the foyer, so far removed from the spectacle that I might have been on the moon looking down at it, I couldn't help but think how unfair this was. I felt like something brittle inside of me was about to break, like the hull of a ship ready to cave under the steady weight of a pressing iceberg. I was on empty; I had no more to give. This was the last great gesture, and it was crumbling depressingly.

Carly approached with a red cup. "Natty Light," she said with disgust. She tipped it toward me, a meager offering. "You want?"

I shook my head. "How long do people usually stay at these things?"

She shrugged and glared. "You're welcome to leave whenever you want. I'm staying."

"No, I'll stay," I told her, taking her hand. She let me without argument, but she wouldn't look at me. "Let's go somewhere quieter."

She cocked an eyebrow. "You going to take advantage of me?"

"No," I said slowly, unsure of whether she was kidding. Carly had never before been entirely a cipher to me, but I couldn't tell if she was being sincere. In mere minutes, she had become inscrutable. I clung to her hand, afraid that if I let her go she would float away. "It's loud."

"It's not so bad," she said, taking my hand and dragging me into the living room. "Let's dance."

We did, and I took comfort in the closeness of her body, the soft weight of her shoulders against my chest. I wrapped my arms around her, buried my face in her hair, and held on.

She pulled away. "Neily, stop it—this isn't a slow song."

"So?"

"People are looking at us funny."

"Who cares?"

"I do."

My chest tightened. "Carly, what's going on?"

"Nothing. I have to go to the bathroom. Watch my drink?"

I nodded and followed her as far as the hallway, which had emptied out into the mansion's many rooms, so I was the only person standing in it. I leaned against the banister and sniffed at the beer. I took a sip. It was disgusting, acrid. The whole scene was foul. But what bothered me most was that Carly wanted all this more than she wanted what we had together. She was changing. Had changed. And that scared me.

After a few minutes Audrey meandered over and knocked my cup with hers.

"Cheers," she said, her face glistening with sweat, her makeup all smudged.

"Cass was looking for you," I told her.

"Oh, don't worry, he found me."

I smiled for her. "Having fun?"

"Tons. You?"

I nodded noncommittally. "I'm all right. I like this song."

"Yeah, it's great." She sighed and then feigned having just remembered something. "Oh, Carly wanted me to come get you. She said she needs you in the other room."

"Okay." I looked around. "Which room?"

Audrey pointed. "Down the hall there's a bedroom to the left."

"Great, thanks." I smiled at her.

The bedroom, like every other room, was packed, and I could hardly make my way through. Cass pushed past me, knocking my drink and spilling a bit on me.

"Hey!" I said.

"Look where you're standing," he snapped.

I watched Cass as he walked away, until I noticed who he was walking toward: Carly. When I caught sight of her, it was as if the crowd had parted and I was standing alone. She had her back pressed up against the wall, and Adam was leaning over her, grinning. She lifted her head and he kissed her, mashing his lips against hers and running his hands up her legs. Then she moved her head and we caught each other's eyes, and I boiled over.

I grabbed Adam and threw him aside. "What the fuck are you doing?" I shouted, but I could hardly hear myself over the music and the voices.

Adam shoved me hard. "Don't touch me, Monroe—don't even think about touching me again."

Carly stepped between us. "Let me handle this," she said to Adam. She dragged me off by the arm to a corner. Everyone was staring, eager to hear us over the crushing noise.

"Neily," she said, her voice void of emotion.

"What are you doing with him?" I demanded.

"I'm with him now," she said, looking me in the eyes unwaveringly. "Adam is my boyfriend."

"No," I said, stupidly. "No, I'm your boyfriend."

"I'm sorry, but—"

"You *told* me you weren't cheating. You told me yourself!"

"I wasn't," she said. I turned my entire body away from her, desperate to get out of there but unwilling to leave her behind. She grabbed my arm and made me face her. "I've been trying to find a way to tell you it's over, but I just didn't think you would listen to reason—"

"So this was your solution?" I had a thought. "Did you bring me here for this? So you could break up with me in front of all these people? Is that why I'm here?"

"I tried to warn you," she said, in a voice so soft I could hardly hear her over the music.

"No, you didn't. Here's what that would've sounded like: 'Hey, Neily, just a heads-up—I'm thinking about kicking the crap out of your heart in front of two or three hundred of our classmates!' "

She said nothing.

"God, Carly," I said, slipping my hand up her neck so that my thumb was resting on her cheek and my fingers were nestled in her hair. "Don't do this."

Carly moved away from me, removing my hand from her face and letting it drop. "I don't know what else to tell you."

I took her hand, but she turned and walked back to Adam, who was glowering at me. When she joined him, he smirked and pulled her into him. As they kissed, cementing my humiliation, Carly opened her eyes and looked at me hard. She was right. There were no words.

I turned and walked away from them, pulling the hood of my sweatshirt up to hide my face from the gawkers as I wound my way through the party. Once I reached the door I took a deep, sharp breath of cold air to stop myself from bursting into tears. I shoved my hands into the pockets of my jeans and took off down the street, walking quickly and listening to the screams and laughter of my classmates fade to silence. I was halfway down the block when I heard somebody call my name, but I didn't turn around.

What happened to me after that? Even I don't have an easy answer to that question. I know I became intimately familiar with the idea of implosion. My life crashed in around me, connections severed, wreckage strewn everywhere as I lay in the midst of it all, waiting to wake up. Anyone who's ever had a person disappear from their life knows the feeling. It's an emptiness that still has boundaries, faint outlines that serve as reminders that something is missing, and all you can do is try your hardest to pretend like it never was. Carly dropped out of the program the following fall, at the start of our sophomore year; I stayed in, until she died a year later. I wanted to leave immediately—it didn't feel the same without her; I floundered; I couldn't do it alone or didn't want to try—but the idea of sitting in classrooms with her was too much. But then she was really gone, and I could no longer even keep a semblance of normalcy together.

From early childhood, I had been told how smart I was, and throughout my life various people had tried so hard to teach me everything there was to know. But it occurred to me then how negligent they had been in teaching me how to love. I had two examples of love in life—my mother's, absolute and overburdened, the trial of love; and my father's, the cold and ambitious pursuit of meaning in love, the desire to turn it into a product with a worth that could be measured. Of the two options, I had skewed toward the former, disappointed with my father's method, and so I had bestowed a sort of unconditional love on Carly without really understanding what it meant. I wished that just one person had taught me a way to love her less. If I had loved her less, maybe I wouldn't have hated her so much. And maybe then I could have forgiven her.

PART TWO

~

Audrey

CHAPTER ELEVEN

Sophomore Year—End of Summer

There are moments in your life that you will remember forever, no matter how bad your recall, no matter how deep you
sink into dementia. It amazes me, though, how many of these
moments don't really happen *to* us but happen outside of us,
and the moment that we see so clearly in our heads is the one
when we *found out.* People in my parents' generation usually
talk about the JFK assassination, remember everything down
to whether or not they had their shoes on as they watched the
Zapruder footage roll across their black-and-white television
screens. People in my generation will almost certainly name
September 11, 2001, as their never-forget date, the day their
lives changed—the day the world became a scarier place.

My life changed forever on an idle Friday night at the end of summer. My mind was filled with stupid trivial things, like which new outfit I was going to wear on the first day of junior year. I was reasonably happy; I had a great boyfriend, a group of fun, if wild, friends, and though my grades had never been very good, I was planning on trying harder in school, which I was sort of excited about. There was no reason to think that my life wouldn't continue exactly as it had been, no omen that things were about to take a sharp, devastating turn.

Moving to Empire Valley had been a huge decision for me. Things were difficult with Mom gone. She had tried, with limited success, to shield me from Dad's exploits, his drinking and gambling and unstable employment. But in the two years since she'd taken off, I had seen everything he was capable of and it was too much for a girl as young as I was. So when my grandparents got together and offered to find us a house and move us to Empire Valley, I accepted on Dad's behalf since he, in his sober, rational moments, knew how much his relationship with his family had disintegrated and also—I really believe this—saw how much I was suffering.

But it wasn't an easy choice, mostly because I felt that if my mom were to come back, it would be to Oregon, but also because loneliness terrified me and I had never been the new girl before. I had no idea what to expect.

From the moment I met her, Carly was the most important person in my life. We didn't have the perfect friendship. We fought a lot, probably more than most people think that best friends should fight. But Carly was loyal, sympathetic, and hilarious. She sensed when something was bothering me, and she knew just how to make it better, carefully drawing me out bit by bit, allowing me my silences but doing her best to demonstrate unconditional support. We were always trying to entertain each other, creating characters and jokes that went on for two years and never got old. We shared clothes and gave each other advice; we kept each other company during the boring but compulsory dinner parties Mams, the grandmother we shared, forced us to attend. We had different parents, but we might as well have been born sisters.

I remember every detail from that night. I'd had a stomachache earlier and spent most of the day napping, but I woke up around eight feeling much better. It was just about midnight and I was sitting in my desk chair, dressed in my pajamas, painting my toenails a deep purple in honor of the new school year. On the desk in front of me sat a nail file, my iPod, and a couple of half-completed dittos—what was left of my summer assignments, which I had naturally put off until the last minute. When the doorbell rang, I figured it was Dad; he often forgot his keys and ended up getting locked out. Glad to be answering the door at this hour rather than at, say, dawn, I hobbled downstairs, careful not to ruin the polish on my right foot.

But it wasn't Dad. It was my mom's mom, Grandma Louise, and her face was unusually grave. She opened her mouth to speak, but I cut her off.

"No," I said, a bit too loud. I was sure she was coming to tell me Dad was dead; it was the sort of thing I had been dreading for years, as soon as I began to see what a mess he really was.

She put her wrinkled hand up against my cheek—it was cold, which was odd since the night was warm and even a little muggy—and said tenderly, "Sweetheart, we need to talk."

I stood aside to let her in, tears already spilling out of my eyes. She took my hand and led me into the living room, where she urged me to sit. She hesitated, taking a deep breath, and I burst out, "Just tell me, please." My mind was a tangle of possibilities—he'd been in a car accident, his body left bent and broken on the side of the road; he'd fallen in the bar bathroom and cracked his head against the sink; he'd started a fight and bled out from a knife wound in his stomach in the parking lot.

"Audrey, honey—Carly's dead."

I shook my head slightly to clear it, not quite sure what I had just heard. "Carly?"

Grandma nodded. "They found her at the bridge. She's been murdered."

"Murdered." It was a ludicrous word; it didn't make any sense when used to describe Carly. How could Carly be dead? She was so alive.

But the look on Grandma Louise's face was so frighteningly serious I couldn't not believe it. I began to sob, my head swimming as if I had been holding my breath for a long time. I leaned forward into my lap, afraid I might pass out. Grandma Louise began to rub my back, but I barely felt it; my whole body seemed to have gone numb.

"There's more," she ventured tentatively. I didn't move; I couldn't bear to look at her. I squeezed my eyes shut and tried to will it all away—this had to be a nightmare, and if I just tried hard enough I could wake up on Monday morning, put on my new dress, and go out into the world I recognized, where everything made sense.

"They're saying that Enzo did it," she almost whispered. "Your father has been arrested. He called from the police station to ask me to bring you home with me."

I shook my head violently and bolted upright. "That's impossible!" I cried. "He would never *do* that."

"I know," she said. "I know, I know. He's got a lawyer, and we're going to straighten this all out, I promise. But you shouldn't be here right now; I'm going to go pack you a bag, okay?"

I didn't respond, but she didn't need permission. I sat on the couch, trying—and failing—to find any kernel of sense in what I had just heard, crying sloppily into my hands as Grandma Louise ransacked my room for things I might need. I never went back to Dad's house after that night. Grandma Louise hired a couple of men to move everything I wanted up to her place in the hills, and that became my home. I didn't go back to Brighton on Monday, and from the next day forward my life was no longer my own. I was suddenly that poor girl whose dad had killed someone—her cousin, her best friend, in fact—and everyone, including Grandma Louise and Grandpa Charles, looked at me with a mix of pity and anxiety that felt like a stain that would never wash out.

Senior Year

I'd been to Carly's house a few times since she died. Paul had a reception there after the funeral, but I hadn't gone to that. Grandma Louise didn't think it was such a good idea, under the circumstances. Dad was already being held at the town jail, awaiting arraignment, and attending the funeral was enough exposure. Paul had called me twice in the past year, asking me to pick up some of the things of Carly's he couldn't bear to look at anymore—all the photographs of us and our friends, glassed in and grinning out of colorful frames; her personal effects when they were released after the trial; etc.—but I used my own key to get in and he was never there when I came. This would be the first time I'd seen Paul since the funeral.

"Why do you want me here?" Neily asked as we stood at the front door, waiting for Paul to let us in.

I shrugged. "I need you, that's all." I did, I needed him. If someone had told me two years ago that I'd be saying these words to Neily Monroe, I would've laughed in their face. I had never hated Neily, but I had never really liked him, either. He and Carly were always so much smarter than me, so much more, shall we say, "accomplished" than I was, and when I moved to Empire Valley the summer before freshman year I felt like a third wheel in the most awkward way. Carly made a huge effort with me, and Neily was never rude, but I could always tell he didn't want me around, or at least he wouldn't miss me if I wasn't. I used to tease Carly about him all the time when they were dating, and even after. But I hadn't been the one to start calling him Think Tank. That was the boys, Adam and Cass, and they had sneeringly adopted it as his code name. After they broke up, Carly wouldn't hear a word against Neily, though the boys said a lot behind her back. Adam was much more jealous of Neily than he ever would have suspected.

"And why do you need me?"

"Shhh, he's coming."

Paul opened the door, looking grim.

He had changed a lot since Carly died. His hair had gone completely gray, and he had gained weight, especially around the midsection and in his face. His teeth had yellowed a bit, and there was tobacco under his nails; despite being a doctor—or maybe because of it—Paul loved to smoke, but Miranda and Carly had hated the habit. He had taken it back up after they died.

"Good," Paul said. "I'm glad you're here." He eyed Neily for a second and then shrugged. "Come on in."

Neily and I stood in the dark foyer while Paul riffled through a box full of papers.

"It'd be nice if you could go through the rest of Carly's things," Paul said. "Pick out anything you want to keep, and I'll toss the rest. I'm going to put the house on the market next month."

"You're leaving town?" I asked.

Paul nodded. "I've lived here practically my whole life. I don't think I'm going to miss it."

"Amen," Neily said under his breath. Paul looked at him. "Sorry. That was probably rhetorical."

"What are you doing here, Neily?"

"I asked him to come," I said.

"Fine." Paul turned to Neily. "I'm sure there's probably a few things up there you'd like to have."

"Oh, I doubt it," Neily said.

Paul put his hand on Neily's shoulder. "I wouldn't be so sure." He disappeared into the hallway, calling back, "There are boxes in the garage and pizza in the fridge." Then we heard a door slam, and Paul's car pull out of the driveway.

Neily raised his eyebrows at me. "Wow."

"I know. Just when you start thinking it's all about you."

"It's easy to say that now, but where was he back then? After Miranda died, he was like this phantom—Carly almost never saw him, and when she did they hardly spoke."

"That's kind of harsh, don't you think?"

"No. Seriously—*where was he?*"

"Where were *you?*" I snapped.

"Oh, don't even start with me—where were *you?*"

"This conversation is getting us precisely nowhere." I started climbing the stairs, and Neily followed.

"You two seem okay. No animosity there?"

"After everything that happened, Paul kept trying to convince me he didn't blame me," I said. "He went out of his way to make sure I knew he didn't hate me. I think he feels sorry for me, for having the dad I do, maybe even a little responsible for how he turned out."

"I don't remember him being that warm and cuddly when Carly was alive," Neily said.

"The thing is, I kind of wish he would blame me," I said. "I feel like a traitor, accepting Paul's forgiveness. Like I'm admitting that my dad is guilty."

"Yeah." Neily paused at the top step. "How come you don't call him 'Uncle Paul'?"

"I don't know," I said. "When I was growing up, he was just 'Paul,' or 'fucking Paul,' although I wasn't allowed to repeat that one." Neily gave a small laugh. He was cute when he smiled. A little nerdy perhaps, but he was, on the whole, a pretty handsome guy. Nothing like Adam—who was an Adonis, and I'm not exaggerating—but the way Neily's face used to light up when he looked at Carly, you would've pegged him for the best-looking guy in the room.

We stood in the doorway of Carly's room, which was a complete disaster.

"This is new," Neily said.

"What?" I asked, wading into the middle of the wreckage. I picked up a couple of blouses and heaped them onto the unmade bed.

"When Carly and I were together, she was really neat."

"I think you mean *Miranda* was really neat. Carly couldn't

have given a rat's ass. You know, I don't think Paul's touched a single thing in here since she died. You see that jacket?" I pointed to a red corduroy lump on the seat of Carly's armchair.

"Uh-huh."

"I lent that to her a month before she died." I picked it up and tossed it onto the bed with the other clothes. "Are you okay? You look sick."

He shook his head. "Is this Carly? This—stuff? Is this all she is now?"

"Of course not."

"I still can't believe that people can exist and then not exist, from one second to the next. And when they're gone, all they are is an accumulation of things. They're reduced to whatever possessions they leave behind."

"People don't have to die for that to happen, believe me." There was already a stack of empty boxes in the corner. I put my hands on my hips and sighed. "So where do we start?"

Neily shrugged and grabbed a box. "Is there anything of Carly's you really want to keep?"

I sucked at the inside of my mouth. "I don't want to say."

"Come on, Audrey. I think we're past acting coy."

"The jewelry. If there's anything of Carly's I want it's the jewelry Mams left her."

He raised an eyebrow.

I glared at him. "I know what you're thinking, and stop it."

"You don't know what I'm thinking," he said. "I'll take the bookshelves."

"Yeah, I do. You're thinking how interesting it is that Audrey's dad kills Carly for her diamond necklace, and then who ends up owning it in the end? Audrey!" I shook my head. "You can stop looking at me like that."

Neily began opening each of the drawers in Carly's desk and sorting through the various papers and notebooks he found in them. "You knew you were Carly's beneficiary, right? I mean, before she died."

"Yes," I said sharply. "And I wouldn't say it like that. It's not like I inherited all her money—just a few things that mean something to me."

"You don't have to get defensive, I was just asking a question." He looked up from what he was doing. "Are you going to help?"

I started shoving the dirty clothes into plastic trash bags, figuring I'd take them to be laundered, then donate it all to Goodwill. To be honest, there wasn't much of Carly's I wanted to keep. We had left each other our possessions because we knew that, in the unlikely event that anything should happen to either one of us, we of all people would know what was important enough to save. I didn't count clothes, makeup, or bed linens among those things.

"I'm just saying, if you think about it, it's a completely brilliant plan," Neily said. "Your father kills Carly, possibly with your help, then you inherit all her valuable property. And *then* you rope me into helping you prove he's innocent, both giving your act a witness and nabbing yourself a coconspirator on your quest to free your guilty father."

"That's not funny," I snapped. For all his smarts, Neily certainly knew how to say the wrong thing at the wrong time.

"What? You can accuse me of murder, but I can't have my own theory?"

I threw a trash bag full of clothes into the hallway and walked out. "I'm going to get more boxes."

The boxes in the garage were unassembled, so I grabbed a roll of packing tape and started to put them together. There was a knock on the door, and when I looked up Neily was standing there, looking penitent.

"I guess I hit a nerve," he said, shifting awkwardly.

"I don't like being accused of murder."

"Yeah, well, neither do I," he barked.

"Point taken." I took a deep breath. "Okay, what if we agree to go easier on each other? If we're going to do this, we can't always be second-guessing and pointing fingers."

"That only works if we actually believe one another."

"I believe you. Do you believe me?"

"Yes," he said begrudgingly.

"What a rousing vote of confidence."

"I believe you, but I don't want to act like we just stepped into this not knowing each other," Neily said. "We have a history. I'm not going to pretend we don't."

"I don't expect you to."

"Yeah? Well, you're acting like everything's fine—forgive and forget. I can't do that. I'm not built that way."

"That's your choice," I said hotly. This was getting ridiculous—maybe I was better off doing this alone. "You can go on hating me—I don't blame you. But can you really trust me if you keep holding on to all that old junk?"

"I don't know," he admitted. "But I'll try. For Carly's sake."

"So, you can forgive her, but not me? I'm sorry, Neily, I really am, for everything I helped her do to you, but I am not the monster you're painting me as. I didn't break your heart, Carly did."

"Of course I don't forgive her, but she's dead. It's kind of a moot point."

"It is not a moot point. It does matter. If you can't forgive her, how are you ever going to move past this?"

"You sound like Harriet," he sneered.

"That woman is a pain in the ass, but she makes sense," I said. "You think those dreams are a coincidence? That's your brain telling your heart that it's time to let go."

"I still can't believe you read my file. I don't know how you expect me to trust you."

"I told you the truth, didn't I?" I sighed. "You're right, I'm sorry. It was a stupid thing to do, and wrong, I get that. But I was desperate. I needed to know if you were who I thought you were."

"And am I? Actually, here's a better question—who did you think I was?"

"I don't know if you remember this, but you didn't take the breakup that well. And after Carly died, you became this wall of solid anger. I needed to know that underneath all that hostility you were still the guy who loved Carly."

"And?"

"And I think you're still that guy, Neily. Under all the sarcasm and resentment and fear, you're still you."

"And the fact that I'm having dreams tells you that?"

"No. The dreams are none of my business," I said.

"Now it's none of your business? You steal my cell phone and read my psychiatric file, but you're not going to weigh in on anything that really matters?"

"You don't even care what I think!" I shouted, throwing up my hands. "I don't know why I bother talking to you at all."

"I do care. I know I might act like I don't, but I do, because you're the only person I know who isn't trying to feed me a line."

I paused. "Well, I don't know what it means. But I have a theory."

"Okay."

"That bit about the dreams made me realize that I could come to you. I took it to mean that, whatever you might have convinced yourself of, you weren't wholly certain that Carly's murder was solved, that you had doubts too."

"I do have doubts. And I'm willing to do this with you, but I need you to be straight. No lies, no tricks, no secrets. I need you to promise that this is going to be an equal partnership."

"No lies, no tricks, no secrets," I said, holding out my hand. He shook it. "I promise."

He held fast to my hand. "Do you realize," he said slowly, "that by doing this we are putting ourselves in a lot of danger? Somebody killed Carly—the same thing could happen to us if we're not careful."

I stared at him for a moment, completely at a loss. I couldn't disagree with him, because he was right, and to pretend that such a thought didn't run through my mind a thousand times a day would be ridiculous. "We'll just have to be careful, then," I said.

As Neily let go of my hand, we heard a loud crash coming from the lawn.

"Neily, I think there's someone out there," I said.

"Let's go see who it is."

We ran out the side door and around to the front. A ceramic planter near the door had been knocked over and smashed, geraniums and dirt spilling out all over the brick.

"Hey!" We turned to see a tall, broad man coming from the direction of the garage and carrying some kind of stick. When he walked into the light, I could see that the stick was a broom and the man was wearing a white collared shirt with a name tag. "What are you kids doing here?" he asked.

"My name is Audrey Ribelli," I told him. "Paul Ribelli is my uncle. He knows we're here."

"Oh." The man switched the broom to his left hand and held out his right for me to shake. "Frank Gordon, private security."

"You're a security guard?" Neily asked.

"Did Paul hire you to watch the place?" I asked.

"On nights he's on call, yeah," Frank said.

"I wonder why he didn't mention it," Neily said.

"Maybe he forgot," I said. "How long have you been working here, Frank?"

He thought for a moment. "Almost a year, I guess."

"Why were you hired?" I asked.

Frank shrugged. "When I started, Mr. Ribelli said something about a break-in. I figure he's trying to keep it from happening again. These Castlewood homes got a lot of expensive shit in them."

"A break-in? When?"

Frank hesitated.

"You're right," I said, smiling at him reassuringly. "I really should be asking Paul these questions, shouldn't I? I'll just go inside and give him a call—would you like me to warn him about all this while I'm at it?" I gestured to the broken planter. "What happened here, anyway?"

"Saw the light in the foyer, but Mr. Ribelli didn't warn me that anyone was going to be in the house, so I stood on the planter to get a look." Frank pointed to a small half-circle window over the door; all the other windows had their shades drawn. "But when I was getting down, it tipped over and broke. Was it expensive?"

"Oh, I don't know. But his wife bought that planter in

Carmel on one of their anniversaries, right before she died. He'll be upset, understandably."

"Upset enough to fire me?" Frank asked, his eyes widening.

"Not sure. I guess I could tell him it was a raccoon or something." I gave Frank a pointed look.

"You're a manipulative little thing, aren't you?" He glanced at Neily, and we both shrugged.

"The break-in happened about a week after his daughter got shot." Frank sighed. "Whoever it was climbed up the drainpipe and got in through an unlocked window. They went through her room, but I don't think anything was taken. At least, nothing I heard about."

"Why didn't Paul report this to the police?" I asked.

"Don't think he wanted to get them involved. All that red tape. Plus, like I said, nothing was stolen. What would be the point?"

Neily shot me a meaningful look; we were having the same thought. Not reporting a break-in that happened the week *after* Carly died served to keep the case against my dad airtight— since there was no way *he* could've broken into the house from jail, Paul chose not to alert the police. Maybe Paul thought it was a coincidence, but I didn't believe in them. One reason for the break-in could've been that the real killer had left something in Carly's possession, some piece of evidence that could prove my dad's innocence and move the investigation in a different direction.

We took our leave of Frank, with me promising to back him up when he said an animal knocked over the planter (though, really, the planter had no sentimental value to Paul that I knew of), and returned to the house. Back in Carly's room, Neily asked, "You think Paul kept this from the police because he didn't want anyone to suspect somebody besides your dad?"

I nodded.

"Why would he do that to his own brother?"

"Maybe *he* killed her."

"You really think that's possible?" Neily asked.

I sighed. "No, I don't. He couldn't have—he was at the hospital all night; he has witnesses for practically every minute of his shift. But my dad and Paul have hated each other my entire life. Maybe he was so certain that my dad killed Carly that he didn't want anything derailing the investigation."

"If that's true, he may have helped Carly's real killer get off scot-free," Neily said darkly.

"*May* have? Oh, I can pretty much guarantee it."

Chapter Twelve

I started going through Carly's closet, which was, of course, very messy. I have to admit, I was much more uptight about the state of my own bedroom, and had been arranging the clothes in my closet by color since I was seven. Carly had always taken sort of an English-garden approach to her life; instead of everything having a place, she believed that things would come to her when she needed them.

My phone began to ring, breaking apart the silence into which Neily and I had lapsed since getting back to work. He was still concentrating on her desk and nightstand, though he didn't seem to be getting much accomplished.

"You going to get that?" Neily asked.

"No need," I told him, shoving a bunch of the school papers that were littering the closet floor into a trash bag. "I know who it is."

"Who?"

"Cass." It had to be. He had his own ringtone. "Third time today."

"Oh." Neily raised his eyebrows. "I thought you weren't talking to him."

"I'm not. I ran into him outside Harriet's office the other day and we spoke for, like, two seconds. It's really no big deal." I tried to sound nonchalant, but it wasn't an accident that today I was wearing my cutest outfit: a pair of tight, ridiculously expensive jeans I had picked up in San Francisco over the summer, a black and white striped tube top with a black sash and white buckle under the bust—made appropriate for school with a lightweight black cotton cardigan—and a pair of black patent-leather flats. Back when things were different, when Carly was alive and I was dating one of the most popular guys in school, I had dedicated a lot of energy—maybe too much—to maintaining my appearance. But since she died and Dad went to prison I had been too distracted and too depressed to make much of an effort. Even though I questioned my own motives in dressing as nicely as possible and making certain my hair and makeup were perfect today, I did feel much more like myself than I had in a long time.

"And he's been calling you? That doesn't sound like no big deal."

"Doesn't matter. Don't care." I wanted so badly for that to be true, and I was trying so hard to make it so. There was this wall inside of me—I could feel it in my chest—and it hid all the vulnerable parts that had been damaged in the past year. I had put my feelings for Cass back there so that he couldn't hurt me again. Maybe that was what was so comforting about Neily's presence, the sense that he was hiding stuff behind a wall too.

"Why do you think he's suddenly so chatty?"

"I have no idea."

"Maybe he's regretting what happened," Neily suggested. "Maybe he wants to kiss and make up."

"And you think that's a good idea?"

"No," Neily said. "But you're the one who just gave me the speech about forgiveness. If you expect me to work through my issues, you should think about working through yours."

"Hey! Don't psychoanalyze me, Freud. I don't expect you to work through anything. Your issues are your business."

Neily rolled his eyes. "Are you going to call him back?"

"Not a chance. He abandoned me," I said, taking a deep breath. "You know how that feels."

"For what it's worth, I think you're making the right choice."

"Yeah. I guess."

"But," he continued, "just because you hate someone doesn't mean you can't still love them." He gestured to himself. "Case in point."

"Okay, let's just stop talking about it." I held up a piece of paper. "Look. Carly's first article for the *Brighton Public Address*."

He took it from me and read it. "An exposé about the parking permit lottery?"

"Don't you remember? She found out that the varsity athletes were getting preferential treatment and flipped her shit. I thought her head was going to explode."

"She was just mad that she didn't get a permit."

"If you asked her, she'd tell you that she was fighting for justice," I said. I pulled the rest of the papers out of Carly's desk. Inside the mound of clippings, catalogs, and receipts there was a manila envelope with IMPORTANT scrawled in bold across the front.

"What's that?"

"It's a letter authorizing Carly to access her parents' safe-deposit box. It's signed by Paul."

"Why would she need that?" Neily asked.

"I don't know. Maybe she put something in it, something too valuable to keep in the house."

"Like what?"

"Mams's jewelry?"

"You know we're going to have to get into that safe-deposit box," Neily pointed out.

"Why?"

"Because even if your grandmother's jewelry is in the box, Carly might've put something else in there for safekeeping."

"Okay, but how am *I* supposed to get access to it? Legally I have no claim on it, remember?"

"Carly apparently did."

"Yeah, but I'm not Carly."

"We'll figure out a way," he said assuredly.

I put my hands on my hips and surveyed the scene. "We're never going to get through all this."

"Yeah we are. Is there a box in that back corner over there?"

I reached past a few empty suitcases and a stack of old fashion magazines and grabbed the edge of a small cardboard box. Inside was a scratchy orange wool sweater that had probably been an unfortunate Christmas or birthday gift from a distant relative. I lifted the sweater out to show it to Neily, and when I unfolded it something fell to the ground with a thud. I picked it up—it was a book, but it had no binding, no spine. It was just the guts of the book.

"What's that?" Neily asked.

"Edgar Allan Poe," I read from the flyleaf. *"The Purloined Letter and Other Stories."*

"I know that book," Neily said, as if from far off. "Carly was reading it the first time we— No." He shook his head. *"The Purloined Letter . . ."* He stood up and went over to examine Carly's bookshelf. After a moment, his face lit up like a slot machine that was about to pay out. He pried a hardcover book off the shelf and held it in his hands as if it were some sort of artifact, an ancient chest he was afraid to open. "She wasn't reading *The Purloined Letter,* she was *writing* in it. Do you know what 'The Purloined Letter' is about?"

I shrugged. "No."

"It's a mystery set in Paris. Somebody is using a stolen letter to blackmail an influential person and the police can't find it. Eventually, a private detective figures out where the blackmailer hid it—with all the other mail in the room, *in plain sight.*" He handed me the book and I opened it up to the first page, where Carly had scrawled her name. "Tell me that's not a journal glued into the binding."

I nodded. "Looks like it."

Neily came to look over my shoulder.

"I had no idea she kept a diary," I said. "I sometimes saw her writing things down, but I always thought it was ideas for newspaper stories." I flipped through the pages carefully. Carly's handwriting was messy and not easily legible, but I had gotten used to copying her class notes and was pretty good at deciphering it. "It doesn't look like she wrote in here very often. Maybe once a month, if that. She started it when she was twelve, but stopped after a few entries. She didn't pick it up again until just after her mom died. Look." I pointed to the date on the left-hand corner.

"Let me see," Neily said, reaching for it.

I turned quickly to the last page. "I think we should read the end. Maybe she wrote something that will help us."

Neily narrowed his eyes. "What are you doing?"

"You'll get distracted," I said. "I know what you're looking for."

His expression clouded. "Okay, let's read the end."

My breath hitched. "The last entry reads: 'Now I know that whatever happened to Laura Brandt was because of me. I'm a monster for what I did to her, and I can't rest until I make things right.' "

"Who's Laura Brandt?"

"I don't know."

"We should read the whole thing," Neily said, taking the journal. "Maybe she says something more."

"I'll take it home tonight. It's not very long." I held out my hand, but Neily refused to give me the book.

"I want to read it first."

I tried to grab it from him. "No way," I said.

"Excuse me?"

"What makes you think that you have any right to read this?" I challenged. "This is *Carly's* diary and now that she's dead it belongs to me. You have no claim on it."

"We had a deal!"

"I'll show you anything I find."

"Audrey, I have—" he began.

I put my hand on his arm. "I know what you're looking for. But now is not the time for that."

Neily hesitated, then nodded with resignation and let go of the book.

I slipped Carly's journal into my bag, then went over to her bureau and took the jewelry box down. It wasn't long, but it was deep, with a top level separated into smaller compartments that could be removed. Everything in the jewelry box was of the costume variety; I wasn't particularly interested in keeping any of it. I took the top compartments out and placed them on the desk. In the lower bed of the jewelry box, there was only a small manila envelope on which Carly had written OLD in black permanent marker.

The envelope contained pictures. They were mostly of Neily and Carly, but there were some of Carly and me, too, and a couple of the three of us together that had been taken by Miranda. In those pictures, Carly was always between the two of us, her arms draped around our shoulders. I called Neily over to look at them.

"I guess that's what Paul meant," I said, pressing them into his hand. "You should keep them."

He handed them back. "No, that's okay."

"You should. You might want them someday."

Neily took the photos and glanced through them. He had made it about halfway through the stack when I realized something. I snatched one of the pictures from his hand. It was one of the three of us, and I pointed to Carly's hand.

"You see that?" I asked.

"Carly's ring?" Carly had a claddagh ring that her mom and

dad had bought for her in Ireland when she was ten. She had worn it on her right ring finger; ever since her mom's death, as far as I knew, she had never taken it off.

I started rummaging through the compartments of the jewelry box. "I don't see it in here, and I'm sure it wasn't in the box of her effects the police turned over after they closed the case." I grabbed the files out of my bag and found the inventory. "It's not listed on here."

"Maybe she lost it."

"She loved that ring. She was always so careful with it—it's not something she would just drop down the drain."

"You're thinking that the person who killed her took it," Neily said.

I nodded. "Nobody thought about it because of the necklace— who would notice some cheap silver ring missing when they were all focused on the diamond?"

"Do you think that would be enough to start building an appeal on?"

"I'll check with Dad's lawyer, but I doubt it. I guess there's really no way to prove she didn't just lose it. Or give it away, or put it somewhere we haven't found yet."

"At least we know that the motive wasn't theft. I mean, the ring is gone, but it's not the sort of thing you'd steal because you could pawn it. It's too personal." He grew silent, shuddering. "It's like a trophy."

"What? What are you thinking?"

"Adam. It has to be him. Who else would want something like that?"

I gave him a pointed look.

"I thought you agreed not to do that anymore," he said angrily.

"I'm just saying."

"I would never do something like that."

"*I* know, but you could forgive someone who didn't know you very well for thinking that you would." I sighed. "I'm not saying Adam's innocent—from where I'm sitting, he looks just as guilty as anybody else—but I'm not going to settle for a simple 'he was her boyfriend, so he did it' solution, and I know that's where you were heading, so I thought I'd cut you off at the pass."

"Who has more of a motive? We know he and Carly fought the night before she died, he has a reputation for having a short temper and getting into fights, and he knew you well enough to get his hands on your father's gun."

"I don't think it's a good idea to jump to any conclusions. I'll read the diary tonight and call you if I find anything."

"What am I supposed to do?"

"Go home."

That night, after dinner with my grandparents, I settled down on my bed and combed through Carly's diary.

January 10

My mother died thirteen days ago. Harriet says that it could help to write the words, to tell some inanimate object what I'm thinking and feeling. Well, I think and feel that this is a waste of my time, but she's going to check to see if I'm writing in the journal, so I thought I'd better give it a shot. It honestly isn't so bad. I've had this journal for years, written stupid little-girl things in it, which I don't read, but

I know that they're there. It's easier to write how I feel than to say it aloud. I can't talk to anybody about this, especially Dad. Mom is the one who died, but he's the ghost in this house. He stays up until all hours, pacing his study. He can't work, and he won't eat. I have to force him, beg him, which is unfair. I'm the child. I miss her too, so much that sometimes I can't breathe, but I can't let him see it because I'm afraid that it will just make him sadder. Sometimes I think that she's coming back, that she caught the travel bug and took off to Mexico, or England, and that next month she'll show up in Empire Valley. Sometimes I let myself imagine it, before I go to sleep, hoping that maybe I'll dream it that way. If it's a dream, I won't have to feel bad for pretending.

After a while, these sorts of entries stopped with no explanation. There were a couple of paragraphs written around the time that Carly broke things off with Neily. I was afraid to let him see these. It would hurt him, and Carly had hurt him enough.

I knew that Neily held me partially responsible for their breakup, but I had less to do with it than he thought. It was true that after I started dating Cass I had tried to draw Carly into my new group of friends. It had nothing to do with Neily. Carly was my best friend, and I wanted her around. When Adam started showing interest in her, I encouraged it. Neily thought I had changed her into someone else, but the truth was that Carly's transformation was her own doing, and her relationship with Adam was a symptom, not the cause of it. I knew Neily resented me for standing idly by while Carly broke his heart and humiliated him publicly, and I was probably guilty of that. She convinced me that it was the only way to make absolutely clear to him that she wanted to end things, and the plan sounded oddly noble.

"I don't want to torture him by drawing it out," Carly had told me the day before. "He'll fight for me—that's the kind of person Neily is—but he shouldn't. I'm not worth it. He needs to see that." The incident was carefully choreographed, and Neily had gotten the message. Even though I knew it was for his own good, when I saw his face, everything changed. I went after him, called his name from the door as he walked away from the party, not knowing what I'd say if he actually turned around.

After Carly broke up with Neily, she'd written only a few entries until August twenty-seventh. "Mams died today" was all that one said. Less than nine months following Miranda's death, and a little more than a year before Carly's, Mams had succumbed to a terrible case of double pneumonia. Losing Mams was awful for me. With Mom gone and Dad the way he was, my grandparents were the only people in the world I could really count on to take care of me, and now one of them had passed away.

But Carly was an absolute wreck. In some ways, I think Mams's death might have been harder on Carly than her mom's death had been. After Miranda's diagnosis, her family was forced to face the possibility that she might not survive. Carly was, in some small way, prepared for what happened to her mom, but Mams's death was a complete shock. We were in Carly's bedroom doing the last of our summer assignments when Paul came in to give us the news, and I remember Carly's expression of utter disbelief. She seemed stunned to find out that one major loss didn't immunize her against others.

Carly didn't speak very much at the funeral, but she did say one thing that's followed me ever since.

"How many people are we going to lose before the universe decides we've had enough?" Carly asked me. I didn't answer, but if I had known what was coming I would have said, "All of them." Horrible, but true.

As I continued on through Carly's diary, it amazed me how young we were then, and how stupid. Carly's decision to get involved with Adam was the biggest mistake she ever made, but of course she couldn't see it at the time. She dated him for the same reason people jump out of airplanes: because it was exciting and dangerous, and she didn't seriously believe she could get hurt.

Adam was already notorious for dealing drugs, which at a school like Brighton, where nearly eighty percent of the students had more pocket money than most Americans make in several months, was a very profitable business. Adam played the part admirably, and he had a sinister presence that made every word or movement seem like a threat. He also had Cass, the only person who could control him. Cass brought out Adam's better side. When it was just the four of us, things were fine, but when Cass was busy with basketball, I knew that Adam wasn't so benign. Carly thought she could handle him. She was desperate for the sort of attention that she got from Adam, and she became reckless in her pursuit of it.

But it wasn't until the summer before she died that I started to understand how much Adam had changed Carly, and how little perspective she had on her life.

Sophomore Year—Spring Semester

It was the Friday night before finals week, and we were celebrating with the Force, Carly's favorite party drink. On paper, it's pretty much the most disgusting thing that's ever been invented—beer, vodka, and a can of frozen pink lemonade concentrate. In actuality, though, it tastes sort of okay. We mixed up a batch in her bathroom and filled two water bottles, taking them into her bedroom to play a drinking game to the movie *Glitter*.

"Okay, here's the rule," Carly said as she pressed PLAY. "Every time there's an aerial shot of New York, we take a drink."

Fun fact: *Glitter* has about thirty-seven thousand aerial shots of New York in it, so we were pleasantly buzzed by the time the movie was over. When the credits began to roll, Carly turned off the TV and turned on the radio.

"I love this song!" she said, flopping down on her bed.

"Me too! What is it?"

"I don't know. Adam will—get me my phone, it's in my bag."

I was still sitting on the floor near her bed, so I leaned over and dragged her schoolbag toward me. My head felt like it was stuffed with cotton and my arms were heavy, as if I had on those weight cuffs that runners wear. I practically dumped the contents of the bag into my lap to find her cell.

"Here," I said, tossing the phone up to her. Carly dialed Adam and had him listen to the song over the phone. I was slowly putting everything back into her purse when a small square plastic bag filled with white powder fell out of her cosmetics case. I picked it up between two fingers, my mind scrolling through everything it could be *besides* drugs. All my fuzzy brain could come up with was flour, but I didn't think Carly was doing any impromptu baking at school.

Carly hung up, laughing. "He was like, 'I can't even hear what you're playing me, but if *you* like it, then it must be horrible.' What an asshole."

"Carly," I said, holding up the bag. "What's this?"

"Hey," she cried, grabbing it out of my hand. "What are you going through my stuff for?"

"Is that cocaine?"

"No! Yes. I don't know. It's not even mine. Adam told me to give it to Jamie Pierson in trig and I forgot."

"You *forgot*?"

"*Yes,* and don't tell Adam, he'll kill me. I told Jamie I'd drop it off at his house tomorrow morning. Unless you want to come with me tonight?" she proposed, grinning.

"No thanks," I snapped. "If you want to let your boyfriend turn you into a *drug* mule that's your business, but don't you dare even think about getting me involved!"

"Aren't you a saint," she said. The look on Carly's face infuriated me. She was clearly dumbfounded by my reaction, as if I were the one being totally irrational. I stormed out of her room and went right to Cass's house, but he didn't respond as I'd expected.

"I wouldn't worry too much about Carly," he said with trademark nonchalance. "It is possible to be friends with Adam and do him the occasional favor and not entirely ruin your life. I speak from experience."

"That's not the point," I fumed.

"I'll talk to her if you want," Cass offered. "And Adam listens to me. I can make sure she doesn't become a delivery service."

I wrapped my arms around his waist and snuggled close to him. "Thanks, Cass."

"Any time," he said.

Carly didn't react well to whatever Cass told her; she resented his interference, and their once casual, good-natured friendship quickly deteriorated into loathing on her side. She even encouraged me to break up with him a couple of times; Carly was good at holding a grudge. In any case, it didn't matter; our own relationship had reached an obstacle it couldn't really overcome. Plenty of our friends used drugs recreationally, but I was scared for Carly. If nothing else, my parents' history had taught me that substance abuse leads to violence, and getting involved with Adam's affairs would only lead to misery.

Senior Year

Carly and I argued a lot in the next few months before she died. It was clear that she didn't think she could trust me anymore, but I couldn't let it go. She didn't want my advice. She was so entrenched in Adam's world that she couldn't see a way out of it; she was secretive, withholding. They fought all the time, but she wouldn't leave him. It was as if she didn't think she was worth anything more than what Adam could give her. She didn't say it quite that way in her diary, but everything she wrote about him was laced with self-loathing and despair.

An entry dated June eighth, the tail end of our sophomore year, caught my eye:

Something happened last night at Cass's party. I took a couple of shots in the kitchen, and when I came out into the hall somebody (?) handed me a drink. I'm afraid it was drugged. I don't remember anything after that, but when I woke up this morning—in my own bed (who drove me home?)—I couldn't find my underwear. There are bruises on my thighs and stomach—I'm afraid something bad happened. I can't remember, but I know this feeling. I want to ask Adam if we had sex last night, but if he says we didn't, I just don't know what I'll do. What will I tell him if he asks why? Who could I have slept with? Who would do this to me? I can't tell Audrey—she'll freak.

I put my hand to my forehead; my fingers were cold. I willed myself to keep reading, but there wasn't anything else. The next entry wasn't until August, and it mentioned nothing about what had happened in June.

I had been at that party. Cass—and, before Cass, his brother, Jerod—had a tradition of throwing a party at the end of the school year; they called it the School's Out for Summer Bash. It was the same party Carly had broken up with Neily at the year before. Cass had gone all out, buying several kegs of expensive beer and creating a sickly sweet pink punch for the girls, most of whom were already drunk. I showed up late, on my way home from Grandpa Charles's birthday dinner, and I couldn't find Carly anywhere. I asked around for her, but nobody could tell me where she was. Cass was in the game room playing beer pong with his buddies; I watched for a while, but after about an hour of spectating and socializing I wandered into the Irvings' spectacular screening room, where I nursed a beer while *The Godfather* played and a few couples made out furiously. I was asleep in a cushy theater chair when Adam woke me roughly and thrust Carly, incredibly drunk and nearly passed out, into my arms.

"Take her home," he snapped. "And tell her not to call me in the morning." Then he walked off.

Carly's hair was mussed and her clothes were tangled, but at the time it seemed like par for the course. She revived a little in the car when I rolled down the windows. I had to pull over to let her throw up three times, but eventually I got her home.

"How much did you drink?" I whispered as I put her to bed.

She covered her eyes with her arm and slurred, "Too much."

I slept next to her in the bed the whole night, and after checking on her in the morning I slipped out and went home. It never occurred to me that something might have happened to her at the party—she always overdid it, especially when Adam was around—and, true to her word, she never mentioned anything to me. I felt sick to my stomach, thinking about how I'd been sleeping in the screening room while Carly was being raped.

How was I going to tell Neily?

CHAPTER THIRTEEN

"I'll wait while you process," I said, folding my arms on the table and squinting behind my sunglasses at Neily. I was wearing them inside the Calamity Diner, not because I thought I was cool or I was trying to be incognito, but because I didn't want Neily to see how red my eyes were.

He jumped out of his chair and began pacing. "I don't want to process, I want to hit something."

"Don't overreact," I warned.

"*Over*react? I don't think that's possible."

"Maybe we should go talk to Harriet."

"No way. She'll tell us to go to the police."

"Well, maybe we should."

"And say what? We think Carly Ribelli was raped? They'd probably laugh in our faces and tell us she got what was coming to her."

"They would not!" I said. Neily was given to exaggeration. Yes, Carly had had a few run-ins with the police—they had once found her sleeping, drunk, on a park bench in the middle of the afternoon after a series of events I'm still not quite clear on; she'd been in attendance at several parties they'd broken up; and she was with Adam the one time they tried unsuccessfully to bust him for dealing marijuana out of his car in the back parking lot of Howard's Yogurt—but she wasn't exactly Public Enemy Number One.

"With the people she hung out with? The only person who made anywhere near the amount of trouble in this town as Adam's gang was your dad. How far did police sympathy get him?"

"That's ridiculous," I said, not really believing it.

"Plus, we don't even know that whatever happened to her that night had anything to do with her death. No," he said firmly. "We can do this on our own."

"I'm going to show the diary to my dad's lawyer," I told him. "Between this and the ring, maybe he can build a strong enough case to justify an appeal."

"A rape that might not have actually been a rape and a missing souvenir ring? Yeah, that sounds like a convincing argument. Maybe your dad should just fire his lawyer and get you to defend him."

"Shut up and sit down, you're making me nervous." I lifted my sunglasses and rubbed my eyes. I had stayed up all night parsing the diary, and had found no other mention of the rape.

He took his seat and a deep breath. "I just don't know what to do with all this."

"I know. Me either." I leaned forward. "Hey, I have a question. Did you send Carly any letters between June and September?"

"No."

"Are you sure?"

"I think I'd remember. Why do you ask?"

"It's just that in the diary she mentions getting a letter from you, but she doesn't say when it came or what it said. I got the impression it wasn't the first."

"Show me."

I passed him the diary opened to the relevant page. He read it twice, then shook his head. "I have no idea what she's talking about."

I sighed.

"So what's our next move?"

"I guess we find out who was alone with Carly the night of Cass's party. Ask around."

"Okay, except who's going to tell us anything? We're a regular little leper colony."

"I'll figure it out. I may not be friends with the in-crowd anymore, but I still know how to push their buttons."

"Want me to come with you?"

"No," I said. "You make people uncomfortable."

"Thanks."

"It's a compliment, believe me, but it's not going to get the job done. Those people are professional secret keepers—the reason they get away with everything is because they protect one another."

"So what's your strategy?"

"Pick out the limping gazelle, isolate it from the herd," I murmured.

"Who's that?"

"Take a wild guess."

"Lucy Miller."

I hadn't talked to Lucy since Carly's funeral. At one time, she and Carly and I had been inseparable, a trio of girlfriends in a social group made up mostly of guys. We banded together, confiding and gossiping about boys, but those days were so remote to me now, it was as if the memories weren't even mine. I felt like my life had started anew the moment I heard that Carly was dead.

I showed up at Lucy's house at around four o'clock, knowing that her parents wouldn't be home from work yet. Her dad was a pediatrician at the hospital, and her mom was a lawyer at a prestigious firm in Palo Alto.

Lucy was surprised to see me. She glared at me like I was an intruder, a stranger whose very presence on her doorstep was grounds for suspicion.

"Hi, Lucy," I said softly, knowing that submission was the only way to ingratiate myself. What Lucy wanted—what she had always wanted—was power and influence over others, though she was neither charismatic enough nor strong enough to demand it. She had always taken a backseat to Carly and me when we were friends, and I knew that asserting myself was the quickest way to shut her off. I needed to earn her trust or her curiosity. Either would do.

"What are you doing here?" she asked, fixing me with a cold stare.

"I wanted to talk."

She folded her arms across her chest. "About?"

"Can I come in?"

"No." But she was wavering. Gossip was her one true love.

"Come on, Luce," I pleaded. "It's about Carly."

She looked stricken. If I had ever wondered if Lucy actually missed Carly, I knew the answer now. She never would've reacted like that if she didn't. "No way," she said sharply.

"I'm not leaving until you agree to talk." I made a big show of sitting down on her stoop and taking out a copy of *In Style*. "Don't worry, I brought a magazine."

Lucy checked her watch, then spent a few moments trying to figure out if I was serious. "Okay. But I don't have a lot of time. I'm meeting someone later."

"It won't take very long," I promised, stepping inside the cool, dark foyer. "Is there somewhere private we can talk?"

Lucy led me out onto the patio and gestured to a pair of lounge chairs. Four feet away, the Millers' infinity pool glistened, the water lapping over the side and plunging, so it seemed, into the valley below.

"Sit," she commanded, taking the chair opposite and stretching out. She was trying to affect some semblance of calm, a cool remoteness she had picked up from Carly. At first Lucy had resented Carly; she had been close friends with Adam for ages and was jealous of his intense interest in a girl who just five minutes before had been one of those bookish weirdos who were too smart for regular classes. But Lucy eventually came to adore Carly. She looked up to her like an older sister even though we were all the same age. Lucy was a cute girl, petite with dark curly hair, a pert nose, and stormy gray eyes; she was always with some guy or another, but she had a hard time getting any of them to fall in love with her. Carly, on the other hand, had had every one of Adam's goons—and Adam, too—wrapped around her finger. She did it by acting distant, which never failed to get the attention she was looking for. Lucy had learned by watching, and was doing a pretty good job of imitating Carly's method, but that's all it was, artificial posing.

"Tell me."

"Do you remember Cass's School's Out for Summer party?"

"Which one?"

"Sophomore year."

"I'm gonna need a little bit more."

I tried to dig up some other notable events from that night. "I think that was the night Stephanie Cohen threw up all over your new shoes."

"The black Balenciaga peep toes?" Lucy asked.

"Uh-huh."

"Yeah, I remember," she sighed. "God, I loved those shoes. Stephanie owes me five hundred dollars. I'm pretty sure that's why she moved."

"Yes, I'm sure that's why." *Not because, you know, her dad got transferred or anything,* I thought. "Did you see Carly at all that night?"

"Sure. We had a few drinks together, shared a joint, and then I went off to talk to some people. After that I lost her. Why?"

"Did you see her with anybody that night? Any guy besides Adam?"

Lucy thought about it. "Well, the Bean was following her around everywhere, but I don't think he really counts."

"The Bean?" Toby Pinto, aka the Bean, was one of Adam's

squadron of drug hustlers, a squat chubby guy who followed him around like a lapdog. He seemed to dote on every girl who ever talked to him, which was why I had always tried to avoid him as much as possible. The boys were pretty cruel to him; when they were bored, they pranked him, taking pleasure in upsetting him. The Bean had a legendary temper, and the smallest things could set him off like fireworks, although he was generally a pretty nice guy. All he wanted was to be liked, and that was why they despised him. His desperation made him an easy target.

"Yeah. She always treated him like her own personal charity case," Lucy said snidely. "He was pretty hung up on her."

"He was pretty hung up on everybody."

"But Carly especially. He once told me that he was in love with her."

"He did?" That people were fools enough to confide anything in Lucy had always baffled me. "And you told Adam."

"Of course," she said. "Adam and a couple of the guys threatened him. You didn't hear about that?"

"No," I confessed.

"Big shock there," she said. "Everyone was always so careful around you—don't tell Audrey, she'll get *upset*. Carly most of all. She was always telling us to keep things secret from you."

"Like what things?"

"She made us promise not to tell you how much she used, for one." Lucy yawned. "She thought you'd tell her dad or turn her in to Finch. Which you totally would have."

"No I wouldn't."

"Oh, come on, Audrey! You were such a good girl," she sneered. "You would've ratted her out in a hot second."

"I never turned on Adam," I pointed out. "He did his thing, I did mine. Cass told me everything."

"That's the stupidest thing I've ever heard. You knew nothing." But she didn't seem so sure. "You should go."

"Just give me five more minutes," I insisted. "So the Bean was following Carly around?"

"Yeah, until Adam had Oz eject him." Sean Ozrick was one of Adam's able-bodied henchmen. I thought he was a good person at heart, but then again, we weren't best friends. I hung out with them sometimes, but I wasn't what you'd call close with most of Adam's goons, Brighton students or not. I spent most of my time with Cass or the girls.

"When?"

"I don't know, around midnight?"

"Did you see the Bean take Carly into one of the bedrooms?" I asked.

She shrugged. "I guess somebody must've—Adam found Carly in one of the guest rooms, half naked and passed out."

"He must've been pissed—he dropped her in my lap and practically demanded I drive her home."

"He figured she cheated on him. He tried to find out who, but he never could. She denied it, of course." Lucy swung her tanned legs over the side of the chaise. "You should ask Cass. He might've seen something."

I wasn't particularly excited to do that. "Could *you* ask Cass for me?"

"Why would I do you a favor?" Lucy said caustically. "I'm already doing you one just talking to you."

"You're a real softy, Luce." I stood up, impatient to leave. Lucy had no more information for me, that much was clear. "Thanks for your help."

"Wait. Now I have a question. What's going on with you and Think Tank? Are you together now?"

"Did Cass ask you to find out for him?"

"Yeah, right." She laughed. "Like Cass cares what you do with Carly's rejects."

"Feel free to tell him that it's none of his business."

Lucy's face clouded over suddenly. "What are you doing, Audrey? Hanging around with Neily Monroe, asking all these questions? Carly is dead—this is all in the past. Why do you have to go dragging it all up again?" Her voice wobbled. I almost felt sorry for her. Sometimes I forgot other people had lost a friend as well.

"I guess I just need to know," I told her.

"Need to know what?" she called after me, but I was already walking away and didn't turn back.

CHAPTER FOURTEEN

The next day at school, Neily met me at my locker.

"Do you remember Toby Pinto?" I asked, pulling a year-book from two years ago out of my bag. I flipped to a flagged page and pointed to a photo.

"You mean the Bean?" Neily asked. "Sure. Carly and I had gym class with him freshman year. What about him?"

"He used to be part of Adam's crew," I said. "Adam and his buddies were horrible to the Bean. They used to pull pranks on him all the time, but poor Toby thought they were all friends. Sometimes they would goof on him and he would lose it and start swearing and flailing and screaming like a two-year-old, and they would all just sit back and laugh at him." I shook my head. "It was disgusting."

"That was a nice group of guys you and Carly got yourselves mixed up with," Neily remarked, but I let it go.

"As far as I can remember, Carly was the only person who was ever really nice to the Bean," I said. "Whenever he got upset, Carly would stick up for him." Carly was like that. With her close friends she could be mercurial, moving in and out of good and bad moods like a car dodging through traffic, but with others—like the Bean, or like Fiona Benson, a girl with cerebral palsy whom she took notes for in all the classes they shared—she was uniformly kind and patient. She was actually quite nurturing, if you watched closely enough.

"You think the Bean had some sort of massive crush on Carly?"

"Well, there was an incident. One time, Carly was trying to talk to him during one of his tantrums and he accidentally smacked her across the face. The guys flipped out, Adam especially. They would've beaten him up, only Carly and I were right there. But he kept bothering Carly, trying to get her to talk to Adam for him, and finally Adam got sick of it, so he organized a really mean trick."

"What a shock."

"Cass told the Bean that Adam and Carly had broken up, and that they had been fighting over him. Cass convinced the Bean that he should ask Carly to go to prom, because it was obvious that she had feelings for him."

"I still can't believe she actually went with him." I said. "It made absolutely no sense to me."

"Well, later she had to tell the Bean some sort of story so that she could 'get back together' with Adam."

"So what does that have to do with Carly's rape?"

"The Bean was at Cass's party."

"Sounds like everybody was. My invitation must've gotten lost in the mail."

"Oh boo hoo. Anyway, as far as I can recall the Bean crashed the party—he was already on the outs with Adam. Lucy said that he was following Carly around until Adam threw him out."

"So where's he now?"

I shrugged. "College?"

"I don't think so. Neither the brains nor the motivation."

"Then I'm going to go with living at home and working at an auto body shop," I said. "He was really big on cars. We just have to figure out which shop."

"How? There have to be hundreds of mechanics in the tri-valley area."

"Maybe somebody knows."

"Did the Bean have any real friends?"

"I don't know. But I think I know who to ask." I glanced across the quad at Cass, who was surrounded by his usual cadre of teammates and bimbo cheerleaders. "I just really don't want to do it."

⁓⁓⁓

My old boyfriend, Cass Irving, was the star of the basketball team, a good student, and an all-around mensch. Cass was very tall and blond, with a mop of curly hair that his coach made him cut every three days during the season. He and Adam Murray had been best friends since childhood, which was how we all ended up being as close as we were. While my relationship with Cass disintegrated as a result of Carly's

murder and Dad's incarceration, Cass and Adam's had remained firmly intact, although recently there had been talk
that the two were fighting. It was difficult to get Cass alone, but
eventually I managed it.

I caught up with him after school as he was walking to his
car. I had already made sure I looked perfect, spending almost
twenty minutes in the bathroom at the end of seventh period
checking myself from head to toe and talking myself into
adopting a strong, impervious attitude for approaching my ex.
Now that I was standing right next to him, though, I felt the
nerves wriggling like worms in my stomach and tried my best
to resist the urge to run away.

"I have a question for you," I said. It felt completely natural
to be walking beside him. My mind started bombarding me
with nostalgia-inducing flashes of my former life. I worked
hard to push it all out of my head, to start concentrating on the
present before my cool exterior crumbled away.

He gave me a strange look and started scanning the sky.

"What are you doing?" I asked.

"Checking for flying pigs," Cass said lightly, putting his
hand on my shoulder.

"Careful," I said, shrugging it off. "You wouldn't want your
friends to see you making contact. They might have to put you
in quarantine."

"I think I'll risk it."

Even though we were no longer touching, I could still feel
the warmth of his hand. "I just need some information. About
the Bean."

"I called you like five times yesterday. You never called me
back," he said, looking a little hurt.

"I'm sorry. I was busy."

"With Neily Monroe?" He raised his eyebrows at me. "I saw you talking to him this morning. Are you with him now?"

"Is Lucy doing reconnaissance for you?"

"I was curious. Sue me."

"Neily and I are just—" Come to think of it, I couldn't come up with a word to accurately describe what Neily and I were. "Partners. We're working on a project for English class together."

"Bummer," Cass said, but he looked relieved. "What do you want with the Bean, anyway?"

"I'm thinking about asking him to prom."

"Funny."

"I'm having a problem with my car," I said. "I heard he was working at a garage somewhere. I thought he might be able to give me some advice, or at least a discount."

"I could take a look at it," Cass offered. He stopped walking and made eye contact with me, which I couldn't avoid.

"Thanks for the offer, but I think I'll leave it to a professional."

Cass ran his fingers through his hair, which hadn't been subjected to its inaugural basketball-season chop yet. "Yeah, well, I don't know where the Bean works, but I could give you his number."

"That would be very decent of you, Cass," I said, smiling and pulling out my phone. He got his out and read the Bean's number off to me. "Thanks."

"So that's it? That's all you wanted?"

"That's all," I said, turning to walk away. Cass grabbed my arm and pulled me back.

"Come on, Aud, when are you going to forgive me?" he asked softly.

"I don't remember you asking for my forgiveness," I said.

"It was implied."

"No it wasn't." He started to say something, but I interrupted him. "And don't bother trying, because it's so not going to happen."

"So you're only going to talk to me when you want something?" he asked. "Is that how this works?"

"Yeah," I said. "That's how it works."

Freshman Year—Fall Semester

The first time Cass Irving ever spoke to me is burned into my brain. It was Halloween, and he was dressed as Count Dracula; he had dyed his hair black and was wearing what looked like stage makeup to turn his skin pale. We were in English class and our instructor had stepped out of the room for a couple of moments to talk to Mr. Finch. Cass, who was sitting right in front of me (later he would tell me that he had chosen the seat on purpose), turned around and asked, "So what exactly are you supposed to be?"

I had no idea that Halloween was such a big deal at Brighton. Even people who normally didn't care about stuff like that—Neily, for example—came to school that day in elaborate outfits. One of the nerdy guys in my third-period history class actually built an R2-D2 shell that he could climb into, sit in, and wheel around campus in. Student Government held a costume contest at lunchtime and people actually cared who won (it was that R2-D2 kid, and I was pretty sure that was the first and last time that anyone popular noticed him, which was probably the point of all that effort). It was a big change from my old school in Oregon, that's for sure.

"I'm not wearing a costume," I told him. "As you can probably tell."

"Why's that?"

"I don't like Halloween," I said.

"You don't like Halloween? That's impossible. Everybody likes Halloween. It's my favorite holiday." He beamed at me. I loved his smile. Every time he turned it on me, I felt my skin tingle.

I shook my head. "Sorry I've let you down."

"You can redeem yourself by telling me *why* you don't like Halloween," he said. "If I know what the problem is, I'll do my best to fix it."

I wanted to tell him—he was just so friendly and warm and open, I instantly felt like I could trust him with all of my secrets—but I wasn't very good at sharing. The truth was that my mom had left us on Halloween. That year I'd dressed as a cat and I stood on the pavement outside school for an hour and a half, waiting for her to pick me up. She never showed. I ended up walking the two miles home in my black leotard and leggings, wiping off the whiskers I'd penciled on with Mom's eyeliner along the way. When I got inside the house it was empty. It had been two years, and I hadn't seen or heard from her since.

Cass was expecting an answer, but instead I shrugged. "I've just never been able to get into the spirit."

"Well, that's tragic, because you can't come to my Halloween party tonight if you're not dressed up," he warned me. "Nobody's allowed inside without a costume. That's the rule."

"I wasn't invited to your party," I told him.

He gave an exaggerated look of horror. "Nobody told you? Massive oversight. The Halloween party is open to the whole school. It's the only nonexclusive shindig I'll throw all year."

"That's very generous of you. Did you just use the word 'shindig'?" I smiled.

"I did. And it *is* very generous of me; thank you for noticing, I don't get nearly enough credit for it. But just between you and me, I don't think you need to worry about getting an invite to any of my parties from here on out," Cass said, leaning close to me and practically whispering. "I think it's safe to say you'll always be welcome at an Irving 'shindig.' "

"There's that word again."

"So what do you say, Audrey Ribelli?" he asked. "Will you be attending the event of the year?"

I paused to consider. I really wanted to spend time with Cass, and he was personally inviting me, but I could see how this would go: I'd show up, there'd be a million other people there he knew better and he'd ignore me. Carly and Neily wouldn't go with me; their holiday spirit had definite limits. I'd probably be stuck in a corner alone, drinking spiked punch and missing my mom. "I don't think I'll be very fun tonight, to be honest. Some other time, maybe."

"How about next weekend?" Cass suggested.

"You're having another party next weekend?"

He shook his head. "I meant just you and me hanging out. We could go see a movie and have dinner or something."

"Are you asking me out on a date?" I was so excited I thought I might choke, but I forced myself to breathe and tried to look calm.

"Yes," he said firmly. "Are you accepting?"

"Yes," I said, feeling so light it was as if I were airborne. "Absolutely."

Senior Year

I called the Bean's number as soon as I shook Cass, but he didn't pick up, so I left him a message. I doubted he would call back. The Bean had only known me through Cass, and it was pretty likely he'd either forgotten me or dodged my call on account of my ex.

Neily and I met up at Paul's house to keep going through Carly's things, and I told him what I had found out. He seemed to find my conversation with Cass a lot more interesting than what Cass had told me.

"So he does want to get back together," Neily said. "And you blew him off?"

"Naturally," I said, folding a sweater and putting it in the Goodwill box. "What did you think I was going to do, swoon? The guy barely even apologized."

Neily shrugged. "You had a really intense thing going for a really long time. I wouldn't blame you if you still had feelings for him."

"Yes you would."

"Yeah, you're probably right. Hey, have you figured out a way to get to the safe-deposit box yet?"

"No. And I'm starting to think it doesn't matter if I do."

"You don't know what's in it," he pointed out. "There could be something important in there."

"I don't even have the key," I told him. "And I can't very well ask Paul for it."

"Maybe Carly had one."

"We didn't find it in her room."

"Yeah, but we haven't gone through everything. Anyway, maybe Carly hid it. It would be like her to do that."

"Maybe," I said. "Or she could've misplaced it. But I wouldn't worry about it just yet—I'm sure it'll turn up eventually."

The Bean never called me back, but that didn't matter. Neily did some recon, visiting every auto body shop in three towns until he found someone who could tell him where the Bean worked.

"There's a place in Danville," Neily told me over the phone on Saturday morning. "Keptow Auto Body. The Bean's some sort of foreign-car specialist."

"Figures," I said. "Only the best spark plugs for an upper-middle-class mechanic."

"You should've heard how they talked about him," Neily said. "Reverently, like he was some sort of BMW god."

"Maybe I *should* have him take a look at my car," I said. "Are you at home?"

"Yeah, why?"

"I'm coming to pick you up. We're going to pay a visit to the Bean."

CHAPTER FIFTEEN

Danville was a few towns away, which in northern California can mean thirty miles with the way the foothills separate everything. They cordon off Empire Valley on all sides, and we had to hop on the freeway to get out. It was Saturday, so the traffic was light, and it only took us about twenty minutes to get to the Bean's garage.

"Wow," Neily said as we got out of the car. "It's like Beamer heaven. The gleam of the sun off the expensive German parts is blinding." He shielded his eyes.

We went into the front office and approached the receptionist. "Hi," I said. "I'm here to see Toby Pinto? He's one of your mechanics."

"I know who he is," the girl said haughtily. She looked about sixteen. "The Bean is my boyfriend."

"So they're still calling him 'the Bean,' " Neily whispered. I swatted at him and he retreated to a corner, burying his face in an old issue of *Foreign Auto*.

"You're Toby's girlfriend? That's really great," I said.

"Who are you?"

"Just an old friend from high school. I wanted to stop by and pay a visit. It's been a really long time."

"Not that long. He graduated in June," the girl said. She was not entirely unattractive, but definitely horse-faced, and her snottiness worked not at all in her favor. Still, my smile never wavered. Probably no one was ever nice to this chick.

"I don't think Toby ever mentioned you. What's your name?"

"Amanda," she said.

"Amanda. Look, I've known Toby for years, and I think he'd like to see me, so if you could just tell me whether or not he's here, I'd really appreciate it. As a favor?"

"He's here," she told me reluctantly. "Just go on back. If Leo gives you trouble, tell him you're a customer."

"Great, thanks," I said, grabbing Neily.

"How'd you get her to back off?" he said.

"It's all about confidence," I said as we wound our way to the garage at the back. "You act like you have all the power, and people will normally give you what you want. Cass taught me that. He does it all the time in restaurants."

"Nice."

"Plus, there's something to say for just being polite. Look, there he is. Let me do the talking, all right?"

Neily nodded and gestured for me to go ahead. I strolled up

to the Bean and gave him a big smile. "Hey, Toby. How's it going?"

"What are you doing back here?" the Bean asked, furrowing his brow in agitation. I couldn't tell if he guessed the reason we were there, but it was pretty clear from his expression and the way he drew himself up as straight as possible as I walked toward him that he was surprised and unnerved to see us.

"I came to have a little chat. I called you a few days ago, but you might not have gotten the message. I was really hoping to talk to you," I said, inching closer to him. I was wearing a low-cut top (one of the reasons Amanda had been eyeing me suspiciously, I'm sure) and I leaned in to the full advantage of my cleavage. Nothing too slutty, just the right amount of interest combined with the right amount of . . . well, let's call them "assets."

"Yeah, Audrey, right?" he said uncertainly, staring at me in the predictable way.

"I thought you might not remember me, since I wasn't in school all last year. It's really great to see you."

"Yeah, you too," he said, still looking befuddled. "But can we sign each other's yearbooks another time? I'm kind of in the middle of something." He pointed to a car that was jacked halfway up to the ceiling.

"This'll be real quick." I held up three fingers. "Scout's honor."

The Bean relented. "Okay, sure. But what's he doing here?"

"He's a friend of mine," I said, unsure how much the Bean remembered Neily.

"You're that guy," he said to Neily. "You used to date Carly Ribelli. We have that in common."

To his credit, Neily didn't make a face. "Yeah, man."

"So what do you want?" The Bean had gained weight since I last saw him, but he was tanner now and he had cut his hair. He was about three or four inches shorter than Neily, and seemed anxious around him.

"Actually, this is about Carly," I said.

He turned away and rummaged through a box of tools. "Yeah?"

"Do you remember the last time you talked to her?"

"Um, I guess it was a couple of days after prom. I got a hotel room that night and she seemed to be really mad about it, so I left her alone and let her cool down." He shook his head at Neily. "Women."

Neily shrugged. "Then what?"

"Then I saw her after school with Adam Murray and I got pissed, you know? I mean, here's my girl, making out with her ex-boyfriend. I had a right to be pissed."

"Sure."

"So I went over to her house that night and confronted her about it. She said that she was sorry, but she was still in love with Adam or some shit. She dumped me. It was brutal." He shook his head. I looked over at Neily, but he had wandered away, pretending to admire a Lexus nearby, still within earshot.

"And that's it?"

"She avoided me after that. What was I supposed to do?"

"You didn't try to talk to her again?" I asked. "Like maybe at Cass's School's Out for Summer party, the one he threw at the end of your junior year?"

"Maybe for a few seconds. Adam told me that if I ever came

near her again he'd kick my ass so bad even my own mother wouldn't recognize me. And you know he could do it. He bench-presses his own goddamned body weight. I knew better than to mess with him." He looked around nervously. "That better be it, because my boss has been riding me lately about my 'commitment' to the job. You should probably go."

I nodded. "We're leaving. Thanks for your help, Toby."

"Okay." He looked puzzled, but I didn't stop to explain further. I just grabbed Neily by the arm and dragged him out of the shop.

"Did you catch that?" I asked him when we got back to the car.

"Yeah, Adam's jacked. All you have to do is look at him."

"No, I mean what the Bean said about Adam bullying him. Do you think he's just being melodramatic?"

Neily shook his head vehemently. "I'll admit, where Carly's concerned the Bean is still living in a fantasy world, but I don't doubt for a second that Adam threatened to maim him."

"What makes you so sure?"

"Because he did the same thing to me."

I raised an eyebrow. "Really? When? How come I didn't hear about this?"

Neily hesitated. "It was at the start of sophomore year, three months after Carly dumped me. I'd kept my distance, but she hadn't dropped out of the program yet and I saw her around sometimes. Once, she came up to me at my locker and asked how I was. I told her where she could stick her concern, but I guess Adam saw us talking and got pissed. Five minutes later I had my head shoved under a faucet in the bathroom, and I was choking on running water. Adam told me that if I ever spoke to Carly again I would seriously regret it."

"Did Carly know about this?"

Neily shook his head. "I don't think so."

I leaned against my car. "Adam's not exactly a teddy bear, but I had no idea he got so out of control."

Neily grimaced. "That's nothing. You know that kid who got seriously beat up in San Leandro last summer?" San Leandro, a notoriously sketchy town where the rich kids from Empire Valley sometimes bought and sold drugs, was about twenty minutes down the freeway. I remembered hearing about it but hadn't really paid much attention.

"Adam did that?"

Neily squinted, pausing as he struggled with how to put it. "I don't know. But that was the rumor. People said it was a bad deal."

"Jesus."

"How could you not know about all this?"

I shrugged. "Nobody ever said anything to me. According to Lucy, there was a whole conspiracy in place to keep me out of the loop. And I'm sure Carly didn't know about it."

"Oh, I doubt that."

"Carly was a good person," I protested. "She may have treated you badly, but she never would have stood aside and watched her boyfriend wreak havoc."

"Seriously? You expect me to believe that? Just because you've got all these warm and fuzzy memories of Carly kicking around in your head doesn't mean you should let them affect the way you look back on her behavior. Carly wasn't always good. Sometimes, she was horrible."

I took in a sharp breath and let it out slowly, trying not to get angry with him. Because he was right, of course. For every act of kindness Carly was capable of performing, there was an equal amount of trouble that she doled out, almost unconsciously, in my opinion. I should know—I was often the receiver of that trouble, those sharp remarks, those impatient outbursts. Still, I felt compelled to defend her, and was annoyed that Neily did not. "Those last few years were really hard. Miranda's death—it changed her."

"That's not an excuse," Neily said.

"No, but it's an explanation," I said. "I can't believe you're being so uncompromising about this. I'm positive that Carly didn't know anything about what Adam was capable of, even if you aren't."

"Fine," he said, in a tone that told me it was absolutely not fine. "What's next?"

"I think we should talk to Adam," I said.

"Are you nuts?"

"Contrary to what you might like to believe, Adam knew Carly pretty well," I said. "He spent a lot of time with her."

"He spent a lot of time jerking her around. That's not the same thing."

"You're awfully protective of someone you say you hate," I pointed out.

"Look, just because I was stupid enough to get involved in all this doesn't mean you get to start making assumptions about how I feel or what I think," he fumed. "When it comes to Carly, it gets complicated, and I don't need you throwing everything I say in my face."

I stared ahead, watching the cars fly past on the street.

"I don't trust Adam," Neily continued. "He's a dealer and a

liar, and I think"—he paused, as if uncertain of whether or not to go on—"I think *he* killed Carly."

"You do." I drew myself up slowly, straightening my shoulders, pushing my hair back from my eyes, like I was preparing for battle.

"Yeah."

"You think Adam shot his girlfriend in cold blood?" Even as I was saying it, I knew it wasn't as implausible as my tone implied.

"Yeah, that *would* be unusual. You almost never see an episode of *Law & Order* where someone is murdered by the person they're sleeping with," Neily said sarcastically.

"You know that the police investigated him, right? They didn't find any evidence. What does that tell you?"

"That they fucked up."

"He has an alibi, Neily, remember?"

"Right. And those have never been known to be falsified."

"He was with Cass the whole night."

"Of course," Neily said, but he sounded unconvinced. He took out his cell phone and checked the time. "Shit. I'm supposed to have dinner with my dad."

I nodded. "We'll talk later."

That evening, Neily called me on my cell.

"I thought you were having dinner with your dad," I said.

"I am. I'm at Casa Orozco and guess who just walked in?"

"Who?"

"Lucy Miller and Adam Murray."

"What would Lucy and Adam be doing together?" I asked Neily the next day. We were sitting at Neily's usual table in the library.

"What do you think?" he asked, raising an eyebrow suggestively.

I shook my head. "No way."

"Why not? They've been friends since middle school. Maybe they're something more now."

"I don't think so. Back when I was hanging out with them, Adam was always complaining to Carly about how clingy Lucy was, how desperate." It had annoyed Cass, too. She was always hooking up with the guys on the basketball team and then obsessing over them to him.

"Maybe that was all a front. If Adam was secretly hooking up with Lucy behind Carly's back, of course he would trash-talk her to Carly's face. They looked more than chummy at the restaurant," Neily went on. "I watched them all night, and they couldn't keep their hands off each other."

"Ugh. Just what we needed—another wrinkle."

"This *is* just what we needed. What if there was something going on between them back then, too? Lucy might know something about why Adam killed Carly, even if she doesn't know she knows," Neily suggested. "Hell, she might be the reason."

"So now we're operating under the assumption that Adam did, in fact, kill Carly?" I gave him a dubious look.

"I am."

I sighed. "We have no proof of that."

"Well, if you want to talk about proof, maybe we should go over all the evidence that your father killed Carly. That should be fruitful."

"Do you always have to go there?" I snapped.

"I thought you wanted answers. Answers that *contradict* the status quo, I mean."

"I do."

"Then why are you fighting so hard against my theory that Adam is to blame? What do we have to lose by exploring that possibility?"

"We'll look into Adam. But don't forget, he has an alibi for the murder." An alibi my ex-boyfriend had given him.

"What? That he was getting drunk and high and playing video games at Cass's house? Yeah, that's rock solid. There's no way that Cass, under the influence, wouldn't have noticed Adam sneaking out of the house," he said.

"Yeah, okay. But we have to approach this very carefully—if Adam is as dangerous as you think he is, we're going to land on his shit list *real* fast if he finds out what we're doing."

"Agreed. So, where do we start?"

"We need to find out who had Carly in that room at Cass's party," I told him. He shot me a dark look. I threw up my hands. "What? We can't just ignore that it happened because you've already got Adam fitted for a noose. I don't believe in coincidence—I'm sure that it had something to do with what happened to her."

"What makes you so sure?"

"It's just a feeling. That's not the sort of thing Carly would be able to let go of. She must have gone looking for answers, and if she became a threat to the wrong person it might have landed her in a lot of trouble."

"Okay, but what about Adam?"

"I'll talk to Cass again about his party, and I'll also try to fish around about the night that Carly died."

"You're going to talk to Cass again?"

"It's the fastest way to the answers we're looking for. Believe me, I don't want to."

"Don't you? Just a little?" he asked.

"No," I insisted, slamming my chemistry book shut and getting up. "Not even a little."

CHAPTER SIXTEEN

I lied to Neily. The way I felt about Cass—the way I had felt about him, the way I still felt about him—resisted definition, and I could hardly explain that to Neily, even though he was likely one of the few people who would understand. But Neily deeply distrusted that whole group, he fundamentally hated the Casses and Adams of the world, and he wasn't going to go through the trouble of trying to understand what was going through my head. Regrettable, yes, but I had learned to handle things on my own.

I had never expected Cass Irving to like me. Back when we were freshmen at Brighton he was far and away the best-looking and most popular boy in our class. I never imagined that he would notice me, but I couldn't help but obsess over him like every other girl our age. It felt more like worshipping a movie star than liking a flesh-and-blood boy—that was how untouchable he seemed to me.

Carly wanted the best for me, even from the beginning, when we were still getting to know each other. When I moved to Empire Valley, she seemed determined rather than inclined to like me, and expected Neily to feel the same way. He never did, as far as I could tell, but he made a good show of it for Carly's sake, and he put up with us patiently. I think it was because he knew how much it meant for her to have some family member she felt connected to as her mom became sicker and sicker. Paul was no help at all; he ignored her and spoiled her and left her to her own devices, trying to combat his depression over his wife's illness by plunging headfirst into his work and rarely surfacing. All Carly had was me, and I her, and Neily appeared to respect that.

After her mom's death, Carly began to change. At first she buried herself in Neily, seeking comfort in him and shutting out the rest of the world, especially me. It was as if she resented me, although I could never figure out why—after all, I was also motherless, except that my mom had left me behind by choice. Maybe she thought I was the luckier one, because my mom wasn't entirely lost to me—there was at least a chance that she might return, and Carly probably assumed this gave me some sort of comfort. It did not. It never has. My mom wasn't coming back, that much was obvious. She may not have been dead, but she was as good as.

But Carly's loss was always threatening to catch up with her, and by the end of freshman year it had. It didn't happen overnight; it happened slowly, progressively, over several months, and we would've been powerless to stop it. Except that I didn't try to. I was dating Cass, and it was like I was part of a different world. I wanted Carly to be there with me, to join me in the popular crowd so that I didn't have to be alone, so that people wouldn't be aware of how much I didn't belong. My runaway mom and my drunk of a dad had made me painfully insecure, but Carly could protect me. She could help me hide it. I used her to my own advantage just like everybody else.

I could tell Adam liked Carly, and I liked the idea of them dating. If she was with Cass's best friend, we'd hang out more. It was a selfish thing to do, but one morning before school I saw her arguing with Neily in the parking lot, and sensing a moment of weakness, I pulled her aside at lunch to float the possibility.

"Fighting with Neily?" I asked, putting a cup of yogurt on my tray as we moved through the cafeteria line.

"Yes," she sighed, grabbing an apple. "I didn't hang out with him on Saturday night like I said I would and of course he's upset with me about it. But what was I going to do, take him to Stephanie's party?"

"Did you even invite him?"

"Have you met Neily? He'd hate it. And it's not even the alcohol! If he was morally opposed to underage drinking I could understand, but it's, like, the *principle* of the thing. He just assumes that everyone who goes to those parties is a self-involved, spoiled rich prick and he refuses to hang out with them."

"I was at that party. Uh, *thanks,* Neily," I said.

"Exactly!" she cried. "That's what I said. 'I went to that party with Audrey, Neily, so what does that say about me?' But, you know, he has no response to that and goes into concern mode—'I'm worried about you, Carly, I just want you to be happy,' blah blah blah. It's like, 'If you want me to be happy, then don't try to guilt-trip me every time I do something I want to do just because you don't like it.' "

"Makes sense to me," I said. "You want to hear something funny?"

"No. I hate humor," she deadpanned. Then she smiled. "Of course I want to hear something funny."

"Well, it's not ha-ha funny, more like interesting funny. Adam asked if you and Neily were still together because *he* was thinking of asking you out."

She raised her eyebrows. "Adam *Murray*?"

"Yep. The one and only."

She grinned. "I think I'm sitting with you guys at lunch today."

"Slow down, Speed Racer. What about Neily?"

"He's my boyfriend, not my warden," she said. "He doesn't get to say who I can and can't be friends with."

"Wow, Carly. That's very girl power of you."

"Damn right it is," she said, taking my arm and tugging me in the direction of my usual lunch table. "Let's go."

Adam Murray was full of problems, and the drugs were only the beginning. He and Cass's brother, Jerod, were superclose, and Adam took over his connections when Jerod left for Los Angeles, bolstering the business with his obscene allowance and unpredictable temper. Cass, to my relief, showed no interest in picking up where Jerod left off—he had basketball to worry about. Funnily, Adam never seemed very interested in doing hard drugs himself, though he liked to get drunk and smoke out whenever possible, but greed is undeniable and drug dealing is a path to power. I was always amazed that he never got caught, but he was smarter than he looked and his boys were loyal to a fault. Nobody would've dared turn on Adam.

After Cass and I started dating, Carly and Adam got closer. She began to disappear with him for hours, spending time at his house when his parents were away, inviting him to her house when her dad was at the hospital, taking long drives with him down the coast to Carmel and up I-80 to Sacramento. I encouraged her to do this, even though she was still with Neily and I knew that she was hurting him. Neily must think that I don't regret it, but I do. I'm not the sort of person who tells herself that regrets are futile. I think they're necessary, to teach us how not to behave in the future. But I didn't know Adam then, at least not as well as I did later; to me, he was just an old, close friend of Cass's, and I was so enamored with my new boyfriend that I considered everything associated with him to be right and good. That's how naïve I was. It wasn't until later that I learned that even decent people can have awful friends.

But I don't flatter myself that my influence swayed Carly very much either way. She was intent on tearing herself down, on recklessly seeking out bad situations and exploiting them to facilitate her self-destruction. Miranda's death had affected her deeply; she had depended upon her mom's opinion for guidance and strength for so long that when Miranda died she lost sight of who she was, assumed that every bit of worth she had amassed in her short life had followed her mom to the grave. She should have stayed in counseling, she should have had someone to talk to and confide in, but she refused and so she had no one. Carly convinced herself that the only recourse was to destroy what she could not preserve.

~~~~~

Adam and Cass held court at the largest table in the quad every day at lunch. Girls like Lucy hovered around them, laughing and tossing their hair in an effort to be noticed, to be singled out. I watched them play from the steps of the library, focusing on the interaction between Adam and Lucy, but they barely spoke, hardly came near each other. Obviously their relationship, whatever it amounted to, was a carefully guarded secret.

I was so intent on observing Adam and Lucy that I didn't notice that Cass was staring at me. Neily was the one who pointed it out. He came out of the library and sat down next to me, squinting into the sun.

"Doesn't that creep you out?" he asked.

"You sitting here? I'm getting used to it."

He rolled his eyes. "I mean Cass. He's been watching you for like five minutes."

I looked up and locked eyes with Cass. My heart sped up and my stomach jumped; I turned away. "Is he still looking?"

"Yeah," Neily said. "And he doesn't seem very happy."

"Huh."

"So obviously his flame's still burning."

"I doubt it," I said. "He's probably just trolling for hot freshman ass."

"Okay, fine. But I wouldn't be surprised if sometime today I find my head under a faucet again."

"You think Cass is jealous? Of you?" I laughed. "You've got to be kidding me."

"What? We've been spending a lot of time together lately, and we haven't exactly been keeping it a secret. We could be dating," Neily said. "Are you saying you're too good for me?"

"Not exactly," I said. "It's just that—well, everybody knows you hate me."

"Oh my God, I don't *hate* you," he said, exasperated. "Would you stop saying that?"

"Yeah, you do." Now I was just teasing him. "You don't do a good job of hiding it, either."

"If I hated you, would I be sitting here right now, risking permanent water damage?" he joked. I smiled. "What?"

"Aw, Neily. I think we're friends now, or something."

"Or something," he said, leaning back against the step and lifting his face up to the sun. "Definitely 'or something.' "

Freshman Year—Spring Semester

As much as I adored Cass, I had a hard time getting up the courage to tell him that I loved him. After watching my parents' disastrous marriage crumble, I was wary of what caring about someone too much could do to you. Still, I thought about him every minute of every single day, and I wanted him to know that. It was just those three little words that were an obstacle; they had so much power, I was afraid of what unleashing them might bring.

At least there was no pressure on Cass's part. He was very

affectionate and sweet, but it wasn't as if he was rushing to say those words either. It was hard to tell exactly what he was feeling at any given time. In a lot of ways, he was just like me: not very good at sharing, which was probably why we got along so well. We were dating for six months and neither of us had met the other's parents. Most of our time was spent on school property; we didn't go to each other's houses unless we would have them to ourselves. I wanted to meet his parents but was too ashamed of my dad to introduce Cass to him, so I didn't press the issue. When I did finally meet the Irvings, it was by accident, and it was a disaster.

It was the middle of the week and Cass and I had a study date. We were in a lot of the same classes and often got together to work on homework or projects, although we did more making out than studying. On Wednesdays we hung out at his house because his dad, a doctor with a private practice, always worked late and his mom had dinner and played bridge with a coven of other rich physicians' wives.

Later Cass swore up and down that he'd told me his parents would be home on that particular Wednesday night, but either he was mistaken or I had forgotten. I walked from Carly's house, where I'd spent the afternoon with her and Neily, to Cass's and rang the doorbell, expecting him to welcome me with a smile and a kiss like any other night.

Instead, it was his mom who answered. Mrs. Irving was a petite blonde with round wide eyes and an expressionless face tightened by Botox injections. She clutched a glass of brown liquid on the rocks and squinted at me blankly. "Can I help you?"

"I'm, uh, here to see Cass?" I said unsurely.

She shrugged and stood aside to give me room to enter. "Upstairs," she said, jerking her head slightly toward a long, wide staircase.

"Thanks."

I went in the direction of Cass's room until I heard muffled shouting coming from the opposite end of the hall. I walked carefully toward the door to his parents' room, which was open a crack. Through it I could see Cass and his dad standing facing each other and arguing.

"I'm sorry—" Cass was saying, but his dad cut him off.

"These grades are bullshit, Cass!" Mr. Irving yelled. "Do you know what happens if you *fail* algebra? You don't get to play ball this year, that's what happens."

"I know that," Cass said. "I'm trying."

"You're not trying! You never try. You're just another lazy, selfish kid who expects everything to be handed to him on a golden fucking platter."

"It's not that," Cass said, his voice wavering slightly. "Algebra is hard for me. I'll get a tutor."

"Algebra is the easiest goddamn subject in the world," Mr. Irving said. "You can't do algebra? What are you, some kind of idiot? You're telling me that I'm sending you to one of the most expensive private schools in the entire country and yet you still fail to grasp basic mathematics? 'Algebra is hard.' You've got to be kidding me!"

"I know."

"You don't know a goddamn thing. First it's your brother, then you. You're both morons. I was a Rhodes scholar and yet somehow I ended up with two losers for sons. The way you're going you'll never amount to anything, you'll just be a washed-up also-ran who can't even do long division. You're so worth-less, sometimes I doubt that either of you are even mine."

I couldn't stand to hear any more. Even though I was des-perately trying to be quiet, I let out a little involuntary gasp.

"Who's there?" Mr. Irving bellowed, stalking toward the door. I stepped away from it and looked around for someplace to hide, but he flung it open before I could do anything and glared at me, enraged.

"Who the hell are you?" he demanded. I was so paralyzed with fear I couldn't respond.

Cass came up behind his dad and stared at me in disbelief.

"Shit," I said quietly.

Cass pushed past his dad and grabbed my arm roughly. "Come on, Audrey, let's get out of here." He ushered me down the stairs, out of the house, and down the driveway before I could even gather myself enough to ask where we were going.

The Irvings had several cars, more than the number of people in the house who could legally drive, and Cass had made himself a spare set of keys a while back. He took them out of his pocket and unlocked the doors to his mother's silver Lexus.

"Get in," he said abruptly.

"Where are we going?" I asked. I wanted to get away from Cass's parents as much as he did, but I didn't think he should be driving as upset (not to mention underage) as he was.

"Just get in," he commanded through clenched teeth. "I'm taking you home."

"Are you okay to drive?" I bit my lower lip. "Won't your mother be angry with you for taking her car?"

"Fine, I'll just leave you here, then." He slid into the driver's side and started the engine.

"No, I'm coming."

He seemed furious and for several minutes we drove the foothill roads in silence as I waited for him to say something.

When he didn't, I finally said, "Cass, I'm so sorry."

He turned on me. "What were you doing there? I told you my parents were going to be home. I told you not to come!"

"I don't remember," I said. "I'm sorry, so, so sorry."

"Yeah, well, sorry isn't going to fix anything, is it?" he snapped.

I looked off in the opposite direction, not really knowing what else to say or do. Tears welled up in my eyes and I tried to keep them back, afraid to cry in front of him, but I couldn't; they slid down my face faster than I could wipe them away. I heard Cass sigh, but I couldn't bear to look at him.

"Audrey," he said, deliberately affecting a calmer voice. "I shouldn't have yelled at you. I'm sure you didn't mean to make things difficult. It was an honest mistake."

"It *was*," I choked out. I couldn't believe what a mess I was, but meeting Mr. Irving, who scared the crap out of me, combined with the shock of being screamed at by Cass, had left me a bit wobbly.

Cass put his hand on my shoulder. "I didn't mean to lose it like that. It's not even that big of a deal—he was already mad at me."

"Your dad is terrifying," I said, drawing in a deep breath.

Cass shrugged. "He is what he is. I'm sorry he upset you, but I'm pretty much used to it."

"Does he yell at you like that all the time?" I asked.

"No," Cass said. "Mostly he just ignores me. He only gets mad when I screw up. Personally I think he's jealous of me. He's always been a mean bastard who everybody hated, so he resents me for being the opposite. He takes every opportunity to let me know when I've failed or let him down. Why do you think Jerod beat it as soon as his trust fund kicked in?"

"What about your mom?" I couldn't imagine that blank, glassy-eyed woman standing up to Mr. Irving, but how could she do nothing while her son suffered?

"The only way my mom can deal is if she pretends nothing is wrong with her life," Cass said. "She's no help, and anyway, I don't need anyone to protect me. I can protect myself."

"Has he ever hit you?" I asked. This was the question I most feared someone would ask *me,* and I could tell that he didn't want to answer it. Always keeping secrets, always burying the truth, that was how Cass got through life. I knew because I was just like him.

"He used to, when I was a kid," Cass told me after a long hesitation. "He was very careful about it, no bruises where anybody could see. But I'm big enough now that I can fight back and cause some damage myself. He'd never touch me today."

"Does anyone else know?"

Cass shook his head incredulously, as if the answer should've been obvious. "Why would I tell anyone about my fucked-up family? What would be the point of that?"

"I don't know, to get some support, maybe."

"No need. As long as I do everything right and stay out of the old man's way, I'm in the clear." Cass glanced out at the horizon, where the sun was setting. He was deliberately avoiding looking at me because he didn't want to see pity. What he didn't get was that it wasn't pity, it was empathy. I knew exactly what it was like and my heart broke for him.

"But all that pressure to be perfect. Doesn't it bother you?"

"No," he said without emotion. "I'm used to it."

"You keep saying that." I took Cass's hand and he put his right arm around my shoulders without taking his eyes off the road.

"I understand what it's like to have a horrible home life," I reminded him. "You can talk to me about anything, I hope you know that."

"I do," he said, but I wasn't quite sure he did.

"Cass, I care about you *so much,*" I said. Then after a pause I added, "I love you, actually." They were hard words to get out, but I meant them, and in the moment I didn't even care if he said them back. All I wanted was for him to know that he was loved by someone who didn't need him to be flawless.

"I love you, too," he said, hugging me closer.

"Pull in here," I whispered, pointing out my window. We were in the valley now, passing a playground with a parking lot that was well hidden from the road. Cass knew what I was proposing and he eagerly followed my lead. There were no other cars and the sun had almost entirely set. The place was so private, we were so alone, it was as if everyone else on earth had been deleted and we were the only two left.

I kissed his cheek quickly and crawled into the backseat, tugging him along by the hand. He was so tall that he had a hard time squeezing through the front seats, so when he finally made it he came crashing into me.

"That was very graceful." I laughed, mostly to mask the nervousness that had set my heart thumping like the backbeat of a techno song.

"Wasn't it?" He kissed me, first a light peck, and then he came back for a long, lingering kiss. He stroked my jaw with his thumb and pressed me up against the seat, pulling lightly at my lips with his, and briefly kneading my shoulder before letting his hand wander down to my breasts.

Overwhelmed by passion and fear, I went into hyperdrive, yanking his shirt over his head and kissing him hungrily. I was terrified that there wasn't enough of me to satisfy him. Yes, there were the words: "I love you," "I'm sorry," "I'm here." And there was this, this thrilling moment of intense desire. It all made me feel less empty, and I wanted Cass to feel that way too.

It made sense that one person couldn't, maybe shouldn't, be everything to another person, but I longed to be that for Cass. He and I had both been neglected by the people who were supposed to love us the most. As I looked at Cass, practically naked now in the light of the streetlamps, I imagined a small child cowering in front of his angry father and I wanted to sob. Instead I wrapped my arms around his warm, bare chest and pressed my lips against his sternum, promising that I would never leave him.

I didn't even realize until much, much later that he never made the same promise to me. ·

Senior Year

After school, as I was throwing my bag in the backseat of my car, Cass sidled up to me, hands in his pockets, looking unsure of himself. I turned around quickly, as if I didn't see him, and subtly checked my hair in the side mirror. Not as good as it had looked after I blew it dry in the morning, but decent enough.

"Hey," he said, shrugging slightly and giving me a small smile.

"Hey," I said, clutching the top of the driver's side door. "What's up?" My stomach churned like a washing machine. I suddenly wished I was wearing something new, or that I had on more makeup than a swipe of mascara and a layer of Chap Stick.

"Can we, I don't know, take a walk?"

"Uh, sure."

"How about we take the creek path?" he suggested. "Just to the overlook."

The creek path went from the student parking lot all the way down to Empire Creek at the bottom of the foothill, but first it wound through the back parts of the affluent neighborhoods, and halfway down—near Cass's house—there was a large overlook where students would park their cars. You could see the whole valley, and Cass and I had gone there many times when we were dating.

"So," I said.

"So." He took a deep breath. He was nervous, which was adorable. "How are you?"

"I'm fine."

"Is that really true?"

"Yeah, I guess."

"Because you don't seem fine."

"Uh, thanks?"

"I mean, you seem upset."

His words broke the spell. Upset? Of course I was upset. In mere seconds, he had gone from the boy I had loved to the boy who had dumped me when I needed him most. "Well, it's been a long year," I snapped.

"I know." He sighed and ran his fingers through his hair. "I guess I'm mostly to blame for that."

I said nothing, because I couldn't assure him that he wasn't. His abandonment had done all sorts of toxic things to me: It had worsened my growing depression over Carly's death, it had increased my anxiety, and it had basically left me completely alone. But I was starting to build my life back up again. I had found a purpose for my existence, and though I didn't yet know who killed Carly, I felt closer to the truth than ever before. What's more, I couldn't blame it all on Cass. I knew deep down in my gut that he hadn't wanted to leave me. He was just too weak and had caved in to all the pressure his family and friends had put on him. And it was my fault, too. I had taken it all lying down; I had let people talk and whisper, and retreated into a self-imposed exile that left me friendless. I had counted too much on the loyalty of those who weren't capable of giving it.

"I hope," he continued, "that we can maybe find some way to get past this."

"You want me to forgive you?"

"I know you don't want to," he said. "But maybe you could? Because I really miss you, Aud. I made a huge mistake, and I'm *really* sorry. I should've said that a long time ago."

"Yeah, you should have." I kept trying to think how Neily would respond, to channel him, because as much as I didn't want to admit it to myself, I *was* starting to forgive Cass. He hadn't wanted to hurt me, I knew that. He was just a coward. And as much as I wanted to hate him for that, I found that I couldn't. I didn't have Neily's fortitude, or his single-mindedness. I wanted to be happy again. I wanted to move on, to live my life without having to constantly look backward into the past. That was why I was doing all this, and I couldn't help but respect Cass for trying to make it right.

But I also couldn't let him off the hook that easily. "What did you think would happen, Cass?" I asked. "What do you want from me?"

He paused, as if unsure about saying what he wanted to say. "I want us to be together again," Cass admitted. I was a bit taken aback. I hadn't seen Cass's shy side in a really long time. The look on his face was sweet and boyish, and though it had never escaped my notice, I was struck by how *good* he looked—how handsome and tall he was, how perfectly our bodies still complemented each other's. We had been the golden couple, and even after the past year the physical chemistry still crackled between us, easily betraying what both of us were feeling.

"No. I'm sorry, but that's not going to happen." It took all of my inner Neily to say it.

"Why not?" he asked, with the expression of someone who knew exactly why not.

"You turned your back on me when I needed you most," I reminded him. "Maybe I can forgive you, but how am I ever supposed to trust you? And how am I supposed to be with a person that I can't trust?"

He pressed his lips together so hard they practically disappeared. "Is this about Monroe? Are you dating him now?"

"No," I said slowly. "We're just friends."

"I thought you said that you were English partners."

"Well, now we're friends. Things change pretty quickly around here."

"But you're not dating?"

"That's none of your business."

"So you are dating?"

"No!" I shouted. "Why are you doing this to me? Why can't you leave me alone?"

"I just can't," he said.

"You were doing such a good job of it before," I said. "And to tell you the truth, I think I liked it better that way."

He stepped back. "You did?" he asked, wounded.

"Did you honestly think I still had feelings for you?" I asked, anger momentarily eclipsing every other emotion. "After everything that you did to me? After the teasing, and the rumors, and the prank phone calls, did you think that I was still interested in having a relationship with any of you? You and your friends made my life hell. I can't believe I ever cared about a single one of you, because it's obvious that none of you ever gave a damn about me."

"That's not true," he protested. "*I* cared. I know I didn't do a good job of being there for you after what happened, but if Adam or Lucy or any of those other assholes ever did anything to hurt you, I didn't know about it. I never would have let them do it if I knew."

"I don't believe you," I said, with less conviction than before.

"That's your choice, Audrey. But it's the truth. And isn't that what you're all about these days? The truth?" He sat down on a nearby rock.

"What are you talking about?"

"Lucy told me you came to her house and started asking questions about Carly," he said. "She didn't know what it meant, but I did. As soon as I found out you were back at Brighton I knew what you were doing. You're poking around Carly's murder, aren't you?"

I suddenly felt exposed, as if I were standing in the middle of the quad completely naked. "No," I said, as forcefully as I could. "Why would I want to open up all those old wounds?"

"Because you're too smart to believe what everybody's saying about your dad," Cass said. "You know he didn't kill her."

Everything inside of me softened like butter. "You don't think my dad killed Carly?" I asked.

He shook his head. "I used to, but the more I thought about it, the more it didn't make any sense. I know your dad. I don't think he had the heart to do something like that."

"Then why did you break up with me?" I asked, eyes tearing. "If you thought he was innocent, why did you leave me?"

"At the time, I believed the police. I believed the papers. I believed everybody in town who was saying your dad was a killer. How could I not?"

He closed the gap between us and put his arms around me. I buried my face in his chest, breathed him in. He smelled like laundry and skin hot from the sun. "You should know," he said, "that I think you're putting yourself in serious danger playing a game like this."

"It's not a game," I insisted. "I know what I'm doing." Yes, I was afraid, but I was not a coward. I didn't need his warnings—I was perfectly aware.

"I know. But I want to help," he murmured into my hair. "You can't do this alone."

"I'm not alone," I said, pulling away. It was something I had to keep telling myself.

Cass nodded. "Right. Neily."

"He's been helping me figure things out," I told him.

"You really trust that guy?"

"Of course I do. Why wouldn't I?"

"He had a huge grudge against Carly. He found her body," Cass reminded me. "For all you know, *he* could have killed her."

"No," I said.

"Why not?"

"Because he wanted Carly back, not dead. Of all the people in this goddamn town, he's the only person suffering as much as I am. I trust him because we're the same. He understands."

"I understand."

"No, you don't."

"I do! I may not have been as close to Carly as you were, but she was my friend and I miss her," Cass said. "Besides, what happened to her separated us, and if you think I'm not suffering because of that you're crazy."

"What do you want me to do? We can't get back together—that would be a disaster. We can't be friends, because you still have feelings for me. What do you want?" I couldn't bring myself to admit that I still had feelings for him. He would never walk away if he knew that for sure.

"Let me help. Give me a chance to prove that I'm on your side."

"I don't think Neily would like that very much."

"Do you care about what he thinks?"

"Yeah, I do."

Cass shrugged. "Then I guess there's nothing more I can say."

"There isn't," I confirmed. He turned to leave, but I caught his arm. "But I appreciate the apology."

Cass smiled the smile of a person who has played all of his cards and has nothing left to lose. Then he leaned over and kissed me.

CHAPTER SEVENTEEN

Fifteen minutes later, I was sitting in the front seat of my car, alone. I wasn't moving; in fact, I hadn't even put the key into the ignition. I was just sitting. Sitting and thinking.

The kiss had brought back a flood of memories, good and bad. I remembered the first kiss I had ever shared with Cass. He had been too much of a gentleman to kiss me during our first date at the Loon, but the next night Adam had his whole group of friends over while his parents were at their second house, in Tahoe. I had been tipsy, but I knew what I was doing. We were sitting on the couch and I was cuddled up against him, my face resting against his chest. I had made the first move, sloughing off my nerves and leaning forward, catching him off guard. When it was over, he looked happy and relieved. We were fourteen.

But I also remembered the last kiss I had shared with Cass, the morning of the day Carly had died. Sick with what was about to become a series of painful stomachaches brought on by stress, I had left Lucy's party early with the promise that I would see Cass in the morning. At noon, he called to invite me to brunch, and though my stomach still hurt I agreed to let him pick me up and take me out. I wasn't hungry, so we ended up not going to brunch, contenting ourselves instead with driving around town and gossiping about what had happened at Lucy's party after I left. Carly and Adam's blow-out fight, I remember, was the biggest topic, but he also told me that Lucy had gotten really drunk and sung a Britney Spears song on top of the dining-room table. He told me funny stories to cheer me up, and I tried to laugh and smile, but by the time we got back to my house all I wanted to do was lie down and sleep for a hundred years. He took me inside and covered me up with a blanket, and before he left he kissed me.

Carly died that night. I wouldn't see Cass again for three more days, and by then he wouldn't even look me in the eye. We had both turned seventeen in August.

"No. No, I'm sorry. I can't," I said a few seconds after our kiss at the overlook.

Now, as I sat in my car, trying to catch my breath and stop my brain from spinning like a Tilt-a-Whirl, part of me regretted having pushed Cass away at the overlook. To his credit, he hadn't followed me or tried to stop me from leaving. He knew what I needed. In all this time, he hadn't forgotten how to read me.

I picked up my phone to call Neily, but he wasn't going to be much help, so I resisted the urge. Instead, I put the car in drive and headed to Carly's house. Paul would be at work, and there were still plenty of things left to sort through and pack up in Carly's room. I could bury myself in that mindless, robotic work and soon, hopefully, I'd forget all about Cass.

Junior Year—Fall Semester

I had always known that Cass's reputation was important to him; my mistake was in believing that I was more important. I honestly don't know how his parents felt about me before Carly's death, because after that first encounter I only spoke to them a handful of times and I never cared much about impressing them because I knew what terrible people they were, at least as far as Cass was concerned. We didn't talk about his parents and I assume he didn't talk about me at home. It took some maneuvering to ignore the issue, but no more than it takes to avoid a pothole in the road. To me, Cass's parents were practically nonentities, to the point where I sometimes forgot he had them. The shock I felt when I realized they had pressured him into breaking up with me was indescribable.

"What do you mean you can't be with me anymore?" I asked, utterly bewildered. After avoiding me for days, Cass had called and asked me to meet him at the overlook. He didn't seem to have gotten much sleep the night before and I could just hear Mr. Irving's voice in my ear: *You had better break up with that girl, Cass. I won't have my son dating the daughter of a murderer! I don't want you to have anything to do with that family, do you hear me?*

Cass took a deep breath and hung his head slightly. "I'm sorry, Aud. It's not me. It's my family. They think—well, I'm sure you know what they think."

"But . . . I *need* you, Cass," I pleaded, reaching for his hand. "I need you now more than I ever have. I love you so much. You still love me, right?"

He nodded at the ground, unwilling to look at me. His fingers were limp in mine.

"Then we should be together, no matter what anybody says," I insisted. "We can keep it a secret, we don't have to tell anybody."

"We both have enough secrets," Cass told me, swallowing hard. "You have to concentrate on yourself right now. I can't help you through this. I just can't."

"Didn't you hear what I said? I need *you*," I repeated. "All you have to do is be there."

"I'm sorry, Audrey," he said quietly. "I'm sorry." He took his hand out of mine and walked away, back toward the life he'd built to cover the bruises. I couldn't watch him leave, so I turned and looked at the valley sprawled out beneath my feet.

I waited until he was gone to cry.

Senior Year

I let myself into the house using my key and headed upstairs to clean out the rest of Carly's drawers. When I was finished, I ran my hand over the back of each drawer to make sure I hadn't missed anything. Checking the last one, my fingers sent something rolling. It was a tiny hand-painted wooden doll, one that

I recognized as belonging to a set of *matryoshka* dolls Miranda and Paul had brought back for Carly from a trip they took to Saint Petersburg when she was nine years old. The set still sat atop Carly's bureau, next to the packet of pictures I had insisted Neily keep but that he had left behind.

The nesting dolls were fashioned in the rough outline of a woman's figure and painted robin's-egg blue. A girl's face, with big, expressive blue eyes and long black eyelashes, had been painted on, and the dolls were adorned with white polka dots and black and yellow pansies. I shook them, expecting to hear the clatter of something inside, but there was no sound. I opened them up, extracting doll after doll until I got to the very last. Inside, wrapped in tissue paper to muffle the sound, was a dull brass key engraved with the number forty-two.

As I stood holding the key, I finally figured out a way to get to the safe-deposit box. It would be tricky, but if I was a good enough liar I could probably pull it off. I left Paul's house immediately and drove home, where I pulled the box of Carly's things I had decided to keep out from under my bed. Inside, buried under photo albums and stuffed animals and a shoebox full of gently worn notes we'd passed to each other in class, was a plastic folder containing an assortment of official documents I couldn't throw away. One was the authorization letter for the safe-deposit box that I'd found earlier in Carly's desk; maybe I should've given it back to Paul, but I hadn't wanted to give away anything that might come in handy. Another was Carly's driver's license.

As I drove into the valley, I remembered the promise I'd made to Neily: *No lies, no tricks, no secrets.* I kept thinking I should call him, that he should be there when I opened the box, but every time I considered this possibility I rejected it. I

would share the contents of the box with Neily if I found anything relevant, but until then it was mine alone.

It was almost closing time when I arrived at the bank. I
strode up to the counter as confidently as possible and handed
over the key and the letter.

"I'd like to open a safe-deposit box," I told the clerk. "It
belongs to my parents, but my dad authorized me to access it."

The clerk read the letter carefully. "Do you have identifica-
tion, Miss Ribelli?" she asked.

"Yeah, sure." I took out my wallet and handed her Carly's
driver's license. Now, objectively Carly and I look nothing
alike. She was short with brown hair and blue eyes; I'm tall
with blond hair and green eyes. But if you strip that all away,
our faces are pretty similar, and when Carly's driver's license
picture was taken she'd just had her hair highlighted, and with
the flash and the crappy quality of the photo it looks blond.
When she'd shown it to us all, several people commented on
how much she looked like me in it, and I was sure that as long
as the clerk didn't get the sense that I was lying she would think
the same thing.

I stood at a distance that was neither suspicious nor close
enough for the clerk to note the exact color of my eyes. Still,
she looked unconvinced.

"It says here you're five-four," the clerk said.

"I know, right?" I smiled and shrugged. "Growth spurt."

After a few more seconds, the clerk handed back the license and the letter and led me into a small room with a table.
She opened and removed box 42 and left me alone with it, in-
structing me to buzz her on the intercom when I was ready to
pack it in.

I lifted the lid of the box and peered inside. Slowly, I pulled things out. Miranda's passport was in there, and so was Carly's, along with three birth certificates—one for each of them, including Paul. All of Mams's jewelry was there, too, each piece kept in a separate velvet pouch.

I worked my way to the bottom, examining family photos and glancing at various uninteresting legal documents until I came to a thick manila envelope sealed with packing tape. There was nothing written on the package, and it wasn't very heavy. I ripped it open with the edge of my car key and took out a stack of letters, all addressed to Carly.

There was a plastic chair in the corner of the room, and I sat down to read. I felt weightless, like the floor had dropped out from under me. None of the letters were very long, and they were all typed, but the person who wrote them didn't feel the need to use capital letters or punctuation. The sentences blurred together, rage-filled rants at Carly's frigidness, interspersed with violent, staccato declarations of love.

I read each of the letters several times. They repeated the same sentiments over and over, making veiled threats. It seemed as if the writer was completely out of control, even delusional. I wondered how these letters had affected Carly, whether she had been scared or moved to pity. When I reached the end of the pile, a small square note in Carly's handwriting slipped to the ground.

Neily,

I'm returning these letters to you because I know you would not want anybody else to see them. I think you should destroy them. I want you to get over what happened—our breakup was less than ideal, but I didn't think you would understand any other way. We're different

people—I have accepted this, and you should, too. I can't
believe you would do anything to hurt me, because I know
how deeply you still care for me. But please don't send me
any more letters. They make me too sad.

Carly

I put the letters back into the envelope and buried it at the
bottom of my bag. I left everything else and drove to the Calamity
Diner, where I ordered myself dinner before reading the letters
again. My food came, but I couldn't eat. I tossed a twenty-dollar
bill onto the table, grabbed the letters, and fled the diner.

Neily called later, and so did Cass, but I ignored both of
their calls and spent the rest of the evening in my room. Carly
had thought that Neily was her anonymous correspondent,
which was why she hadn't shown anyone the letters or told
anybody she was being stalked. She was trying to be kind. I
couldn't believe what she believed, that Neily had written
them, that he was following her and feeling the kind of anger
that exploded onto those pages. Even though he had never
been able to shake the pain of what had happened between
them, Neily was capable of restraint. Still, I didn't relish the
thought of having to show him the letters, of having to see his
face when he realized just what sort of person Carly had understood him to be.

The next day at school Neily and I didn't get a chance to talk in
private, so I asked him to meet me at the Calamity Diner
around four, when there would be few people around. He sat
down and grabbed a menu from the edge of the table.

"Is it too late for brunch?" he asked.

"You look well rested," I said, trying to keep my voice light.

"Yeah, well, Harriet prescribed me sleeping pills and last night I decided to give one a try." He closed his menu and looked at me. "No offense, but you *don't* look well rested. Have you been crying?"

I shook my head. "Not in the past ten hours."

"What happened?"

"Awkward confrontation with the ex-boyfriend, he kissed me, blah blah blah." I waved my hand dismissively and popped open a menu.

"Blah blah blah?"

"Yeah. Whatever."

"He kissed you?"

"Just once."

"Audrey, come on."

"I told him that I didn't want to be with him, but it was so hard."

"I get it," Neily said.

"I'm sure you do," I said.

"I do," he insisted. "You can talk to me about stuff, you know."

I let out a deep breath. "Yeah, well, I don't really want to talk, so just drop it."

The waitress came then and took our order. When she was gone, Neily asked, "So what's up? I mean, besides Cass's heart rate." When I didn't smile at the joke, he turned serious. "Okay, what's going on?"

I reached into my bag and brought out the packet of letters. "I found the key to Carly's safe-deposit box. And this was in there." I slid the letters across the table and he took them. "I'll give you some time. Just let me know when you're done."

It took him almost a half hour to go through the letters. He pored over them, reading each several times, tracing the words with his fingers. Finally, when he was finished, he passed them to me and took a deep breath.

"That's not good," he said.

"No kidding." I handed him Carly's note. "There's more."

He read the note, shaking his head. "This is—this is—"

"I know."

"This is—you know what? I'm *offended*. I really am. I'm not upset, just totally insulted." He crumpled up the note and tossed it away.

"You can't blame her—"

"The hell I can't! When she broke up with me I thought it was because of her own issues, but it turns out that she didn't even understand me. I never would have done something like this. Follow her around, send her creepy unsigned letters— threaten her? What did she think I was, some kind of psycho?"

"Did you read the letter? She didn't think you were a psycho."

"No, that's right, she pitied me. She *pitied* me, Audrey." He put his hand to his forehead. "That might be worse."

"You need to calm down. You can't let this freak you out— you have to think rationally. If you didn't write these letters, somebody else did, and that person is obviously unstable. We have to figure out how Carly's assault in June, these letters, and her death two months later are connected. Do you think you can put aside your incredulity for maybe an hour so that we can make some headway? Huh?"

He hesitated. "Yeah."

"Great." I chewed my lip. "I have a theory. I think that the person who attacked Carly at Cass's party is the same person who wrote these letters."

"And what led you to that conclusion?" he asked. "Just to play devil's advocate."

I shrugged. "I don't know. It's just a feeling."

"So you're psychic now?"

I shook my head. "That's not it. It just seems like the kind of person who would write those letters would also trick a girl and rape her."

"But the assault happened first."

"We don't know that. The letters don't have dates on them, and Carly didn't keep track of when she got them. I checked the diary again—there's no other mention of them."

"But if Carly was getting them before she was raped, she would have been on her guard."

"Not if she thought you wrote them," I pointed out. "She trusted you not to hurt her. She didn't know there was some-body else to look out for."

"So what next?"

"We trail Adam and the Bean. One of them is going to make a move, and when they do we need to be there to follow."

"Fine."

"Which one do you want?"

"I can't believe you even have to ask."

PART THREE

❦

Neily

Chapter Eighteen

After Audrey showed me the letters, I went back to Empire Creek Bridge. I didn't want to go home and face my mother, whose hopeful expressions and mild encouragements were growing more meaningless as the dark mystery surrounding Carly's murder unfolded. Audrey wanted to be alone, and so did I, free to pace the winding corridors of our minds in search of answers to questions we had just started to learn how to ask. There was only so much that talking about it could do for me, and I was grateful that Audrey understood.

I missed Carly. It was the first thought I had as I stood on that bridge, watching as the sun dipped below the foothills and splashed stripes of orange and pink across the water. As the air cooled—summer was almost over, and fall was coming—I thought about the last time I had stood on this bridge with her. It was some months after her mother's death; she was withdrawn and moody, but things were still good between us, or seemed to be. We were looking out on a sunset just like I was now, and Carly was clutching my hand, her head on my shoulder. Without looking at me, eyes trained on the horizon, Carly asked, "What are you going to do, Neily?"

"About what?"

"When you graduate. What do you want to do?"

I shrugged. "College, I guess. Like everybody else. Why? You want to do something different?"

"My dad would kill me if I decided not to go to college."

"It's your life, Carly. You should do what you want."

"That's not really my style, is it?"

"What do you mean?"

She shook her head. "My mother always had the last word."

"But she's gone now—"

"I don't want her to be gone, I want her to be here!"

"I know," I said. "I didn't mean it like that. All I'm saying is that your decisions are up to you now."

"Stop saying it like it's such a good thing."

"I'm not—I . . ." I took a breath.

"I miss her so much."

"I know."

"And I keep taking it out on you—I don't know why." There were tears creeping into the corners of her eyes.

"Maybe it's because you know that whatever you do, whatever you say, I'll always be here."

She nodded. "That's what I'm afraid of."

"What does that mean?"

"You shouldn't be with a person who treats you like her own personal whipping boy—you deserve better."

"You don't treat me like that."

"I'm starting to. I'm so angry all the time, every little thing sets me off and I'm afraid that I'll end up really hurting you. I don't want that. That's the last thing in the world I want to do. I don't want to turn into some kind of a monster."

"You're not a monster."

"I feel like that's what I'm becoming." She looked up at me, searching my eyes as if she thought there might be answers in them—or absolution. "Do you know who I am? Because I don't, not anymore."

"You're going through something big. It's normal to feel lost. But I love you, I believe in you, and I'm not going anywhere, even if you try to push me away."

"*Why* do you love me?"

"I just do."

She shook her head. "That's not an answer."

"Because ever since I was a kid, people have had all these expectations of me, and I've always been so afraid I wouldn't be able to deliver. But you make me feel good enough just the way I am and that means a lot. To me." I knew I should stop talking, but there was no easy way to say what I felt, so I went for a surplus of words to cover it. "You know me, Carly. You know me in a way that nobody ever has, and it's just so comforting to be with a person who gets you. Before we met, I felt like there was no place safe where I could think and feel and say whatever I wanted. That's why I love you. Being with you feels like being home to me."

She said nothing.

"It's true," I said, afraid that she thought I was just making it up.

"That's a really good answer," she said. One tear dropped, and then another. I kissed her wet cheeks and she put her arms around my neck, pulling me close. I ran my palms up and down her back slowly, the way my mother used to soothe me when I was ill or upset. We hugged tightly, almost bracing each other; I bent my mouth to hers and we kissed there on the bridge until it was dark.

As I walked back to my car, I thought about the journal Audrey and I had found, and how she was trying to prevent me from reading all of it. She knew what I wanted to read, what I had long imagined Carly felt but had been too afraid or too proud to admit: that she still loved me, that she missed me, that she needed and wanted me in a way that only we could need and want each other. Before meeting Audrey at the diner I had resolved to push her into giving up the journal, to beg or demand as much as necessary to get my hands on it, but she ambushed me with the letters. Now I was afraid to read what Carly had written, because for the first time in a long time I was unsure that any feelings other than pity—or possibly remorse—had lingered in her for me. I decided to drop the matter of the journal for the time being—until I knew that I really did want to read it, whatever it said.

After leaving the bridge, I followed up on something that was bugging me. Audrey was bent on investigating the hell out of Toby Pinto, but the last entry in Carly's diary was still ringing in my ears: *Now I know that whatever happened to Laura Brandt was because of me. I'm a monster for what I did to her, and I can't rest until I make things right.* Neither Audrey nor I had any idea who Laura Brandt was, but I was certain that I could find out. All I needed was access to the Internet.

My first search on the name turned up swimming records from a high school in Tulsa, Oklahoma, and the personal Web site of a professor at the University of Florida, but coupled with the name of a local newspaper I got just one hit: an article, dated almost a year and a half ago, about an eighteen-year-old girl living in Lafayette, a town about twenty minutes north of Empire Valley. According to the article, Laura Brandt had been rushed to the hospital after suffering from a cocaine overdose while her parents were away on vacation. The OD landed her in a coma for five days, and when she awoke, parents at her bedside, she refused to give up the name of her dealer. The girl had no priors and was allowed to trade jail time for a voluntary stint in rehab.

How was Carly responsible for Laura Brandt's overdose? The article asserted that while Laura had never been picked up by the police for possession or driving under the influence, she was a veteran drug abuser. And another question: How had Carly even known Laura Brandt? It wasn't such a leap to connect them—Laura was a drug addict, after all, and Carly had been dating a drug dealer. Carly clearly felt guilty for something, but as yet it was unclear what. I supposed that the only person who might be able to tell me was Laura herself.

I called 411 and got the number of her parents' house in Lafayette, but when a man answered and I asked to speak to her, his only response was a sharp "Laura doesn't live here anymore" before hanging up.

Audrey and I met before school the next day in the senior parking lot, in full view of everyone on our hit list. We hadn't been particularly careful about hiding our friendship—partnership, whatever it was—convinced that nobody at school gave a damn about what we were doing, but now we were an object of interest. Somebody, maybe Cass or Lucy, had revealed what we were up to. We got stares from all directions, but the most pointed and poisonous of those stares came from the side of the lot where Adam's posse parked. Cass was not with them; I mentioned it to Audrey, but she just shrugged.

"Why do you think that is?" I asked.

"Let me just consult the schedule he gave me . . . ," she said, reaching for her bag. "Oh, wait." I gave her a look and she sighed a little. "I did hear that he and Adam had some kind of falling-out."

"Who told you that?"

"I overheard some girls talking in the ladies'," she said.

"Haven't they been friends forever?"

"You know, I really don't care. I always thought it would be better for Cass to just stop hanging around Adam, and now he has. Two years too late."

"Maybe it's because of you."

"Why would it have anything to do with me?"

"You told Cass you couldn't trust him, he knows you don't

really like Adam, he stops hanging around Adam because he wants to prove to you that he's serious about giving your relationship another shot," I proposed. "Or, Adam found out Cass still has feelings for you and told him in no uncertain terms that he's not to see you anymore—Cass refuses and gets the cold shoulder. You want more? I can do this all day."

"No, thanks, that's quite enough."

I filled her in on what I'd found out about Laura Brandt, and my inability to track her down. "What now?" I asked.

"I guess we try to find somebody who knows her."

When I sat down with Harvey at lunch that day, he looked surprised.

"What?" I asked, unwrapping my turkey sandwich.

"Nothing. I was just wondering where Audrey is."

I shrugged, taking a bite. "I don't know," I said with my mouth half full.

A moment of silence passed before Harvey spoke again. "Okay, I pretty much resolved not to ask this, seeing as you like your privacy and I usually don't care, but it's getting a little weird for me, so I'm just going to ask. What is going on with you and Audrey?"

"What do you mean?"

"I mean, I see you together all the time at school, and people are talking about how you two are hooking up or whatever. I just want to know: Are these things I should, as your friend, be actively denying, or is there something to all that?"

"I thought you didn't listen to gossip."

"I don't, but sometimes you can't avoid it."

I put down my sandwich. "Okay, I'll tell you, but you have to promise not to say anything."

"Sure, of course."

"Audrey asked for my help investigating Carly's murder."

Harvey's eyes went a little wide. "You're kidding me. No, you're not kidding me at all, are you?"

"No."

"Isn't her killer in prison? In fact, isn't her killer Audrey's *dad*?"

"That is the official story, yes. But Audrey doesn't believe her father could've done it, and neither do I."

"And so you're looking into it by yourselves?"

"Yeah."

"Wow, man. That's brave." He shook his head in disbelief.

"You're not going to lecture me about how stupid it is for us to be doing this?"

"Do you know me, like, at all?"

If Harvey had pointed that out, though, I couldn't have disagreed with him. It felt like Audrey and I were playing detective, but the article about Laura Brandt brought things back into focus. I was almost positive Adam had killed Carly, and if he had somehow been involved in Laura's overdose, then I was starting to see that it went much deeper than Audrey and I could conceive. It felt as though we were stepping into a lion's den; in the pitch darkness it was impossible to see where the danger was coming from, but it was there all the same, lurking in the shadows. But how could I back down? The closer we got to answers, the more I wanted to uncover; I no longer wanted to know, I *needed* to know. It was a pull like an addiction.

"Hey, I have a question for you. Have you ever heard of a girl named Laura Brandt?"

Harvey thought for a moment, then shook his head. "No. Never."

"Yeah, me neither. You do know the Bean, though, right?"

"He was a senior last year."

I nodded. "Remember anything about him?"

"Precious little, and that's enough for me. You know he got in trouble a few years ago for stalking a girl."

"What?"

"Yeah. She was a friend of Lila's, which is how I heard about it. Apparently he got suspended for, quote, harassing her, unquote," Harvey told me. Lila, his older sister, had also been a Fund kid at Brighton, for all four years of high school. She had graduated two years ago.

"What did he do?"

"I'm a bit fuzzy on the details. Why are you so interested?"

"We think he might've been stalking Carly. According to a couple of people, he was completely obsessed with her and is pretty much still delusional about it. Carly got these really creepy anonymous letters in the three months or so before she died. Audrey thinks they may be from him."

"Wow."

"Yeah. Who is this girl the Bean stalked?"

"Her name's Allison Kessler. She transferred midway through her junior year to Athenian, and the last I heard she was at Stanford. She and my sister still keep in touch."

"Do you think you could get her number? I'd like to talk to her."

Harvey nodded. "Sure, I could try."

Audrey and I agreed that after school we would each start tail-
ing our primary suspect. Adam and his friends hung around
the quad for about a half hour after school, so I sat inside the
library near the front doors, watching them through the glass.
They tossed around a football and were approached by several
different students, most of whom I recognized as stoners. After
a while they went to the parking lot and got into three different
cars. Once they left, I followed Adam's truck at a safe distance
all the way into the valley. There was a large empty space on the
east side of town where the mayor's office had recently installed
a meandering nature walk, a jungle gym, and a basketball court.
It was pretty far away from everything, and surrounded by a
thick ring of trees, so people rarely brought their kids there,
preferring the sunnier parks close to the center of town. It was
the perfect place for Adam to conduct business.

I parked my car at the farthest corner of the lot and
slouched down in my seat so that I could just see Adam if I
peeked over the top of the dash. My car was rather inconspicu-
ous, but it was possible that he would recognize it, or that it
would attract his attention by virtue of being one of the only
other cars in the lot. I decided to take that chance—after all,
what could he do to me that I couldn't avoid simply by gunning
the engine and getting the hell out of there?

For a while, Adam and his friends lolled around on the
basketball court, smoking what may have been cigarettes,
halfheartedly knocking one another around. In about fifteen
minutes, though, cars started rolling into the lot carrying

people I recognized as the same dopeheads who had approached Adam earlier in the quad. Money and packages surreptitiously changed hands, and I was secretly a little thrilled to be witnessing a drug deal—several, actually—firsthand, like an undercover cop in a movie.

As Adam went about his business, I considered his cohorts. There were some whose faces I knew but whose names I couldn't place, students a couple of grades lower whom I had never met or had classes with. There was one guy, Dick Brenner, who was in my grade; his sister had been two years ahead of Carly and me in the program and was now at Yale. Dick, however, had displayed none of his sister's academic aptitude, only a pretty big appetite for trouble, which explained why he was part of Adam's crew.

I also recognized a quiet, muscle-bound junior who hovered on the edges of the assembly, watching the proceedings with an unwavering eye and looking uncomfortable in his own skin. This was Sean Ozrick, known around campus as Oz; he was Adam's enforcer, although Adam was quite capable of causing his own damage. Oz had a juvenile record and a notoriously abusive father, but he was relatively smart; he was in my English class.

Suddenly, in the middle of a transaction, Oz paused and looked straight at me. I started, then reached for the ignition. I was well hidden, but it was possible that he had still seen me. He leaned over and said something to Adam, who didn't look in my direction but wrapped up his conversation with a kid I didn't recognize and took his keys from his pocket. The rest of the group stirred at a word from him and everyone headed toward the three cars they'd arrived in. In a minute or two, they were gone. My heart was beating wildly, and I decided to wait till they were clear before venturing out of the lot.

This, it turned out, was a really bad idea. While I was still slumped behind the wheel, eyes closed, trying to even out my breathing, the passenger-side door opened and Adam slid into the seat next to me.

I sat up. "What the fuck—?"

Adam pressed the muzzle of a handgun up against my rib cage. I recoiled instinctively. Adam had a trigger-happy temper, but it had never occurred to me that he would be carrying a gun. Things were getting very real very quickly. "What're you doing here, Think Tank?"

I inhaled sharply and held my breath, my mind racing with fear. I suddenly wished I had told someone, anyone, where I was.

"Don't bother lying—I know what you're doing. You're spying for Finch, aren't you?"

"No," I croaked.

He stared at me. "Then why are you following me?"

"I'm not."

"You think I'm some kind of idiot? Is this your idea of revenge—you narc on me for taking Carly?"

I shook my head. "I'm not—" He pressed the gun harder against my side. "For fuck's sake, put that away."

"Not until you tell me what you're doing here." He thought for a moment. "This have something to do with Audrey?"

"What?"

"Lucy told me Audrey's investigating Carly's murder. You know something about that?"

"She's not."

"You think I killed Carly?" He was nervous now; his hands

were shaking, and the gun pulsated against my ribs. "Is that what you think?"

"I don't know."

"Enzo Ribelli killed Carly."

"Maybe."

"I've got an alibi," he said, his voice rising. "I had nothing to do with that."

"Okay. God, put the gun away!"

He hesitated, then slipped it in his waistband. "This isn't a toy, Think Tank. I see you around here again, you're going to find that out the hard way."

"Fuck."

"Are we clear?"

"Yeah, we're clear."

"You see me at school, you don't even look at me. I get called into Finch's office, I'm going to assume you had something to do with it. Got it?"

I nodded, praying he'd leave. He opened the door and climbed out, leaning in for one final word.

"It's not just me in this. You try to take us down, there's a shitload of people who'll make you suffer. You're in way over your head."

I said nothing, staring ahead, desperate to leave. I had never thought of myself as a coward, but all I wanted to do was run and hide. How could Carly have gotten involved with this psycho?

"Hey!" he yelled.

"I know, I heard you."

"Fine. We're done here."

When he was gone, I left the parking lot as fast as I could, and didn't stop driving until I was safe at home.

CHAPTER NINETEEN

Audrey's evening was a lot less eventful. After school she drove to Keptow Auto Body and waited for the Bean in the Starbucks parking lot across the street. When he left at seven o'clock, she tailed him to a house in Danville where he picked up his girlfriend and took her back to his apartment in Empire Valley. Audrey sat outside for three hours, but the shades were drawn on all the windows and the two of them didn't come out, so she left shortly before midnight, empty-handed.

When she asked me how I'd done with Adam, I told her where I'd gone and what I'd seen, but not how Adam had accosted me in my car. I figured she'd just worry, insist we call the cops or something, and I wasn't going to back down that easy. I was more convinced than ever of Adam's guilt. The way his voice rose, the way he shook when he contemplated the idea of us launching our own investigation—he was scared shitless. But I wasn't about to freak Audrey out, and anyway, she'd just think I was on yet another anti-Adam tirade. I needed more proof before I told her what had happened.

"I think they might've seen me," I said. "I'd probably better back off for a while, see what happens."

She nodded, biting her lip thoughtfully. "Do what you have to do, Neily."

"Are you mad?"

"No. It's good that you're being careful. There's no telling what he might do if he found out you were following him around."

I nodded. "Yeah. No telling."

We had a substitute teacher in Phyllis's class that morning; she handed us a few problem sets and told us to work quietly at our desks, while she flipped through a fashion magazine at the podium.

"Hey," Harvey whispered, leaning over.

"Don't bother looking at my paper—I haven't even started yet," I said.

"Like I would ever cheat off you. Listen, I talked to my sister about getting ahold of Allison and she gave me her cell number." He passed me a note and I stuck it in my pocket. "Tell her you're a friend of Lila's."

"Good work," I said, patting him on the shoulder. Then I raised my hand and asked for the bathroom pass. We weren't supposed to be on our phones during school hours, but the bathroom was a loophole to that rule—the teachers rarely used the students' facilities, preferring the ones in their own lounge. Once I was satisfied that nobody was hiding in any of the stalls, I dialed Allison Kessler's phone number. It rang twice before she picked up.

"Hello?" She sounded wary, like a girl who wouldn't normally answer a call from an unfamiliar number.

"My name is Neily Monroe. I'm a friend of Lila Rosenberg's."

"Oh." She paused. "Is Lila okay?"

"She's great. Listen, I wanted to ask you about Toby Pinto."

"What?"

"Toby Pinto. I think you knew him at Brighton."

"Is this some kind of sick joke?"

"No joke, I promise. I heard you got the Bean suspended three years ago. I need to know why."

"I'm hanging up now."

"Please don't. Look, Allison, I know this is a major invasion of privacy, but you accused the Bean of stalking you and I'm afraid he might have done the same thing to another girl— my ex-girlfriend. So if you could just help me out here . . ."

"Another girl?"

"Carly Ribelli."

Allison repeated the name, then stopped suddenly. "Isn't she that girl who died?"

"Yeah. Are you starting to see why this is so important?"

She hesitated. "I barely knew the Bean. He asked me out a couple of times and I kept saying no, I had a boyfriend, but he wouldn't stop. And then he just started showing up random places where I'd be. At the grocery store when I was there with my mom, at the diner, at the gym. He was everywhere. Sometimes I'd look out my window at night and his car would be parked across the street. I even called the cops once, but he left before they got there."

"Did he ever write you any letters?" I asked.

"E-mails, yeah. Creepy ones. That's how they proved it was him—they traced the e-mail address back to him. I filed for a restraining order, then I left school—I thought this was all over."

"You're sure that he never sent you anything besides those e-mails? He never dropped notes in your locker or your mailbox at home? Slipped something under your door?"

"Nope. Just the e-mails."

"And it stopped when you transferred?"

"Pretty much."

"Have you heard from him since then?"

"No. Thank God."

After fifth period, on my way to lunch, I stopped by my locker to drop off a few books and found a note folded at the bottom. It wasn't another article—it was smaller, handwritten. It said: *If the fall doesn't kill you, the crocodile will. 4:30 today.* I read it twice, then folded it up and put it in my pocket. There was no telling who wrote it—I wouldn't know until I met them— but I was sure I knew what it meant.

I hadn't been to the Oakland Zoo since I was ten years old. I had gone on a school field trip there once, and I remembered just where they kept the big reptiles. I knew what the note meant because I'd seen the words before, on a sign hanging over the crocodile pit at the Sydney Aquarium. The biology teacher had a photograph of it in his classroom. I must've passed it at least twice a day while walking through the science building, just like everybody else at Brighton.

At four-thirty on the dot, I felt a tap on my shoulder.

"Oz?" He squared his shoulders and stared at me but didn't speak. Trying to lighten the mood, I gestured to the pit. "You know that's an alligator? They don't have crocodiles here."

He shrugged, but still said nothing.

"Did Adam send you?"

"He told me how he pulled a gun on you yesterday."

I nodded, backing away slowly. "We're not going to have a repeat of that, are we? I got the message the first time."

Oz shook his head. "That's why I had you meet me in a public place. So you'd know I wasn't here to beat you up or anything. I just want to talk."

"Look, I'm not going to turn you guys in," I told him. "Your business is . . . your business. I'm not looking to mess things up for you."

"This isn't about the drugs," Oz said. "Or, it is, but not directly."

"Okay. So talk."

He took in a deep breath and let it out slowly. "Did you ever hear of a girl named Laura Brandt?"

"No." It seemed smart to keep a lid on my knowledge. Any explanation of how I knew a girl who lived several towns away and with whom I had no friends in common would inevitably lead back to Carly's diary, and I didn't want anyone to know that Audrey and I had found it. "Does she go to Brighton?"

"No. She was homeschooled."

I waited, but he said nothing else. "What does she have to do with me?"

"I heard you're investigating Carly's murder. Is that true?"

"Why are you asking?"

"I think I have some information for you."

I tried to gauge his expression. "Then I am. Well, sort of. Trying, anyway."

"Laura and I go back a long way. We were both home-schooled when we were younger, and we were both in this social group some of the mothers set up to help us make friends."

"I guess you knew her pretty well, then."

"Yeah, we were close. Even though I ended up going to Brighton and she stayed homeschooled, we hung out a lot."

Something told me that Oz and Laura were more than friends, or at least Oz had wanted them to be. "What happened to her?"

Oz ran his fingers through his dark hair, fidgeting. "I don't know. She just—disappeared."

"She didn't tell you where she was going?"

"A couple of years ago, I introduced her to Adam and they got to be friends. She'd hang out with us a lot, even got close to Carly. She'd been doing drugs for a little while, but Adam got her hooked on some strong stuff."

"You just let him do that to her?"

"I figured it was her choice, and who was I to tell her not to? I mean, I deal the stuff, I'm not exactly innocent here."

"Fine. She was hooked on, what, coke?"

He nodded. "About three months before Carly died, Laura ODed on cocaine—or, what she thought was pure cocaine. The doctors at the hospital told her that the coke she bought from Adam had been cut with Special K."

"Special K?"

"That's its street name—the medical term is ketamine. Adam gets it over the counter from a vet in Tijuana."

"A vet?"

"Yeah. They use it to put down big animals. Anyway, Special K in powder form looks like cocaine, but it's a pretty powerful hallucinogen, sort of like PCP. It can do some pretty horrible shit to you when you mix it with as much coke as Laura had in her system that day."

"What did it do to her?"

"Put her in a coma. She was lucky. Most of the time, people who OD on ketamine and coke end up brain damaged or dead. Anyway, at first she pretended not to remember who sold her the junk, but once she found out about the ketamine she got really angry. She started talking about turning Adam in, about going to the police and providing testimony that would get him locked up."

"He probably could've wriggled his way out of it," I said bitterly. "Daddy's money would've gotten him off the hook."

"Maybe, if he was some small-time dope dealer, but Adam's into some pretty big shit. He's partners with this guy named Barton; you'd never believe how big."

"So?"

"So I wasn't the only person Laura mouthed off to about this. I told her not to say anything, that I'd ask Adam about the Special K, but she wouldn't listen. She was going into rehab, and she kept saying that when she got back she was going to blow the lid off Adam's entire operation. She was crazy. She wouldn't listen to reason."

"Who else did she tell?"

Oz said nothing, but from the look in his eyes I could guess. "Carly?"

"Yeah. For whatever reason, she trusted Carly. I told Laura not to, that it was a mistake, but she kept saying that Carly was planning on leaving Adam and was going to help her bring him down."

"You think Carly tipped Adam off that Laura was going to talk to the police?"

"She must've, because he definitely found out."

"If Carly was going to break up with Adam, why would she warn him about Laura's plans?"

"Maybe," Oz said, "she *lied.*"

"How did Adam react?" I asked.

"He lost it, started threatening her. He got the Bean to run her off the road one day when she was driving up the freeway— she almost rolled her car into a ditch."

"The Bean?"

"Yeah. Anyway, she was shaken up, but right before she went to rehab she swore to me she was still going to do it. She begged me to get out before she did, and I was going to, but then—"

"Then?"

"She was in rehab for three weeks in Arizona, then she checked herself out and never came back."

"She just vanished?"

Oz shrugged. "She committed herself voluntarily, so she could leave whenever she felt like it, but she was really serious about getting clean. I can't believe she would just disappear, unless somebody talked her into it."

"Like who?"

"I don't know. The Bean, maybe."

"Why would she listen to the Bean if he ran her off the road?"

"She didn't know who did it, and I didn't even find out until a couple of months ago. She liked the Bean; she thought they were friends. The people she trusted the most in the group were me, Carly, and the Bean, and I didn't do it. I thought Carly might have, but she was in town that whole week."

"What do you think happened to Laura?"

"At first I thought that maybe they offered her money to disappear. She was eighteen, so it wasn't like she would be considered a runaway. And she was hard up for cash, which Adam knew. If he couldn't intimidate her, I thought maybe he'd bribe her to shut up and go away."

"What changed?"

"Nothing really, except the night before Carly died, she and Adam had a fight at Lucy Miller's End of Summer party. Everyone heard them yelling at each other, and I'm pretty sure I heard Laura's name come up. Carly said something about Adam turning her into a monster, and she screamed, 'What happened to Laura?' "

"Man."

"Yeah." Oz stared at the ground.

"Why don't you go to the police?"

"I don't have any proof. And if I betray Adam, I might disappear too."

"So why are you telling me all this?"

"I don't know. I just thought that maybe, if Carly found out what happened to Laura and got pissed enough to do something about it, that might be the reason she's dead."

"You don't believe Enzo Ribelli killed her?"

He shook his head. "This makes more sense to me, with what I heard and what I know."

"What else did you hear that night?"

"Not much. The music drowned out most of what they were saying, and Adam took Carly into a bedroom once she started to get really upset. I didn't see either of them after that."

Remembering Audrey's theory about the Bean, I asked, "Was the Bean at the party?"

Oz paused, then said, "Yeah. He left sometime around two o'clock. He was so drunk, he hit a mailbox backing out of the driveway."

I got the phone message from Carly around two-thirty. I was fairly certain that she had left the party by then. "Did he leave with Carly?"

Oz shrugged. "I don't know. She did leave, though, because I stayed the night and when I woke up she was gone."

"Who was there with you in the morning?"

"Just Lucy, Adam, and Cass. Cass went to brunch with Audrey, and I went over to Cass's house later. When I left at five, they were on the couch playing video games."

Adam's alibi was that they had stayed on that couch, playing video games, for the rest of the night, and it hinged on Cass's testimony, which he had given eagerly, if not truthfully. Enzo's lawyer told Audrey that the whole time the DA was arraigning Enzo and building up the case against him, the police were running a concurrent investigation into Adam, but if that was true it must've been a pretty cursory affair—they hadn't dug up anything about Adam's drug dealing, or so I assumed since the papers hadn't gotten wind of it and he wasn't behind bars. That made sense to me; nobody with an ounce of self-preservation would've rolled over on Adam. It all came down to his alibi—they could neither prove that Cass was lying about being with Adam that evening nor prove that Adam had been anywhere else during the hours surrounding the murder. Eventually, under pressure from the district attorney's office, which already had its criminal behind bars, they dropped it. I was not so easily put off.

It was my belief that Cass was lying to cover for his friend. I couldn't quite figure out why, unless it was under duress—maybe Adam had threatened him, or Audrey, if Cass didn't keep his mouth shut about where Adam really was that evening. Somehow Cass must've been compromised, and taking into account their most recent rift and his lingering feelings for Audrey, she was now in a prime position to drag it all out of him—if I could convince her to see things my way.

"I'll look into it," I told Oz. "I just have one more question."

"Sure."

"You said Special K was a powder?"

"Yeah, but you can also get it as a liquid. Lots of people pour a dose into a drink, but that's not really smart. Special K mixed with alcohol can knock you right out."

"Sean Ozrick?" Audrey raised an eyebrow. We met at the diner after school. This was, obviously, not a conversation I wanted to have at Brighton. "Somehow he doesn't strike me as the cloak-and-dagger type."

"I think he's totally freaked."

"I would be, too, if I were him." She stared at her hands.

"Do you really think Carly told Adam about Laura Brandt's plan to rat him out?"

I thought for a moment. "Yeah, I do."

Audrey shook her head slowly. "I can't believe she would do that."

"But look at it from her perspective. She had feelings for Adam. Laura started talking about how she was going to turn him in, and an operation of that size could get him tried as an adult, even if he was a lackey for somebody else."

"Do we know who that could be?"

I shook my head. "Oz said it was some guy named Barton. I'm guessing he's not in high school."

"Could you find out?"

"Maybe. But do you really think it's a good idea to be attracting that kind of attention?"

"No. But we need all the facts. Try to meet with Oz again—maybe he'll spill, if he thinks you'll help him figure out who vanished Laura."

"I wonder what really happened to her."

"Let's hope that whatever it is, it's better than what happened to Carly."

I told her what I had found out earlier that day from Allison Kessler, then said, "I think we should probably go find the Bean tonight—see what he has to say about Allison and Laura."

"Sounds like a plan."

"Hey, are you sure you've never heard of Laura Brandt? I mean, if she was a friend of Carly and Adam's, wouldn't you have met her, or at least heard of her?"

Audrey shook her head. "I think you overestimate how much a part of that group I was. Carly and Adam were friends with a *lot* of people, people like Laura Brandt, but I wasn't involved in all their activities. I didn't do drugs and I didn't take an interest in that side of their lives. Cass and I tried to stay away from that as much as we could, and Carly was apparently careful about keeping certain things secret from me."

"I think you're giving Cass too much credit," I insisted, growing frustrated with her. "His brother used to be the biggest drug dealer in Empire Valley. At the very least, he must know something about Adam's operation."

"Look," Audrey said, "Cass and I were together for two years. He's always been busy with basketball. Not drugs."

"So you say."

Audrey's phone rang. "Oh, hi, Grandma," she said, holding up a finger. "Well, I have this school project—uh-huh." A sigh. "Okay. Seven-thirty. I know, I promise."

"Late for cocktail hour?" I smirked.

"Sort of. Grandma Louise wants me home for dinner tonight—apparently, my absence has been noticed. I should go," Audrey said reluctantly. "I've been trying so hard to be a good daughter lately, I've been a shitty granddaughter."

"Go. I can handle the Bean."

✦

Around five o'clock I headed to Keptow Auto Body and parked across the street, waiting for the Bean to get off. When I saw him leave around eight o'clock, I left my car and jogged toward him.

"Bean!"

He looked up and rolled his eyes. "Can I help you?"

"Yeah. I've got a couple of questions."

"Well, hurry up, because I've got somewhere to be."

"Meeting the girlfriend?"

"Yeah."

"It won't take too long. Do you remember a girl named Allison Kessler?"

The Bean's eyes widened and he looked down at the ground. "No."

"Come on, I know that's not true."

"Then why did you ask?"

"I wanted to see what you'd say."

"That stuff with Allison was a long time ago."

"You stalked her, Bean. Why?"

He threw up his hands. "I don't know. Because I liked her and I wanted to get her attention."

"Oh, you got her attention. I think she's scarred for life."

"Look, I never wanted to scare her. It was a misunderstanding. I followed the restraining order. I haven't gone near her or spoken to her in three years."

"I believe you."

"Then can I go now?"

"Just one more thing. I want to know what you know about Laura Brandt."

The Bean struggled to keep his face blank, but I could see the panic rise in his eyes. "Never heard of her."

I leaned against the door of his car and he backed up a little. "See, you lied about knowing Allison Kessler, which makes it really hard to believe that you're telling the truth now."

"I am. I didn't know her."

"I know you knew her. More than that, I know that Adam got you to run her off the road."

"No way, man. I wouldn't do that."

"Don't try to fuck with me, Bean. You know I don't believe you."

"Dude, who do you think you are?"

"I'm not here to bust you. You were always somebody's tool—you didn't do it for your own reasons. I just need to know the truth. What happened to Laura Brandt?"

"I told you, I don't know her. Now get off my car. That's an expensive paint job."

"Did Adam send you to Arizona to lure her out of rehab and pay her off? Did you abandon her someplace? Did you kill her?"

"I didn't have anything to do with Laura!" he nearly shouted.

"So you did know her?"

He hesitated. "Fine, yeah, I knew her. Barely. I met her a couple of times, but I never even talked to her."

"I heard that you were friends."

He narrowed his eyes. "From who?"

"I think something really bad happened to her. I think somebody killed her, and if what happened to Laura had something to do with what happened to Carly, I need to know about it. So did you do it, Bean? Did you kill Laura Brandt?"

"I told you I didn't. Don't you listen?"

"I'm not convinced."

"That's not my fucking problem. You're not the police—you can't do anything to me."

"Well, if you didn't do it, you must know who did. Was it Adam?"

"I don't hang with Adam anymore. If he had something to do with Laura's disappearance, I don't know about it. Now get off my car. And don't come back here, or *I'll* call the cops." He was gripping his car keys so hard his knuckles were turning white. I shook my head.

"I wouldn't do that, Bean," I said, getting up and walking off. "I really wouldn't."

CHAPTER TWENTY

After first period the next day, Harvey and I swung past the vending machines outside the cafeteria. We were heading back to class when I caught sight of a freshman I barely recognized pushing a piece of paper into my locker.

"Hey!" I called, about ten feet away, and when the kid started to run I gave chase, dropping my bag and books at Harvey's feet. I grabbed the kid by the collar and spun him around. He panted in my face.

"What the fuck, you little weasel?" I yanked him over to my locker and opened it up. "What's that, huh?" I pointed to a piece of paper at the bottom. When he didn't answer, I picked the paper up and unfolded it.

Harvey caught up to us. "Jesus, Neily, let him go."

It was another article, which read along the same lines as the first, except this one mentioned Audrey's father as Carly's alleged killer. "Who gave you this?" I asked the kid, who was squirming to get out of my grip.

"A-Adam Mu-Murray," he stammered, and I let go. He scurried down into the quad and out of sight.

I leaned against the lockers and crumpled the article into a ball. Harvey took it from me and read it. He raised his eyebrows.

"Adam Murray?"

"It's not the first one," I told him. "He's trying to fuck with my head."

"Why?"

"To scare me?"

"Sounds more like he's scared *of* you. This is a sign of a desperate man."

"A desperate, guilty man."

"Yeah, maybe. What are you going to do?"

"I'll think of something."

⟿⟿

As it turned out, it didn't require much thinking. I tracked Adam down right outside his first-period classroom and slammed him against a row of lockers. I wasn't as big as Adam, but I was strong and angry and full of adrenaline. Shoving Adam felt like pushing over a trash can.

"What the fuck is this?" I shouted, thrusting the article into his face.

He shoved me off. "What's your problem?"

I shoved back hard. "You had a freshman put articles about Carly in my locker? What the fuck is that, some kind of scare tactic? You just trying to shake me up?"

"Don't touch me again, Monroe, or it'll be the last thing you do."

"I'm not scared of you. You've got everybody else fooled into thinking you're some big tough, but the truth is that you're just a little boy with a gun. And now you don't even have that, so what's there for me to be afraid of?"

"Neily!" Harvey grabbed me. "Don't be crazy. You want to get expelled?"

I ignored him. Adam tried to leave, but I was too quick. I punched him. He punched me back, landing a nice right hook on my cheek. I stumbled and fell against a pole, clutching my face. Adam shook out his hand and glared at me.

In a moment, two rough hands were pinning my arms at the small of my back. I glanced behind me and saw Finch, enraged, glowering down at me.

"Come with me, Neily," he said in his coldest, most you're-so-fucked voice. Adam was shaking his head; he had put on a shocked expression just for Finch.

As Finch hauled me off, I glared at Adam and said, "I know what you did. And I swear to God, if it is the last thing I do, I will make sure that you pay for it."

※

"What the *hell* were you thinking?" Finch yelled.

"Jesus, Finch, my ears?"

"Don't you dare," he said. "Fighting? What has happened to you, Neily?"

"I guess I'm sick of taking everybody's shit."

"Oh yeah? And what shit did Adam Murray give you today that justified slamming your fist into his face?"

I struggled to keep calm. "Ask him yourself."

"I will, rest assured. But until then, I'm suspending you for a week. I don't want to see your face within a mile of this campus. Am I understood?"

"Yes, sir," I said.

"If I were you, Neily, I'd wipe that look right off your face, because I called your father. He should be here any minute." Finch smiled. "That's better."

***

"A fight? You got in a fight?" my father screamed. He had been silent all the way to my mother's house, but now that we were home he was letting loose. "Are you a lunatic? Do you know how a fight is going to look on your permanent record?"

"Might want to call those Ivies, Dad," I said. "Do some damage control."

"You think this is funny? Are you enjoying this? You're going to ruin your life, Neily. First you let your grades slip, now this. You're going to end up flipping burgers at the diner and you'll have nobody to blame but yourself."

"And you."

"That's perfect. Blame me for your problems. What haven't I given you, Neily? And you throw it all back in my face like it's garbage."

"I'm supposed to be grateful you walked out on us?" I challenged. I knew that would rile him up. He hated to be reminded he was anything less than a god. "I'm supposed to be *grateful* that you put all that pressure on me to be a genius, to be the best? I was drowning at that school, Dad, and you couldn't care less so long as I get into Harvard. That's what this is really all about, isn't it? I let you down, so you write me off?"

"That's ridiculous. When have I ever written you off?"

"The second I dropped out of the program you acted like you barely knew me," I said. "My best friend is dead and you can hardly even look at me. Do you know how hard it was for me last year, with the investigation and the trial? But instead of talking to me about it like a real father, you just throw me to a therapist once a week and pretend it'll make it all better."

"Neily—"

"It is *not* all better, Dad," I said. "Because I'm still drowning."

He just stood there, afraid to look me in the eye. We sat in silence after that, waiting for my mother to get home from work.

That night, Audrey paid me a visit.

"Are you insane?" she said when I opened the door.

"Hello to you, too." I went out onto the porch and closed the door behind me.

"Attacking Adam on school grounds? Tell me you weren't suspended."

"I'm suspended. For a week."

"Jesus, Neily, is this your idea of low profile?"

"He provoked me. I had to show him who he was dealing with."

"I don't care if he put bamboo shoots under your toenails

and made you kick a door, you should never have done what you did. Now he knows how to get to you and he won't let up." She shook her head. "You are such a chump. And what if you're right, and Adam did kill Carly? Now you've attracted his attention and if you weren't at the top of his list before, you certainly are now. How could you be so careless? After what happened to Carly?"

"At least I'm not sleeping with the enemy," I said, knowing she was right.

"Shut up. You don't even know what you're talking about."

"I know that you're considering getting back together with Cass. Anybody who's seen you the past few days knows that."

"That's none of your business. And he's not the enemy. We went to the auto body shop this afternoon, and guess what? The Bean's gone, his girlfriend says for good. Cass is going to use his connections to help track him down. You need more proof that he's on our side?"

"The Bean has left town?" I shook my head. "I talked to him yesterday, asked him about Allison Kessler and Laura Brandt, just like we planned."

"What did he say?"

"He admitted to stalking Allison, but he claimed he didn't know anything about Laura. He was lying, I could tell, but I'm pretty convinced he didn't do it. Do you still think he killed Carly?"

"I think that if he was as messed up as those letters say he was, he's definitely capable of it."

"You don't know that he wrote those."

"You don't know that he didn't. He wrote to Allison."

"Yeah—e-mails, not actual letters."

"So he's finally learned how to use a printer. That doesn't prove anything."

"It seems like an important distinction to me."

"Can you think of anybody else who might have written them, then? And don't you dare say Adam—that can't be your answer for everything."

"Yeah, well, Cass might have the connections, but I'm the only person getting anything done around here."

"Don't give yourself too much credit," Audrey said. "You're probably the one who scared the Bean off."

"He didn't look scared."

"His behavior would seem to indicate otherwise."

I couldn't argue with that. "Who are these 'connections' of Cass's?"

"He didn't say."

"No shit. Well, good luck with that one. He's slippery."

"Fuck off, Neily. And the next time you want to hit something, put your fist through a wall." With that, she split.

✦

Suspension agreed with me. I had never understood why the punishment for troublemakers—who clearly hated school—was to force them to stay home. I spent the weekend and the first few days of my punishment lounging around, watching television and reading, but by Wednesday afternoon I was bored, and relieved when Harvey offered to drop by to play video games.

"I hate to tell you this, but I saw Audrey and Cass making out in the quad today," Harvey told me.

"Yeah. I figured that was going to happen."

"Why does it bother you so much?"

"Because the last time I lost a friend to that crowd, she ended up dead."

"You sure you don't have feelings for Audrey?"

"No. Her love life is her own business—I'm just trying to look out for her. Let's change the subject."

"So, exactly how are you going to continue investigating from in here?" Harvey asked, stuffing his mouth full of Cheetos.

"I can leave. I'm not under house arrest."

"I see. And have you left the house today?"

"No," I said. "The problem is, with the Bean gone, the best I can do is follow Adam around town. Except—"

"Except you can't go near the school. Remind me again how getting suspended works into your master plan?"

"Eh, it doesn't. But at least I've only got a couple of days left." I sighed. "Audrey's right. I never should've let Adam know he was getting to me."

"So what are you going to do now?"

I pulled a note out of my pocket. "Can you leave this in Oz's locker tomorrow?"

Harvey nodded. "Will do."

꙳

The zoo was practically dead when I met Oz the next day. He lumbered up behind me looking somber, like a man going to his execution.

"What did you find out?" he asked without even saying hello.

"Nothing much. The Bean denies having anything to do

271

with Laura's disappearance, but he took off yesterday and we have no idea where he's gone."

"Jesus." Oz sat down on a bench and put his head in his hands, elbows resting on his knees. "How did you do it, Neily?"

"Do what?"

"Lose the girl you loved like this. Doesn't it just kill you?"

"Interesting word choice." I sat down on the opposite side of the bench. "Yeah, it kills me. I went through this whole period where all I wanted to do was hit something, all the time. I may actually still be going through that period."

"I heard about the fight."

"Yeah, it was pretty stupid."

"That's a bit of an understatement. Adam's got blood in his mouth now. You're his number one target."

"Maybe that's a good thing. If he makes a move, we can nail him."

"We?" He shook his head. "Uh-uh, Neily. I'm not stepping into this thing."

"You came to me," I reminded him.

"For help, not conscription. I'm risking everything just talking to you right now. Which reminds me." He pulled my note from his pocket. "You got something to say?"

"More like a question to ask. Who's Adam's business partner?"

Oz shrugged. "No idea. Adam always calls him 'Barton,' because that's apparently what he calls himself, but I've never met him, never even heard his real name. Supposedly he's an old connection of Jerod Irving's. All I know is that he helps Adam bankroll the whole operation, he gets most of the drugs, and he calls a lot of the shots. I'm pretty sure that it was his idea to do something about Laura."

"So you can't get me a meeting with him?"

"Have you been smoking something?"

"I'll take that as a no." A thought occurred to me. "How does Adam keep track of his deals?"

"He's got a BlackBerry he carries on him with every number of every client he has. He keeps a calendar full of stats—type of drug, ounces, money owed and exchanged, buyer. It's all in code."

"That's pretty high tech."

"It's digital so that he can back it up, but he can also get rid of the info with the press of a button."

"How can I get my hands on Adam's BlackBerry?"

"If you're willing to risk your life, pretty easily."

"Let's say I don't have a death wish."

"Well, then I'd say the chances are slim to none you'll ever get near enough to Adam to snag it."

"He carries it with him at *all* times?"

Oz nodded. "Pretty much."

"What about during weight lifting?" Adam, like most of the senior guys who couldn't stand the idea of taking chorus or drama for their elective, sought the comforting presence of other sweaty slackers in the weight room during eighth period.

Oz's eyes widened. "He probably leaves it in his locker."

"If I got my hands on the BlackBerry while Adam's working the butterfly press, do you think you could crack the code for me?"

"I think so. What exactly are you looking for?"

"I want to know precisely what Adam's movements were

the night Carly died. If he had some kind of deal to make that evening, maybe I can find a way to prove he wasn't at Cass's when she was killed. But I won't be forcing it out of Cass. That way, everybody wins."

"Except Cass, who'd get in trouble for lying to the police. I don't think Audrey would consider that 'winning.' "

"They'd let him off if he agreed to testify. Anyway, I'm not worried about Audrey's feelings right now. All I care about is watching Adam go down for what he did."

"And if it wasn't him?"

"Oh, believe me," I said. "It was him."

CHAPTER TWENTY-ONE

The next evening, Audrey called and asked me to meet her at the diner. I had to sneak out of my house to do it—I might not technically have been under house arrest, but my mother was no amateur. She had taken my car keys, but I had an extra set, and when she fell asleep on the couch watching TV, I slipped out the back door, put the car in neutral, and pushed it to the end of the block before hopping in and driving off.

Audrey gave me a tight smile. "How's your hand?"

"A lot better than my face," I told her, pointing to my black eye. "I'm guessing you're not mad at me anymore."

"I wasn't mad."

"Then somebody call the Academy, because that little performance the other day should've earned you an Oscar."

"I'm scared. A guy like Adam isn't going to let you get away with what you did."

"So I've been told."

"Did you talk to Oz?"

I nodded. "Yeah. He said that he has no idea who Adam's partner is—only that his nickname is Barton and he calls a lot of the shots. Oz thinks that Barton had something to do with Laura Brandt's disappearance—which means that the Bean is officially off the hook."

"Not so fast. I asked Cass if he knew anything about Adam's supplier, but he doesn't, only that the guy isn't in Empire Valley and that he's a bit of a shadow. Nobody's ever met him, but Adam complained to Cass last year that Barton was doing a lot of stuff behind his back—having people roughed up, sending Adam's toadies out on special assignments, bringing stuff over the border without telling Adam, et cetera. He didn't say so, but I got the impression it might've been this Barton guy who cut the cocaine he sold Laura Brandt with Special K."

"So?"

"So we know that Adam kicked the Bean out of his circle after Cass's School's Out for Summer party, but the Laura Brandt stuff didn't go down until after that—in July and at Lucy's party in August. Both Adam and this Barton character had a lot to lose if she actually went to the cops. Maybe the Bean agreed to freak her out on the freeway or dispose of her permanently to get on either or both of their good sides."

"Maybe. You seem to be consulting a lot with Cass lately. Is he part of this investigation now?"

"That's what I wanted to talk to you about, actually," she said, ripping open a packet of Sweet'N Low and pouring it into a tall glass of iced tea. "Cass and I are back together."

"I've heard."

"That's it? That's all you have to say?"

"What do you want me to say? That I think it's a big mistake?" I looked her straight in the eyes. "Fine. I think it's a big mistake."

"Why?"

"You really want to do this?"

"Do what?"

"You really want to have this conversation about how I disapprove of your boyfriend? We just started becoming friendly and this is how you want all that to end?"

"I know you don't trust him because he's friends with Adam, but he told me that they hardly even speak anymore and I really think—"

"Here's what I think. I think he lied about being with Adam the night of Carly's murder, and I'm about to prove it. Are you going to stand by him when you find out he impeded a police investigation and he gets arrested for aiding and abetting?"

"If that's what happened, then yeah, I am going to stick by him."

"Because he did such a fine job of sticking by you," I said. "I thought a girl like you would prefer to return the favor."

"I love him, Neily. If Carly had come to you and said, 'I'm sorry, I've made a mistake, I want you back,' what would you have done?"

She had a point. "It's your life. But for the record, I wasn't going to say anything."

"You said you were about to prove that Adam wasn't where he said he was the night of Carly's murder. How are you going to do that?"

I hesitated. "I don't think I can trust you with that information."

"You've got to be kidding me."

"Nope. I'm willing to play the understanding, sympathetic friend who supports all your decisions no matter how stupid they are, but you're compromising the whole investigation by getting back together with Cass."

"How?"

"There. Right there, that look."

"What look?"

"That panicked look you had on your face when I talked about proving that Cass is a liar. You're either on board a hundred percent or you're not. But if you're not, I can't use you."

"You can't use *me*? Whose idea was this in the first place?"

"Yours. Which is why I'm surprised that you would give it all up to make out with Cass in the backseat of a car."

"It's a really nice car," she snapped.

"Oh, good one. Right where it hurts."

"I'm not giving it all up. I still want to find out who killed Carly—I still want to clear my dad."

"Sure doesn't look like it. But I guess that you were just doing this to exorcise your daddy issues, and now that you have, the rest is gravy."

"Excuse me? 'Daddy issues'?"

"Don't act like you don't know what I'm talking about."

"Enlighten me," she said, seething.

"This all started because you wanted to win back the love of a man who abandoned you," I said, on a roll now. I didn't want to hurt her, but I also didn't want to let her off easy for walking away from this. It had been comforting, knowing that some-body was there with me, believing the same things I was, fight-ing for the same cause, but all she was doing was launching a campaign to get back her ex-boyfriend. What annoyed me most was that I saw this coming, but I thought she would make the right decision. It just showed how little I knew her. "Now you have. It's a different man, but he'll do, I'm sure."

"You're such an asshole."

"Well, at least some things don't change."

"How can you say that to me? After everything we've both been through, how can you deny me the one scrap of happiness I've had over the past year and a half? You're so goddamned selfish it makes me want to throw up." She threw a few dollar bills on the table and left the restaurant. I didn't watch her leave. It was too sad.

~~~

I saw Audrey Monday morning at school, but she didn't look at me. Instead, she dove right for Cass, as if to show me that she knew what she was doing. I wanted to give consideration to Audrey and Cass, but unfortunately I had bigger things to worry about. First of all, I had to figure out how to get into Adam's gym locker without using the bolt cutter I'd stashed in my own locker in case of emergency.

"If I had to get into somebody's locker, how would I do it?" Harvey repeated for clarification. "I'm assuming this is not just a hypothetical question."

"Let's pretend it is."

"Okay," he said. "Well, I guess the best way to compromise a combination lock would be to use a shim."

"A shim?"

"Yeah. You can buy them on the Internet, I think."

"Wish I had known that yesterday."

"Relax, dude." Harvey walked over to the soda machine and dropped a handful of coins into the slot. A can of root beer tumbled out and he picked it up. "You can make your own out of an aluminum can."

"Tell me you know how to make a shim."

"As a matter of fact, I do."

I grinned and shook my head. "Unbelievable."

"What? I get bored a lot and I used to be a Boy Scout."

"No, it's brilliant. What else do you need?"

"A knife, some scissors, and a Sharpie."

"I have a Swiss Army knife in my car and I'm sure we can get a marker from Gert."

"Well, what are you waiting for? Let's get hacking."

"You are having way too much fun with this," I said as I watched Harvey chop up the soda can and draw lines on it with a chunky blue Sharpie we'd borrowed from Gert the librarian. We were in the back of the library at my usual table, where nobody would stumble across us unexpectedly.

"I'm thinking about being an FBI agent when I grow up," Harvey said. "What's all this about, anyway?"

"I'm really close to figuring out who killed Carly," I told him. "To do that, I need something in a certain locker."

Harvey raised an eyebrow. "You sure you want to do this? It seems like a long way to go for a girl you claim to hate."

"I don't hate her," I said softly, watching his hands work the aluminum instead of looking him in the face.

"Dude, you burned all her pictures."

"I don't hate her," I said. "I was just so angry at her. She broke my heart, she humiliated me, and then she went and got herself killed. How am I supposed to deal with that?"

"So she had some flaws, and she made some big mistakes," Harvey said. "Everybody does. You can't be perfect, and you definitely can't expect other people to be."

I scoffed.

"Seriously. You know, my grandmother used to say that flaws are God's greatest gift to humanity, because they give us the opportunity to learn from ourselves and from each other. She said they're not obstacles to perfection, merely signs and guideposts on the path we take in pursuit of it."

"But if nobody's perfect, no matter how hard we try, then what's the point?"

Harvey didn't look up; he was concentrating hard on his work. "The universe is infinite; we'll never map its edges, yet NASA keeps on sending up spacecrafts," he said, folding the metal precisely. "The *point* is just to get a little closer."

He smiled and held up the handmade shim. "Now, this may or may not work—the metal is a little too thin to be one hundred percent, but those combination locks are pretty weak. Still, you might need to use some brute force."

"So I do what? Jam this in where the lock closes and give it a tug?"

"Exactly."

"What are you doing seventh period, Harv?"

"Well, I was going to go to government class, but seeing as you'll be otherwise engaged, I guess I can tag along, play lookout."

"Great."

"You look a little terrified, Neily. You sure this is a good idea?"

"No. But it's the only idea I have at the moment."

"Whose locker are we breaking into, by the way?"

"Adam Murray's."

Harvey let out a low whistle. "You might want to keep that knife on you, just in case."

Shortly after the bell announced the start of seventh period, the men's locker room emptied out and all the muscleheads started doing rotations in the weight room down the hall. When we were sure that the coast was clear, Harvey and I went into the locker room and jammed the door closed with a wedge.

"Do you know which one's his locker?" Harvey asked as we walked along the aisles.

I stopped in front of locker 214 and pointed to a large round sticker that had been affixed to the door. "Where else in northern California would you find a Pittsburgh Steelers logo than on the private property of the great-great-great-grandnephew of Andrew Carnegie?"

"And here I thought being a Niners fan was heresy. You know way too much about the people in this town."

"Yet another sign that it's time to get the fuck out of here," I said. "Give me the shim."

Harvey handed it to me. It took me a couple of tries, but eventually the lock popped open.

"Sweet," I said in a low voice. I pawed through a pile of dirty laundry, trying not to inhale, and found the BlackBerry in its case near the bottom. "Got it. Let's get out of here."

After I stole Adam's BlackBerry, we booked it to the Mac lab on the second floor of the library to peruse its contents. I hooked it up using a cable from my father's BlackBerry that I had accidentally taken with my cell-phone charger the last time I stayed with him.

"Good thing I kept this," I remarked as all of Adam's data uploaded to the computer.

Harvey shook his head. "I don't get this. What are all these calendar entries?"

"Oz told me he wrote them in code. I'm going to print this out so I have a copy to show him. He thinks he can figure out what the code means if he can take a look at it."

"All right, you'd better hurry. You only have"—Harvey checked his watch—"ten minutes until the meatheads get back to the locker room."

"Ten minutes till busted." I got up and went to the printer. "God, it's like this thing was made in the seventies. Hurry up, you piece of crap."

The printer finished three minutes before the BlackBerry had to be back in Adam's locker. "Let's go," Harvey said nervously.

"I just have to check one thing." I scrolled through the BlackBerry's phone book until I landed on Carly's number. I selected EDIT and then RINGTONE—Pat Benatar's "Hit Me with Your Best Shot" screamed out into the library's emptiness. The same ringtone was set for her home phone. *Good,* I thought. *Not Cyndi Lauper.*

"What the hell are you doing?" Harvey asked.

"Nothing. Let's go," I said, grabbing the lock and Black-Berry and running out of the library with Harvey close on my heels. As we passed down the corridor toward the locker room, I glanced into the weight room—it was empty.

"Shit," I said under my breath. "What now?"

"Sometimes Coach Wilson makes them do a couple of laps on the field before hitting the showers," Harvey said.

"How do you know that?"

"I took weight lifting over the summer. Thought I'd try and bulk up."

"Uh . . ."

"I think I'm doomed to remain a skinny white guy," Harvey said. "All I got from that class was insulted."

"I admire your commitment, though," I said. "Meet you at the lot."

Harvey was right—the weight lifters hadn't come into the locker room yet. I jogged over to Adam's locker and replaced the BlackBerry and the lock, only moments before the door swung open and a group of Adam's cronies swarmed in. I walked quickly toward the door, hoping to God Adam wouldn't notice me, but he wasn't among them. Oz, however, body-slammed me into a row of lockers.

"You lost, Think Tank?" he asked gruffly, searching my face with his eyes.

I nodded once and said, "I think I am. I was looking for the Oakland Zoo, actually. Looks like they moved it."

"You better get out of here," he said.

"Oh, I'm going. I have a four o'clock appointment at the reptile house. Don't want to be late." And with that, I slipped out the door and ran all the way to the student parking lot.

I wasn't quite sure that Oz had gotten the message—extemporaneous code creating wasn't exactly my strong suit—but at four-fifteen he lurched up to the alligator pit looking nervous.

"Sorry I'm late. You got the BlackBerry?" he asked.

I handed him the printout I'd made of Adam's calendar. "A reasonable facsimile thereof. Can you tell me what it all means?"

"I can try." Oz sat down on a bench and pored over the document. After about fifteen minutes, he said, "I think I've got it."

"Great."

"You see this?" He pointed to a small box, marked June seventh, that read JON TRAJILLO—BIRTHDAY, 18. "Jonny Trajillo is one of Adam's clients. His dad—"

"Owns that chain of Mexican restaurants," I said. "I know."

"Right. Okay, so that's his birthday. Now look at this. March fourth of last year—Roman numeral VI-VII-VIII-IX. Six seven eight nine."

"June seventh, 1989," I said. "Along with the time they met, what he bought, and how much money he owed."

"That's it. That's how he keeps track. And then the numbers are in his phone under people's real names."

"What if there's a duplicate?"

285

"Well, then he adds an extra dash and another number—one, two, three . . . however many he needs."

"So another person listed beneath Jonny on June seventh would be VI-VII-VIII-IX-I."

"If they were born in the same year."

"Wow."

"Adam knows what he's doing. He's no amateur."

"That sounds like admiration."

"It is a little."

"There's just one more thing I need to check." I flipped to the page with the month that Carly died, and there it was—a meeting with XI-XI-VIII-VIII. "Whose birthday is November eleventh, 1988?"

"I don't know. Look it up."

And there it was, under November 11, 1988: Freddie Kramer.

"Who's Freddie Kramer?"

"You wouldn't know him. He went to Brighton for, like, a minute before he got kicked out for fighting. Last I heard, his parents sent him to live with his grandparents in Stockton."

I looked up Freddie's number in Adam's files and dialed it.

"No answer?"

"The phone's been disconnected. Give me a second." I called 411. "Empire Valley, California. I need a listing for Kramer."

"There are two listings for Kramer in Empire Valley," said the woman from Information. "A Bonnie Kramer and a Fred Kramer."

"Fred Kramer," I said, reasoning that Freddie was probably a Fred Jr.

The Kramers' phone rang three times before a woman—I

assumed Freddie's mother—picked up. "Hi, Mrs. Kramer? My name is Joe Neiland. I was a classmate of Freddie's at Brighton Day and I was trying to get ahold of Freddie, but his cell phone's been disconnected. Is there another way I could reach him?"

Mrs. Kramer snapped, "He's not here." Then she hung up. I closed the phone and gave Oz an exasperated look. "Mother of the Year, that one."

"Joe Neiland?"

I shrugged. "It's my uncle's name. Who were Freddie's friends? Do you know anybody else who might have a clue as to how to get in touch with him?"

"I do. Freddie didn't have a lot of friends, but there was one person he did hang out with pretty regularly: the Bean."

CHAPTER TWENTY-TWO

Audrey had told me the Bean had fled, but his girlfriend was still around and I figured there was about a fifty-fifty chance he was in the area too. I thought about calling Audrey to come along on the stakeout, but now that she was back with Cass it didn't seem like a good idea. Still, it felt weird doing something without Audrey. I kind of missed her.

I sat outside Keptow Auto Body until six o'clock, when young Amanda Richardson, the Bean's sullen girlfriend—who I had learned that day, with a few pointed questions to the right people, was actually twenty, though she looked about fifteen—emerged from the office. She locked the door behind her and shuffled to her car, an ancient BMW with vanity plates that read 2HOT4U. Besides the Bean, I doubted that there were many men out there who would agree.

It turned out that stealth was not one of the Bean and Amanda's best qualities, because following her for a half hour through traffic led me to a run-down apartment building in San Leandro. She had been inside for about fifteen minutes when I finally turned off the ignition and headed up the stairs to knock on the door of apartment 2A.

To my surprise, the Bean himself answered. When he saw who it was, he tried to shut the door in my face, but I was quicker and wedged myself in to stop it.

"I'm not going anywhere until you talk to me, Bean," I told him.

"I didn't do anything. You got the wrong guy."

"I think you're right. But I have a couple of questions, if you don't mind."

"Why should I tell you anything?"

"Because you're afraid Audrey's going to pin Carly's murder on you, and we both know that you didn't kill her. I just need you to help me prove it."

"How?"

"Can I come in? I'm starting to feel like a Jehovah's Witness."

"Fine. But don't get comfortable. You're not staying long."

The Bean's hideout was just as nice and cozy on the inside as it was on the outside. Empty pizza boxes and empty cans of Coors Light littered every surface, and it looked like he and Amanda had been sleeping together on the couch, which wasn't a pullout.

"I know that Adam had a meeting with Freddie Kramer right before Carly died. The problem is that I'm having a hard

time getting ahold of Freddie. Oz told me you were friends—
have any idea where I can find him?"

"Freddie moved."

"You think I don't know that? That's why I'm here, Bean.
Try to keep up."

"If I get you in touch with Freddie, will you promise to
leave me alone?"

"I promise."

"Okay. Give me a second."

Fifteen minutes later, the Bean came out with good news.
"Freddie's agreed to meet you in town tonight while his grandparents are at bingo."

"Which town?"

"Empire Valley, at the Howard's Yogurt downtown."

"At the Ho-Yo? I haven't been there since I was, like,
ten."

"Cool story."

"One more question: You did try to run Laura Brandt off
the road, didn't you?"

The Bean paused. "Adam told me to scare her a little. I
didn't mean for her to go into that ditch. I swear, I didn't want
to hurt her."

I nodded. "I believe you."

"That's it?"

"Yep, that's it." I glanced at Amanda. "Are you really running, Bean?"

He nodded. "Amanda's psycho ex-boyfriend keeps harassing her. We're going down to L.A. to throw him off."

"Wow. That's kind of ironic, don't you think?" The Bean
didn't seem to find it funny. "Well, good luck with that."

"Uh, thanks. And Neily?"

"Yeah?"

"Don't tell Adam I told you." ·

✧✧✧

The Ho-Yo was sort of an Empire Valley landmark. It'd been there for years and was run by a friendly Vietnamese family that lived down the street from my mom. When I was younger, my parents used to take me there all the time before the divorce. The owner, Mr. Nguyen, had an uncanny memory for regulars' orders. After all this time, he handed me a cup of chocolate and vanilla twist two minutes after I stepped into the shop. I didn't have the heart to tell him I'd lost the taste for frozen yogurt, so I paid for the cup and chose a seat in the back of the shop, farthest away from the counter and the door.

I had no idea what Freddie Kramer looked like, but I recognized him instantly when he walked through the door. Freddie was short but stocky, twenty pounds overweight and with arms that looked as though he had been working out. There were freckles all over his face and his hair was red; he looked exactly like the sort of kid who ought to have been named Freddie.

"Neily Monroe?" he asked, sitting down across from me and eyeing my yogurt. "That for me?"

I nodded and pushed it toward him. "Sure."

"The Bean said you had a couple of questions."

"Yeah. Thanks for coming, by the way."

"No problem. I hardly ever get out of the house anymore. It's sort of a nice change. I miss this town."

"That makes one of us. Listen, Freddie, do you remember Carly Ribelli?"

"Yeah. She's that chick who got killed on the bridge last year, right?"

I chafed at the word "chick" but tried not to react. "She was murdered, yeah. Do you remember where you were the night she died?"

His face fell. "Oh. Um, yeah, sort of."

"You *sort of* remember?"

"Well, things are a little fuzzy. That was the night I got my face scrambled by Adam Murray and a couple of his boys."

"Why did they beat you up?"

"Well, I was supposed to be picking up an eight ball I'd ordered, but a friend of mine owed them money and they decided to send him a message by kicking the crap out of me."

"Where did this happen?"

"At the overlook." Just ten minutes away by car from the scene of Carly's murder.

"What time?"

"We were supposed to meet at seven forty-five, but Adam was early. They jumped me as soon as I got out of my car. It was over by eight, because I remember hearing the bell in the clock tower ringing as I counted what was left of my teeth." He opened his mouth and pointed to his two front ones. "See these? Fake."

"And they just left after that?"

"Yeah. Adam told them to stop and then they took off."

"Do you remember anything else? Did they stay together, or did Adam leave on his own?"

"He got a phone call right as they were getting back into

their cars. He picked it up, listened, said, 'I'll call you back,' and kicked everyone out of his car. Then he took off."

"You don't by any chance know who the call came from, do you? He didn't mention it to any of his buddies?"

"No, but I remember thinking the ringtone was really weird for a guy like him. You know Adam, he's all tough, but the ring was pretty girly, like from the eighties or something."

"Like the kind of song a girlfriend would program into your phone to play when she calls?"

"I guess. I wouldn't really know."

"Sorry, man. I've got to run, but enjoy the ice cream."

"Frozen yogurt."

"Whatever."

I readied myself for a confrontation when Adam opened his front door, but instead of getting up in my face he just eyed me warily, as if I were an unidentified species of insect.

"What do you want?" he demanded, gripping the door with one hand and the frame with the other.

"I have something that belongs to you." From my backpack, I pulled the printout I'd made of the files on his Black-Berry.

"What the hell is this?" He grabbed it from me and his eyes widened. "Where did you get this?"

"You should really look into password-protecting that thing—it was stupidly easy to get all the information the police are going to need to convict your sorry ass. Keep it. I made copies."

"Do you have a death wish? Do you know what I could do to you?"

"You could get some thugs to beat me up," I said. "But you won't."

"If that's what you think, you're in for a big surprise." He made a move in my direction, but I didn't flinch. Honestly, I didn't find him all that menacing. My knowledge made me feel invincible.

"We both know I can take you," I said. "I think I proved that the other day at school."

"You're such a dumb shit," he sneered. "I could've put you in the hospital."

"Maybe you should just kill me, like you killed Carly. That would probably be smarter, because I can still talk with broken bones."

"I didn't kill Carly."

"Very convincing. I guess I won't tell the police about your falsified alibi, then. I mean, why stir everyone up if you say you're innocent?" I was trying to stay calm, but seething anger is a difficult thing to suppress. I turned and started to walk away, but Adam reached out and grabbed the collar of my shirt.

"What makes you think I lied about my alibi?" he asked. There was barely any color in his face, and I could tell he was afraid.

"I just had a conversation with Freddie Kramer." Adam stiffened. I continued, "You might remember him—he's the guy whose ass you kicked right before Carly died. And he told me that you were done by eight, giving you plenty of time to get to the bridge, meet Carly, and then kill her. I know you had a phone call from her, and I know you left the overlook alone."

Adam took a step backward. "No way. Look, man, I cared about Carly. I would never have hurt her."

"That's bullshit!" I shouted. "You weren't even faithful to her. What about Lucy Miller?"

"That doesn't prove that I didn't care about her. Things with Carly were complicated, and Lucy, she was easy."

"I'm sure she was. Probably still is, in fact."

"Look, Lucy and I have known each other a long time. She was comfortable and undemanding. I didn't mean for it to happen, it just did. I didn't want to be with Lucy, I just didn't know how to be with Carly. But I did care. I might not have treated her great all the time, but that doesn't mean I killed her."

"If you cared so much about her, why did you drag her down to your level, huh? What part of your sick, corrupt little world did you think was good for her?"

"Dude, calm down," Adam said. "It was her choice to get involved with me. I didn't force her to do anything."

"You took advantage of her at a point in her life when she was looking for an escape," I said. "You gave her drugs so you could get what you wanted out of her."

"No, I loved her—"

"No, *I* loved her! I wanted what was best for Carly. All you wanted was someone to manipulate, someone to do whatever you wanted. That's not love."

Adam stopped protesting. All he said in response was, "I didn't kill her," so softly that I barely heard him.

"Tell it to the police," I said. "I'm turning you in."

"No, Neily, you cannot do that," Adam begged. "Yes, I admit, I did have my guys beat Freddie up, but I swear I went to Cass's immediately afterward. My alibi wasn't a lie; I just neglected to mention the deal because I knew that if the police had me on record as confessing to dealing and roughing up some punk, they'd put me in prison and bring down my entire operation. I would've been fucked."

"I don't fucking believe you." In my mind, I could piece together how it all happened. According to guests at Lucy's party, Carly and Adam had argued the night before she died. If Freddie was right and Carly called Adam around eight o'clock, she had probably arranged to meet him at the bridge. Carly was planning on exposing him—I was convinced that was what the digital recorder was for; why else would she have had it?—and Adam knew it.

He could count on his size and strength to overcome Carly if necessary. On his way to the bridge he noticed Enzo Ribelli's car by the road. Adam knew Enzo well enough to figure out that he was parked near the creek for one reason: to get drunk. In that moment, it all fell into place. He must've lost it completely when he saw the tape recorder. The only thing that bothered me was the gun. I could believe that Adam would take it from Enzo's glove compartment, but how could he know that Enzo had it on him? My head started to spin: Of course—*Carly* had brought the gun. Carly had her own key to Audrey and Enzo's house—I had seen her use it once to drop something off when Audrey was at her grandparents' house—and she knew where Audrey stashed the gun. If she wanted to protect herself, there was no better way than to bring along a firearm. My heart dropped deep into the pit of my stomach. She should've known he was big enough to turn it on her.

As if a dam had burst, my mind flooded with images and I could see instantly what had happened on the bridge: Carly instigated the whole thing. She brought the gun, and she threatened him with exposure, and with her suspicions about Laura Brandt as well. As soon as Adam said something incriminating, she taunted him about the tape, telling him that he was finally going to get what he deserved and that she was going to get her life back. He couldn't let her turn him in—he was only seventeen at the time, but he was no small-time dope dealer. It was quite possible that they'd try him as an adult. Even if they didn't, his whole life would be ruined. He couldn't let her do that to him. He moved to strike her, but she pulled the gun on him; he took advantage of her hesitation and got it away from her, shot her, wiped the gun clean, and threw it and the digital recorder into the river. When he was sure she was dead, he stole the necklace and planted it in the mud next to Enzo's car before going to Cass's house and making him agree to give him an alibi.

"You must've been really angry to shoot her four times," I said quietly.

"What the fuck are you talking about?" he snapped. He was a mess of rage, his whole body tense and shaking, like a big cat waiting to pounce, but I knew he wouldn't touch me. There was fear in his face.

"Why did Cass lie for you?" I asked.

"He's my friend," Adam said, rubbing his eyes and forehead anxiously. "I didn't want to get busted for the deal, so I asked him to say I was at his house all night. But I didn't kill Carly, man, I swear on my life."

"Yeah, well, unfortunately that's not worth very much," I said.

"What do you want from me?" he cried.

"A confession," I told him. "Pick up the phone, call the police and tell them what you did, and believe me, I'll be the least of your problems."

"I'm not going to do that," Adam said. "I'm innocent. What is it going to take for you to believe me?"

"The truth," I said.

"I've told you the truth!"

"You didn't go to Cass's at all that night, did you? Carly called you. Freddie told me that."

"Carly called me back, I admit it."

"Called you *back*?"

"Yeah. I'd called her a couple of times that day, but she never picked up."

"Same with me," I said, realizing something: "Carly was lying low. Handling things on her own, after all."

"What for?"

I ignored him. "Why wasn't your phone number on her cell phone's call log?" I asked. This question had been bothering me. If I'd known they talked before she died, it never would've taken me this long to prove it was Adam who killed her.

"She called me from her home phone. All she said was that she'd left a box of my stuff on my porch and that I was never to speak to her again as long as I lived. I told her I'd call her back, but she'd hung up by then."

"What happened after that? Who did you go see?" I went on. "Where did you go if not to the bridge?"

"I went for a drive."

"Where?"

"San Francisco."

I narrowed my eyes at him. "Why?"

Adam sighed. "Just to clear my head. Lucy kept trying to get ahold of me and I needed some space to process."

"Lucy?"

"Carly found out I was sleeping with Lucy at that last party. It was one of the things we argued about."

"And she was upset."

"Well, yeah, but not for the reason you'd think."

"What do you mean?"

"She was mad at me because everybody knew but her," Adam said. "But she wasn't upset about losing me, because she said she was planning on breaking up with me anyway."

"Why?" It was possible that it wasn't really true. Carly could've just been trying to save face.

"She didn't say. My guess was to get back together with you."

"No way."

"Even though she was with me, she never stopped missing you," Adam said sharply. "She talked about you all the time, always compared me to you. I could tell that she would have gone back to you if she thought she deserved you, but she didn't. I hated you, plain and simple, and I've never stopped."

"Is that why you had that kid put those articles in my locker? Just to fuck with my head?" I asked.

"I wanted you to suffer," he snarled. "Nobody ever asked how her death affected *me.* It was all you, getting special treatment and being babied by everybody. Like you were the only person it happened to."

I couldn't think of anything to say to that.

"She was cheating on me, too, you know," he continued. "I practically caught her at Cass's School's Out for Summer party."

"She wasn't cheating. She was raped that night," I told him.

"No," he said hoarsely.

"Somebody dosed her drink, probably with some of that Special K you've been smuggling in from Tijuana. She wrote about it in her diary." I paused to think. "What else did you argue about?" He said nothing. "Laura Brandt?"

"I had nothing to do with Laura's disappearance. I still think she took off on her own."

"But you did have the Bean run her off the road?"

"Just to put a scare in her. I didn't think she'd have the nerve to pull what she was threatening."

"But Carly thought you had her killed, didn't she?"

"She did. But she was wrong."

"Think back to Cass's party," I said. "Lucy said you found Carly alone in a bedroom later that night. Did you just stumble upon her accidentally?"

"I went looking for her, and when I got to the top of the stairs Cass came up to me, pointed to the bedroom right behind him, and said, 'Your girlfriend's passed out in there. You might want to wake her up and get her home.' "

"Cass?"

Adam nodded. "He's always looking out for his friends."

I barely heard him. I saw it all for what it really was. "No, he wasn't. He was stalking Carly, writing her creepy letters. He raped her. And now he no longer has an alibi for her murder," I said. "How could you not have known?"

"No," Adam protested. "He's my best friend. We protect each other. He did me a favor."

"No, you did him one. He took advantage of *your* desperation for an alibi for the night he *shot* and *killed* your girlfriend. Did you ever think to ask him where he was that night? Or did you just accept his offer to perjure himself for you?"

"It doesn't make any sense," Adam insisted. "Cass has always had my back."

I took a deep breath in an attempt to calm down. "I don't have time to list the countless ways in which you are responsible for what happened to Carly. Do yourself a big fucking favor and go to the police with the truth about your alibi." I held out my hand. "Give me your gun."

"What? Why?"

"Just give it to me!"

Reluctantly, he went inside, then came back and handed me the gun. It was heavier than I thought, and I had no idea what to do with it or what I planned to use it for. I stared at it blankly and shoved it into Adam's hand. "Show me."

He gaped at me. "You want to take a gun with you but you don't know how to use it?"

"Just do it."

"This is the safety," he told me, turning the gun over and pointing to a latch near the trigger with the word SAFE etched into the metal casing. He switched the safety on. "You leave it like this, and don't you dare put your finger anywhere near the trigger unless you're willing to shoot something. If you are— and *don't*—then switch the safety off, lift, aim, and pull." He demonstrated. "But like I said—*don't*."

"Thanks." I took the gun, trying desperately to keep my hands from shaking.

"Wait, man, where are you going?" Adam called after me. "There's something about Cass you should know!"

I didn't stop. Audrey was probably with Cass at that very moment.

PART FOUR

Audrey

CHAPTER TWENTY-THREE

I was sprawled out on Cass's unmade bed wearing a T-shirt and a pair of his boxer shorts. Cass stroked my palm with his fingers and smiled at me.

"Well," he said, climbing out of bed and grabbing a clean pair of jeans and a shirt from a chair nearby. "I'm going to take a shower. I'll be out in a couple of minutes. Don't take off on me."

"I'll stay right here, I promise." He kissed me and headed into the adjoining bathroom.

I didn't care what Neily believed, I trusted Cass. The afternoon before Neily attacked Adam at school, Cass called my grandparents' house and asked to speak to me.

"Hi," I said, trying to squelch my nerves.

"You didn't answer your cell when I called."

"I didn't know what to say."

"It's okay. I just wanted to apologize for kissing you the other day. It was way out of line."

"It was. But I forgive you," I said.

"Good. Hey, can I come over? I'd like to talk—in person."

I hesitated.

"Audrey?"

"Yeah. Come over. I'll be waiting on the porch."

He arrived fifteen minutes later and joined me on the porch swing. "What's up?" he said.

"Nothing. Just enjoying the last warm days," I said, leaning my head back.

"Weather report says the rain is coming. Not really looking forward to dodging idiots on the freeways," Cass said. We were both looking out across the lawn onto the street, where a couple of kids were playing with their dogs. "What are we going to do about this?" he asked.

"About what?" I asked.

"Our feelings."

"*Our* feelings?"

"Pretend all you want, but there was something in that kiss—I know it, and you know it. Acting like those feelings don't exist is not going to make them go away."

"Your friends will never be okay with you and me getting back together," I pointed out.

"Oh, who cares? I'm over them. All they want to do is party and hook up. I don't want that life anymore." He put his hand over mine.

"I heard you and Adam had a fight," I said.

"He thinks you're bad news. I told him to go fuck himself."
He smiled and leaned in as if to kiss me, but I pulled away.

"I can't do this right now. I have other things I need to
focus on," I insisted.

Cass's smile faded. "What, like what happened to Carly? I
can help, Aud. I know you say that Neily's the only person you
can trust, but if you just let me in a little you'll see that you can
trust me, too."

"Can I ask you a question?"

"Sure."

"Who do you think killed Carly?"

He sat for a while in silence. "Honestly? I think the Bean
might have done it."

"Why do you say that?" I thought so, too, but I didn't want
to influence him.

"The Bean doesn't have the best track record with girls. He
stalked this one girl a few years ago."

"He told you he stalked Allison Kessler?" I asked dubi-
ously.

"Well, not in those words. He told me he was writing her
these e-mails but that she wasn't responding. I was like, 'Bean,
maybe she thinks you're crazy and *that's* why she's ignoring
you.' " Cass laughed. "Poor guy. All he ever wanted was somebody to give a damn about him."

"Oh, yeah, poor guy," I said sarcastically.

"Same thing with Carly. She was nice to the Bean and he just
got totally wrapped up in it, spinning these wild fantasies about
how they were going to go away with each other after she graduated and get married—crazy stuff. I tried to talk him into keeping quiet about it, but it got back to Adam and he was pretty
pissed off. That's how the Bean got tossed out of his gang."

"How come you didn't say anything to the police about the Bean being obsessed with Carly?"

"I thought he was over her." Cass shrugged. "After Adam kicked him out of the group he stopped talking about it. Besides, the case against your dad seemed rock solid. Who was I to argue with the Empire Valley Police Department?"

"I found some letters in her family's safe-deposit box. She thought Neily had written them, but he swears he never did. I think they're from the Bean."

"Really?" Cass asked. "Do you have them here? Can I see them?"

"Yeah, sure," I said. "Give me a sec." I went to my room and retrieved the letters. Cass read through them all thoroughly and recognized something.

"This sounds a lot like those e-mails the Bean sent to Allison. No capitals or punctuation, questionable spelling and grammar . . ."

"That's what I thought," I said, triumphant. "He was at your School's Out for Summer party at the end of sophomore year, right? Lucy wasn't making that up?"

"No, he was there. Why?"

"I think Carly was raped that night. I drove her home from the party, but I hadn't seen her in hours and she was so out of it. I think she might've been drugged."

Cass ran his hand through his hair. "And you think the Bean raped her?"

"There doesn't seem to be any better explanation. The Bean knew where to get Special K—I read on the Internet that it's sometimes used as a date rape drug. Carly didn't know who gave her the drink that knocked her out. Her entire memory of that night was erased."

"I'm confused. Did she tell you about the rape?"

I paused. "No. I found a diary when I was going through some of her stuff. She wrote about how she felt the next morning. She wasn't sure at first."

"But she didn't say who did it?"

"I don't think she knew. But I think she figured it out, or remembered it, the night of Lucy's party. I think she realized what the Bean had done to her, and what he had done to Laura Brandt—"

"Wait, who's Laura Brandt?"

I summarized the situation briefly. Cass let out a low whistle. "I can't believe that Adam would tell the Bean to kill her."

"He beat the shit out of the Bean just for telling everybody about his feelings for Carly," I pointed out. "You think he wouldn't do whatever he could to protect his operation?"

"Well, yeah, he's big on covering his own ass, and he's got a bad temper, but murder?"

"I don't necessarily think Adam sent the Bean to kill Laura. I have this theory that he was doing it on the orders of Adam's partner, that guy Barton. You sure you don't know anything about him?"

Cass shook his head. "Only what I told you."

"Well, the Bean had been kicked out of the gang and had lost his drug connections. Maybe he was trying to get on Barton's good side by taking care of the Laura Brandt problem himself."

"Yeah, maybe. You seriously think that the Bean is smart enough to pull all this off?"

"It's the only scenario that fits."

"So what are you going to do about it?"

"I don't know. I can't really prove it. I can go to the police with the letters, but even given the Bean's record there's no way of being positive that they were from him—unless they have his fingerprints on them. My hope is that I can gather enough evidence to convince the police, and that when they question the Bean he caves and confesses."

Cass sighed. "It sounds like you're getting into some dangerous territory, Aud. If this Barton guy had Laura Brandt and Carly rubbed just to keep his operation under wraps, what makes you think he won't come after you once the Bean is picked up?"

"Maybe I can get police protection, or hire a private security detail."

"What, you're going to get armed guards to follow you to school and sit in on your classes?"

"If it keeps me safe."

"You always have a plan." He glanced at his watch. "Look, I've got to go, but call me if you do anything. I want to be there with you when this all goes down, okay?"

"Okay. I'll see you tomorrow."

I watched him go down the stairs and walk toward his car and it hit me: Neily was never going to get a second chance with Carly. I would be a fool to give up my second chance because of pride or hurt feelings. I got up and chased after him.

"Cass, wait!" I called. He turned around and smiled.

"What? You gonna tell me where Jimmy Hoffa is buried?" he asked as I reached him.

"Not exactly." I leaned into him and put my lips to his. A shiver went up my spine as we stood on the lawn, kissing and pulling away and touching and kissing again. My mind seemed blank and all I could remember was how happy this had once made me. We stood there for what seemed like forever as the last rays of late-summer sun burned out at the horizon.

CHAPTER TWENTY-FOUR

The sun had gone down and Cass's bedroom had grown chilly. I switched on a lamp on the nightstand and went to the bureau across the room to dig through his drawers for a pair of socks. I rummaged around, pushing aside a couple of belts and a bunch of handkerchiefs that were embroidered with his full name: Casper Barton Irving.

"Barton?" I said aloud. It occurred to me that during my entire relationship with Cass, I had never known his middle name. He wouldn't tell anyone what it was, he claimed that it was embarrassing and he hated it. I told myself it was just a coincidence that his middle name was the name of Adam's psychotic business partner, but I don't believe in coincidences. I dropped the handkerchiefs and kept going through the drawer; a moment later, my hand brushed against something heavy and metal. I reached in and wrapped my fingers around the cold barrel of a gun.

I pulled my hand away as if burned. What was Cass doing with a gun? Unable to stop myself, I pulled out everything, dumping the drawer's contents on the floor until all that was left was the gun and, in the very back right corner of the drawer, a small plastic bag. I grabbed it; inside the bag was a tarnished silver ring, one that I recognized immediately.

Bile rose in my throat; I barely made it into the hall bathroom, shaking as my stomach turned itself inside out over the toilet. When I was finished I rinsed the taste of vomit out of my mouth with water from the sink, then walked slowly back into the bedroom to get a better look at the ring. Placing the gun on top of the bureau, I shook the ring out of the bag and into my palm, turning it over in the light. It was definitely Carly's—I couldn't believe it, but it was indisputable. I slipped the ring onto my finger. It fit. Carly and I had the same ring size.

I picked up the gun. It wasn't the one that killed Carly, that I knew, but it was as good as. Thoughts raced through my mind, images flashed, and the final pieces of the puzzle fell together with a resounding *click*.

"What are you doing?" Cass was behind me, his voice so soft and sweetly confused I couldn't believe it was all an act. I turned on my heel.

"Is this your gun?" I asked, my voice wobbling with terror.

"No." He took a step toward me and I raised the gun.

"Don't come near me." Cass was between me and the door, and I knew he wasn't going to let me leave.

"Audrey—"

"Is this your *gun*, Cass?"

"I said no."

"*No?* Then what is it doing in your sock drawer?"

"I mean, yes, it's mine, but it's not what it looks like."

I held up Carly's ring. "What are you doing with *this*?"

"I don't know what that is," he insisted.

"It's Carly's ring," I almost shrieked. "The one she never took off her finger. Why do you have it?"

"I must've found it somewhere."

"Where?"

"Christ, I don't know. You need to calm down."

"Don't you *dare* tell me to calm down. You killed Carly."

"That's ridiculous."

"No. No it isn't. *You* wrote those letters. This whole time I thought it was the Bean, and Carly thought it was Neily, but those letters were from *you*."

"I didn't write Carly those letters. Why would I do that? Give me the gun, Audrey. You're going to hurt yourself."

"I'm going to hurt *you* if you get any closer."

"You'd never shoot me. You don't even know how to use a gun."

"I'll figure it out!" I shouted. "Why did you write those letters? Were you in love with her?"

"Of course not. I was in love with you. I still am. Give me the gun, come on."

"No, you weren't in love with her—you were *obsessed* with her. So obsessed that you drugged and raped her the night of your party."

"Audrey, just listen to yourself. Does that sound like me?"

"No," I said weakly. "I don't understand how you could be this whole different person on the inside. I thought I knew you. Did you ever love me?"

"Of *course*. I still do," he insisted, but his eyes were dead. His words were empty and worthless, and now that I could see him for what he was, I realized they always had been.

"No, you don't. You've never loved anybody, have you? You're so good at faking it, being charming and normal, but you don't feel anything for anybody. What happened, Cass? You made a pass at Carly and she wouldn't give you what you wanted, so you took it, just like you take everything?"

"This is crazy."

" 'Act like you have all the power, and people give you what you want.' Isn't that what you taught me? But that wouldn't work with Carly. Maybe she was too good of a person to betray me, or *maybe* she just didn't want you, so you drugged her and forced her to have sex with you."

"I would never do something like that."

"You did. And eventually she figured out it was you."

"Keep your voice down. And stop pointing that gun at me. I didn't *do* anything."

"I don't believe you."

"I don't know what you want me to do about that."

"Tell me the truth!"

"I don't want to talk about this while you have a gun pointed at me."

"You're Barton, aren't you? I saw those handkerchiefs in your drawer—Barton is your middle name. You're the one who took over from your brother, not Adam. You bankroll the drug operation and you call the shots. Isn't that how it works?"

"Fine. You want the truth? You're right. I am Barton."

"Did Carly know that?"

"Yes," he said.

"How?"

"She was suspicious for a while, then one day she followed Adam to the park and saw him hand me a wad of cash in exchange for about fifteen grams of coke. She badgered him about it until he spilled. Carly could be very manipulative, if you remember," he said. "But that doesn't mean I killed her."

"That's exactly what it means."

"How do you figure?" Cass *smiled.* Not a big, villainous grin, just a tiny little smile that curled the corners of his mouth. That smile used to turn me to jelly, but now it made me sick. I was amusing him with my accusations. He actually found this funny.

The things I'd overheard Mr. Irving screaming at Cass years before rang in my ears. *First it's your brother, then you. You're both morons. I was a Rhodes scholar and yet somehow I ended up with two losers for sons.* "You couldn't turn out just like Jerod. You had to be perfect so that the things your father said about you would never be true. You had to be Cass Irving, the basketball star, golden boy of Empire Valley, because that was the only way to prove to your father you weren't worthless. But you couldn't just give up control of Jerod's business, either, not when it came with such power and influence and money. So you invented Barton and made Adam your front man because you knew you could control him better than anyone else."

"What's the big deal?" he asked. "Even if everything you just said is true, it doesn't make me a *killer.*" He was so insincere. I couldn't believe how long I'd been snowed by the persona he'd constructed to hide who he really was. It was horrifying to realize that I'd fallen in love with an absolute lie.

"Carly had you all figured out in the end, didn't she? It wasn't just that you were Barton. She knew you weren't who you appeared to be, what you were capable of. She tried to talk me into breaking up with you multiple times, but I wouldn't listen."

"Carly was a bitch," Cass said.

"No, Carly was smart. So you had to subdue her. Scare her, take advantage of her, ruin her relationship with Adam by making him believe she cheated on him. She had figured out who you really were, what you had done to her and to Laura, and when she tried to take you down you killed her."

Cass didn't respond. Instead he said, "So, what? We have a Mexican standoff until my housekeeper comes in and offers us milk and cookies?"

"Or until you pick up that cell phone and call the police to confess."

"Not going to happen."

"Fine, I'll do it." I moved around the bed and picked up my cell phone from the bedside table, the gun not wavering for an instant. I had left the phone on silent, and there were five missed calls from Neily and a text that read: IT WAS CASS. No shit.

"Audrey, you have no idea what you're doing."

"For the first time in a long time I know exactly what I'm doing." I dialed 911 and someone picked up immediately.

"What's your emergency?"

"I'd like to report a crime—" I began, but was interrupted by the sound of a window breaking and Neily calling my name.

Cass mobilized instantly, taking advantage of my distraction and attacking me, throwing me to the ground and yanking the gun from my hand. Neily ran into the room just as I was getting up off the floor. I looked up to see Cass pointing the gun right at us, and then at Neily, who was pointing a gun at Cass. Suddenly, everyone was armed but me.

"Did you really need socks that badly?" Cass sneered, closing my cell phone and ending the call. "You've done a very stupid thing, Aud, you really have."

"Put the gun down, Cass," Neily said. "There's no point—everyone will know it's you."

"Did you ever think that the point is to shoot you just to watch you die?"

"Don't," I warned Neily. Provoking Cass now was not a good plan.

"Fine. Shoot us. I think four murders officially constitutes a spree."

"Neily!" I hissed.

Neily reached over and gave my hand a quick squeeze. His eyes stayed on Cass, and the hand holding the gun didn't shake. "Why did you kill Carly, Cass?"

"He's Barton," I said. "And Carly knew it. She also knew he killed Laura Brandt, or had her killed. Eventually she must've realized he was the one who raped her."

"Did she threaten you that night on the bridge?" Neily asked. "Did she threaten to expose you, just like Laura did?"

"Audrey's dad murdered Carly," Cass said. "She was shot with his gun. How would I have gotten my hands on that?"

"Good question. *Carly* brought the gun. She had a key to Audrey and Enzo's house and she knew where the gun was stashed; she must've sneaked in that afternoon before Enzo came home. Audrey was sleeping off her stomachache." He turned to me ever so slightly before zeroing in again on Cass. "She knew you were crazy; she knew you would hurt her if you found out she was taping your confession, so she brought the gun to protect herself."

"Considering the position you're in right now, that was probably a safe bet on her part." Cass smiled and shook his head. "And for the record, I didn't rape her. Carly was a slut, and she was high on Special K. She practically *begged* for it."

Neily's hand was shaking, but his voice was calm. "We read her diary. She felt violated and betrayed, but the ketamine wiped her memory and you were off the hook. You couldn't keep away, though, huh? You stalked her, wrote her those creepy letters. She kept them, you know—we've read them."

"You've got all the answers, don't you, Think Tank?"

"Not all of them. I still don't know how she got you down to the bridge in the first place."

Cass's eyes flicked over to my cell phone, which he'd tossed on the foot of the bed.

"She sent him a text," I said. "It wasn't in the sent folder, but he probably deleted it after he shot her. There were no prints on the phone—he must've wiped it down so no one would suspect someone else had touched it."

"Nancy Drew 2.0," Cass said. "Very clever."

"Sometime between the night that you raped her and the night that you killed her, Carly must've figured out that it was *you* who controlled Adam's operation, and when Oz told her that Laura Brandt had disappeared, she knew you had something to do with it," Neily deduced.

"You can't prove that."

"Carly thought she could."

"Carly was an idiot. That's what got her killed. She trusted the wrong people."

"I'm pretty sure she didn't trust you."

"I'm talking about Enzo."

"My dad—!" I cried, but Neily interrupted me.

"Come on, Cass. We all know Enzo didn't kill Carly. You did. She went to Lucy's party the night before she died and confronted Adam about Laura. Then he took her into a bedroom and all those bad memories came flooding back and she knew—she *knew*—you had killed Laura using the information she gave Adam. But she needed proof. So she lured you to the bridge under false pretenses and taped you confessing. What did she tell you? That she wanted you? That she was glad Laura was dead? Anything so you'd spill."

"You think I'd really be stupid enough to confess to her?"

"Carly could be pretty persuasive. And you would've done whatever it took to get at her, to have her under your power. You'd even believe, despite all evidence to the contrary, that she would ever want you."

"Shut up!"

"So that *is* what she told you. And in exchange you told her, what? Everything? How you drove to Arizona and convinced Laura to check herself out of rehab—how? By telling her that her life was in danger, that you were going to give her the money to make herself scarce? I'm no detective, but I'd bet you weren't smart enough not to use a credit card to buy gas, or to use a pay phone instead of a cell phone to call Laura at the rehab center. I'm pretty sure that's the kind of stuff the police can check up on."

Cass went pale, and whether or not Neily actually knew what he was talking about, he had obviously hit a nerve.

"Not that it matters. I talked to Adam, and he's going to go on record shredding your alibi to pieces. And when he does, the police are going to start looking for witnesses who saw your car on Empire Creek Road that night, and they'll probably find one."

"Don't forget this," I said, holding up the ring. "He took it as some kind of sick trophy."

"You think I'm just going to let you walk out of here with that?"

"It's over, Cass," Neily said. "It was over the minute you decided to get rid of Laura Brandt."

"She was going to ruin my life!" he screamed. "They both were! You know what Carly said to me? She said she was going to erase me. So I erased her."

Neily scoffed. "I'm sure that defense will hold up nicely on the witness stand."

"I'm not going to jail!"

"Yes, you are." Neily reached into his pocket with his free hand and pulled out a tape recorder.

Cass's face twisted with rage and his finger tightened on the trigger.

"Get down!" Someone yelled.

I grabbed Neily's arm and yanked him to the ground. Two shots rang out and three police officers stormed into the room. I looked up and watched Cass fall backward onto the bed. The gun tumbled from his hand and onto the carpet.

"Oh my God," I breathed.

"Is he dead?" Neily asked the officer who was hunched over Cass's body, feeling for a pulse. "Officer Bryson?"

The officer exhaled. "Lopez, get the paramedics in here."

"Oh my God," I repeated, trembling. I pressed my face into Neily's shoulder and he put his arms around me.

"Get them out of here," Bryson barked to another officer, who took the gun out of Neily's hand, tugged at his arm, and led us out of the room. I glanced back once at Cass, then looked away. Neily and I held on to each other as we went down the stairs and walked out of the house. The officer packed us into a patrol car and drove us down to the station. It rained the whole way.

CHAPTER TWENTY-FIVE

Cass died that night from complications relating to a gunshot wound to the chest. The police claimed that Cass turned his gun on them, leaving Officer Bryson no choice but to shoot to kill. I had to hand over everything to them—the letters, the ring, the diary—but tucked in between the end pages and the cover of Carly's journal there was a letter addressed to Neily. I shouldn't have read it, but I did. I gave everything else to the police, but this I kept. It belonged to no one but him.

> *Dear Neily,*
>
> *Things have gotten so out of control. I've made some terrible decisions, hurt people I never could have imagined*

hurting. A few months before she died, my mother gave me a book called An Unknown Woman, *by Alice Koller. I never read it, not until last week, when I devoured it in one night. The author wrote something that made me cry. She wrote, "I've arrived at this outermost edge of my life by my own actions. Where I am is thoroughly unacceptable. Therefore, I must stop doing what I've been doing." I knew then that I had to do what was right to fix the mistakes I've made and turn away from the terrible person I'm becoming. I have the inclination and the desire to be good, but I haven't been acting like it. Long before this horrible mess, you became the first casualty of my personality revolution. You'll want to know why. Here it is: I broke up with you because I wanted to realign myself with the world, to distract myself from the fact that I was falling apart by creating a whole new facade to hide behind. I didn't realize that you were the only thing holding me together, that the fact that you cared about me, that you knew me and understood me, was all I needed to rediscover who I was. My mother's death—it wasn't something I wanted to think about, much less talk about. All I wanted was escape—mindless, overwhelming, indulgent escape, and I found it in Adam. Maybe I thought that once I got over my loss I could come back to you, but of course that's ridiculous—you could never forgive me. Still . . . when I've done what I need to do I'm going to go to you—I don't know what I'll say to convince you to take me back, in any way that you can; labels mean nothing when it comes to you and me. I know you still care about me—if you didn't, you wouldn't work so hard to hate me. I miss you so much. I wish you knew how much.*

I have a lot to answer for. You'll want to know why I

did what I did the way I did it—why I found it necessary to corner you, then humiliate you, in front of a million people you can hardly tolerate. The truth is that I was born with a mean streak. I believed I was doing the right thing by pushing you away, but believing it is different than feeling it. At that moment, all I felt was anger and the anticipation of loss, and I wanted to hurt you as much as I was hurting—not to punish you, but to make you feel my pain. It sounds crazy, it sounds cruel, but it's a little bit of who I am—it always has been. I know you'll understand this, because unlike most people in my life, you're capable of loving all of me, even the rotten bits. That's what made you so special to me, but it's also what made you a liability. Please don't misunderstand me—I don't plan on repeating this mistake again. If you let me back into your life, I promise to be better in the future—perfect, or as close as I can get.

Love, Carly

They kept Neily and me at the police station for hours that night, questioning us about our investigation until I practically fell asleep sitting at the interrogation-room table. Grandma Louise wouldn't let me leave the house for days after that, not even to go to school—she was terrified somebody might kidnap me in retaliation. Finally, after a week of confining me to the house for my own protection, she granted me temporary leave to go see Neily.

When I went to his house, his mom told me that he had gone to St. Raymond's cemetery to visit Carly's grave. I found him sitting in front of her headstone, his legs pulled up against his chest, oblivious to the fact that the ground was soaked and muddy.

"Hey," I said, shoving my hands inside the pockets of my raincoat.

"Hey," he said, not looking at me.

I glanced around; the place was empty except for us. "How long have you been here?"

He shrugged. "Few hours."

"A few *hours*?" I crouched down next to him.

Neily nodded. "I needed someplace quiet to think."

"Are you okay, Neily?"

He turned his head to look at me with a blank look. "Are *you* okay?"

I shook my head. My throat felt like a clogged drain. "Definitely not."

He turned back to the headstone, gesturing to it. "I like that quote."

I bent forward, wiping the rain from the smooth stone and tracing the etched letters with my thumb. " 'To unpath'd waters, undream'd shores,' " I read aloud. "What's it from?"

"It's Shakespeare," he said. "From *The Winter's Tale*."

"Oh." Tired of squatting, I slid my legs out from under me and sat down in the mud beside Neily. "It's not your fault," I said, putting a hand on his shoulder.

"If I hadn't—"

"You don't know that. You can't know how things would've worked out."

"Are you saying you don't feel guilty? That some part of you isn't screaming that you should've known all along?"

I swallowed hard. "Of course it is. But it's all over now. We've done all we could."

"I really miss her," he said, struggling against tears.

"Me too." I left off struggling; they were running fast and

hot down my face now. I pulled a stack of papers out of my inside jacket pocket. "I brought this for you."

"What is it?"

"A copy I made of Carly's journal. I don't think we'll be getting the original back from the police for a while, so this is the best I can do." I put the letter on top of it. "This letter was in the journal. It's addressed to you. You should read it."

He shook his head. "I don't think I can."

I pressed it into his palm. "You can." I pointed toward a bench under a nearby tree. "Can I have a minute? I have a few things I'd like to say in private."

"Okay." He hoisted himself to his feet and trudged to the bench. I saw him start reading, then I turned back to face the gravestone, inching closer until the toes of my shoes were pressed right up against it.

"I feel a little stupid, talking to a grave," I said. "But I believe you can hear me—I believe you're listening. I thought a lot about what I would say to you here, but I could never bring myself to come, to give you bad news. But we found your killer, Carly, I'm sure you know that. And I'm sorry. I'm sorry Cass hurt you like that. It's my fault you even knew him at all and I'm so—you can't understand how sorry I am. But I'm so angry at you that it's sometimes hard to feel sorry. Why did you take it all upon yourself and put yourself in danger like that? We would have helped you, Neily and I, if you had just told us the truth. You kept so many secrets. I had no idea you were still in love with Neily, all that time."

I hadn't shown Neily all those tearstained passages where Carly told the truth about who she was—her guilt, her pain, her desire to be better, her weaknesses, her impulses to be worse.

I was afraid it would damage him more, knowing that the whole time he was licking his wounds and tearing out his stitches over his love and hate for her, she was secretly pining for him. I was afraid he would never forgive her. But now I could show him. One more thing I could stop feeling guilty about.

"I don't know what else to say," I continued. "Except that I miss you so much. You were my best friend, and even when we were fighting you got me more than any other person in the world. I leaned on you for everything—I just wish you would've leaned back a little more."

I got up off the ground and walked over to the bench. Neily was sitting with the journal in his lap, staring out over the lawn. "Did you read it?"

He nodded. "I had no idea she still felt—"

"Me neither." I sat down beside him.

"I wish she had told me," he said. The anguish in his voice was unmistakable, but there was strength in it. He would be okay. We both would.

"I know you do," I said.

Neily broke down, clutching the pages so hard that his knuckles turned white. He pressed his face into my shoulder. Unable to stop myself from sobbing, I rested my cheek against the top of his head and put an arm around his back. We cried ourselves dry, and when we were finished, Neily pushed the pages into my hands.

"No, you should keep it."

He shook his head. "I'll just use it to torture myself with what-ifs. It's better if you have it."

I took the diary and the letter from him. I would keep them safe. He would want them back someday.

A sharp chill ran through my bones; winter had come, and with it, the cold, insistent rains that would make everything that had died over the hot summer grow. The rain would green the hills and wash the roads and muddy up the Brighton athletic fields. As Neily and I walked away from Carly's grave together, the sky split and the rain came, soaking us to the skin.

EPILOGUE

◞〜◞

Neily

At the end of the following summer, Harvey and I packed up a U-Haul truck and took the I-5 down to San Diego, where he was starting at the University of California. Somewhere outside of Harris Ranch we heard on the radio that Adam Murray, who was charged with distributing cocaine and other narcotics, had plea-bargained his way into seven years of jail time, three and a half with good behavior. We didn't listen to the pundits discuss the case further; as soon as the announcement was made, Harvey changed the station.

"At least that's finished now," he said over some mind-numbing hip-hop as I stared out the window at the cars streaking past.

Harvey was right; things finally felt over. Audrey and I had spent our last semester of high school with a private tutor, safely out of reach of reporters. We couldn't go back to Brighton, nor did we want to. Finch tried his best to convince us that everything would normalize, that Brighton was our home, but neither one of us believed that. The last time I ever saw him was on television, assuring the good people of the Bay Area that what had happened was a tragedy, yes, but an anomaly, and that he would do everything in his power to make the school safe for their children. Finch was no fool. He knew it was impossible to stamp out darkness, that Cass and Adam left a space that would be filled again someday. But you can't tell people that. What would be the point?

Other than leaving Empire Valley, I didn't have any concrete plans of my own. Find an apartment, get a job, those were the first things on my list, but I did end up enrolling at San Diego State. Audrey went, as we all expected, to USC. We talked on the phone a few times, exchanged a few e-mails, but soon our correspondence dropped off as we carved out new lives a little more than a hundred sleek California-freeway miles apart.

I had begun to think we would never see each other again. This was something I was learning to come to terms with, knowing that we had shared something vital and frightening and altogether too real to keep reminding each other of, recognizing that we both needed room to process what had happened, possibly forever. But in the spring of that first year, I got an envelope in the mail. There was no note inside, no card, no expression of sentiment, only a picture of the three of us—Audrey, Carly, and me—that had been taken the summer

Audrey moved to Empire Valley. I remembered posing for that picture under duress, still uneasy about the changing dynamics of my relationship with Carly as a result of Audrey's sudden arrival, so I was surprised to see that I looked happy in the photograph, and remarkably relaxed. I went out and bought a frame and placed it in a position of honor, on the top of my television.

That summer I got a job working with a sailing company that organized pleasure cruises up the coast to Coronado. It was hard, physical work, but I liked it—it gave me time to think. One morning, I was on the boat, cleaning the cabin in preparation for the day's trips, when someone called out to me from the dock below.

"Cruise starts at nine," I shouted from inside, wiping a coat of Windex off the glass. I could see the shadow of my visitor from where I was standing, and I could tell that he or she wasn't leaving. After waiting a moment, I went down to the deck to send the person away.

"Hi," Audrey said, looking up at me and shielding her eyes from the glare. "Well, aren't you just a regular Gilligan."

I smiled. "And who are you supposed to be, Mary Ann?"

She rolled her eyes. "Duh. Ginger. The movie star?"

"Give me a second." I climbed down the ladder onto the dock and she wrapped her arms around me.

"It's good to see you," she said, stepping back. She squeezed my bicep and nodded appreciatively. "Wow. San Diego's been good to you."

"It's all this manual labor. You look great," I told her, because she did. She had toned up, and gotten a lot of color. She was wearing a tight red tank top and a pair of white capri pants with matching sandals. Her blond hair was shorter, and in pig-tails. I felt a surge of attraction, which was only natural, and had to remind myself that I sort of had a girlfriend.

"Thanks," she said. "I joined a sorority. We all look like this."

"Philistine."

She laughed. "I like it. It feels like being part of a family. It's nice to have that again."

"I can imagine."

"You look really great."

"You said that."

"I mean, you look like you're sleeping well."

"No nightmares."

"Well, that's good to hear."

There was a bit of an awkward pause, which I broke by ask-ing an equally awkward, but obvious, question: "So . . . do you have a boyfriend?"

She shook her head. "Nope. Too soon, I think. I'm still in therapy to deal with . . . well, you know. But I'm working through it."

"That's good."

"What about you?" She punched me lightly in the shoul-der. "Do you have a girlfriend?"

"No." I smacked my forehead. "I don't know why I said that. I do—sort of. Her name is Ellie. And we're not technically, well, we're not exclusive. We're just . . . dating, I guess." Friends with benefits was probably closer to the truth, but I was seriously thinking about making it official. I liked Ellie. She was fresh and interesting, and best of all, she didn't re-mind me of the past, not one iota.

"I'm proud of you," she said, smiling.

"So how's your dad?"

Audrey frowned and tugged at one of her pigtails. "Well, you know, it was hard on him. The adjustment. People staring at him in the grocery store, that sort of thing. Long story short, he started drinking again."

"God, I'm sorry."

"Don't be. He's in rehab now. Going on five weeks. I went to visit him last weekend, and he's doing well."

"That's good."

Audrey nodded. "I'm afraid he'll never get better. I don't know that he has the heart for it."

"He should do it for you."

"Yeah, he should." She kicked at some pebbles on the ground. "I got a letter from my mom a couple of months ago. She sent it to my grandparents' house. Apparently they're talking again."

"Yeah?"

"Turns out she's been living in Bakersfield for the past year or so." Audrey gave a little uncomfortable laugh. "She has a boyfriend, and a house. And a dog, which is sort of annoying because she would never let me have one. She sent me a picture."

"Did you answer the letter?"

"Nope." She gazed at me. "Thought about it, but couldn't. Does that make me a bad person?"

"No way. The fact that you thought about it, that's step one. You'll get there when you're ready. Or you won't, but that still won't make you a bad person. In my opinion, we've both racked up enough good karma to last a lifetime."

She smiled. "I've missed you. You should call me more."

"*You* should call *me* more," I countered.

"Fair. But I didn't know if you wanted to talk to me, or see me."

"So you came down here to surprise me with an unwanted visit?" I teased.

"I wanted to see you, and I figured that if I left it to you I never would," she said. "I stopped by your place. Harvey told me you'd be here."

"I wish I had known you were coming; I would've taken the day off. I'd just bail, but the boss man would fire me, and I like to eat, so . . ."

"Daddy's not bankrolling the whole vagabond thing?"

"Well, he wasn't so thrilled about some of my choices."

"Speaking of, how's San Diego State?"

"I like it. Great place to meet chicks."

"Such a romantic."

"Plus, my roommate doesn't walk around wearing a *semper ubi sub ubi* T-shirt, so I can't complain."

"He does follow that advice, though, right?"

"As far as I know. So what are your plans for the day while I toil on this here dinghy?" I asked, patting the hull of the *Sea Breeze.*

"Does it leak?"

"Not on my watch."

"Well, perhaps I'll join you. Strictly in a leisure capacity, of course—you can fan me and feed me grapes."

"Dream on."

She laughed, the open, happy laugh of a healing heart, and I got a flash of who she would be when she got older. It was only a flash—I couldn't reproduce it in words for anything—but it left me feeling safe, and that's something.

Audrey flung her arm around my shoulder. "So where are we headed? Someplace exotic? Uncharted waters?"

"Coronado," I said.

She pretended to consider it. "Good enough."

When we were fourteen, Carly and I took turns reading to each other from *The Winter's Tale,* and while Carly favored the quote that Paul had etched on her gravestone, I found comfort in another: *What's gone and what's past help should be past grief.* Carly wrote it in her diary, in one of those passages where she talked about how she still loved me, and I can think of no other reason why she would do this unless she really believed that what she and I had, what she had destroyed, was not past help. And so she grieved. And so I grieved. But the truth of the matter is that it's over now, so I no longer grieve—I only hope. That hope is enough for me.

ACKNOWLEDGMENTS

I've come to the conclusion that the longer it takes to write a book, the more people you are indebted to for having helped you write it, even if they have no idea how they've done so. Since it took me six and a half years to write this book, a period that, for me, has encompassed three universities, three degrees, nine residences, five cities in four states, three computers, six jobs, and countless friends, family members, and teachers, I have a lot of people to thank:

My parents, Jim and Barbara Jarzab; my brother, James; my sister, Alicia, and my cousin, Emma Molinare, who together are my first and most reliable readers. Christine and Mike Molinare and Helena Bieniewski, for their love, support, and encouragement, and the extended use of their guest bedrooms, as well as the rest of my family—I couldn't hope for a better one.

My wonderful agent and friend, Joanna MacKenzie—this book is truly hers as well as mine—and Danielle Egan-Miller, whose notes on the manuscript were incredibly helpful, although it seems that, try as I might, I will never fully break my dependence on dashes, as evidenced by the last two paragraphs.

My editor, Françoise Bui, whose enthusiasm for this book and faith in me were a touchstone during all those moments (and they were numerous) when I felt like a total hack, and everyone at Delacorte Press, for their support, excitement, and hard work.

The faculty and staff of the University of Chicago, where this novel was reborn, especially my thesis adviser, Nic Pizzolatto, and my preceptor/cheerleader, Jon Enfield.

Carol Fitzgerald and everybody at The Book Report Network, especially Wiley, world's best boss.

My roommate, Eesha, who always takes time out from saving the world to wax poetical with me about life and love.

Brendan and the entire Dempsey's staff for making me feel at home.

My best friend, Cambria, who read many versions of this story, gave invaluable feedback, and encouraged me not to give up on it.

And, finally, the rest of my friends: Kim, Jenny, Maggie, Scott, Eric, Carmen, Shannel, Brigitte, Nickie, Abby, Nikki, Doug, Brett, Monica, Mary, Alex, Marisa, David, Brian, and Sandra, who fill my life with laughter and never threaten to sue me for stealing their best lines. God love ya.

ABOUT THE AUTHOR

Anna Jarzab grew up entirely in the suburbs, first outside Chicago and then in San Francisco's East Bay area, where *All Unquiet Things* is set. She graduated from Santa Clara University, earned her master's degree from the University of Chicago, and currently lives in New York City. This is her first novel. Visit Anna online at www.annajarzab.com.